The Sybil in Her Grave

SARAH CAUDWELL

LARGE PRINT
Oxford

First published in Great Britain 2002
by
Constable & Robinson Ltd

Published in Large Print 2004 by ISIS Publishing Ltd,
7 Centremead, Osney Mead, Oxford OX2 0ES
by arrangement with
Constable & Robinson Ltd

British Library Cataloguing in Publication Data
Caudwell, Sarah, 1939–2000
    The sybil in her grave. – Large print ed.
    1. Tamar, Hilary (Fictitious character) – Fiction
    2. Legal historians – England – Oxford – Fiction
    3. Detective and mystery stories
    4. Large type books
    I. Title
    823.9'14 [F]

ISBN 0–7531–6991–6 (hb)
ISBN 0–7531–6992–4 (pb)

Printed and bound by Antony Rowe, Chippenham

The Sybil in Her Grave

**Books should be returned or renewed by the
last date stamped above**

_____

_____

_____

Awarded for excellence

Kent
County
Council

Prologue

For certain of my academic colleagues — I resist the temptation to refer in this context to the Bursar — the chief purpose of publication appears to be self-advertisement. Were it so for me, I should no doubt modify my account of the recent curious events in Parsons Haver in such a way as to reflect more credit on myself, for at more than one stage in my consideration of them I reached conclusions which afterwards proved erroneous. It was not until after the last of three mysterious deaths that finally the truth became clear to me.

I fear, however, that I myself cannot think it right to attempt to enlist Scholarship in the service of personal vanity or worldly ambition: she is the servant of Truth and can own no other allegiance. Though I may do less to promote my own reputation than I might hope would be to my advantage, and less to enhance the academic standing of my college than some will consider to be my duty, I cannot bring myself to place before you, dear reader, anything but a strictly accurate account of the events I have mentioned. If I thereby have the misfortune to displease the Bursar, I must be resigned to enduring his displeasure.

By the same token, I cannot think that it would be seemly for me, as the historian of these events, to present myself as if I had played a leading role in them, thrusting myself on the attention of my readers like an amateur actor, cast as a spearbearer, ineptly trying to shoulder his way into the spotlight. The place of the historian is not at the centre of the stage but in the shadows at the side, observing and explaining the actions of the protagonists in the drama. I shall not, therefore, take up your time and attention with any description or account of myself.

Some of my readers, it is true, have been kind enough to say that they would like to know more about me — what I look like, how I dress, how I spend my leisure hours and other details of a personal and sometimes even intimate nature. I do not doubt, however, that these enquiries are made purely as a matter of courtesy and that to take them *au pied de la lettre* would be as grave a solecism as to answer a polite "How do you do, Professor Tamar?" with a full account of the state of my digestion. Of what interest can it be to the reader of a work of history whether the writer of it is tall or short, thin or fat, of fair or dark complexion? It would seem to me an impertinence on my part to claim the attention of my readers for such trivia. Maintaining, therefore, that modest reticence which I think becoming to the historian, I shall say no more of myself than that my name is Hilary Tamar and that I am the Tutor in Legal History at St George's College, Oxford, of which I have the honour to be a Fellow.

In particular, I shall not explain my reasons for deciding, shortly after the end of the summer term, to spend a few days in London: suffice it to say that the Bursar was still in residence at St George's and enough is enough. As I have mentioned elsewhere, Timothy Shepherd, a former pupil of mine now in practice at the Chancery Bar, has a flat conveniently situated at the top of Middle Temple Lane: I telephoned him, knowing the generosity of his nature, in reasonably confident hope of an offer of hospitality.

Timothy expressed his regret that he himself would be absent during the period I mentioned and thus unable to entertain me in person — he was appearing in a case in Manchester or Brussels or some such place. He kindly invited me, however, to treat the flat as my own during his absence and promised to leave a set of keys for me with Selena Jardine, a member of the same Chambers, to be collected on my arrival in London.

At about four o'clock in the afternoon on the Thursday before midsummer, I mounted the steps of 62 New Square and opened the door of the Clerks' Room, intending to ask Henry, the senior clerk, to tell Selena of my arrival.

Midsummer

CHAPTER
ONE

The two men struggling on the floor of the Clerks' Room differed widely in appearance: one young, of slender build, dressed in cotton and denim, with honey-coloured hair worn rather long and a pleasing delicacy of feature; the other perhaps in his sixties, tending to plumpness, wearing a pinstriped suit, with the round, pink face of a bad-tempered baby and very little hair at all. They rolled this way and that, as it seemed inextricably entwined, uttering indistinguishable cries and groans, whether of pain or pleasure I could not easily determine. A ladder was also involved in the proceedings.

I concluded after a few moments that their entanglement was neither hostile nor amorous, but of an involuntary nature on both sides, the result, very possibly, of an accidental collision between the older man and the ladder at a moment when the younger was standing, perhaps imperfectly balanced, on one of its upper rungs.

"Sir Robert — Sir Robert, are you all right?"

Selena's voice, as she ran forward to assist the older man to his feet, conveyed a tactful mixture of deference, apology and concern — it seemed likely that he was one of her clients. If so, this was not the moment to lay claim to her attention: I withdrew, thinking that a pleasant half-hour or so could be spent in visiting Julia Larwood in the Revenue chambers next door.

At 63 New Square I found Julia sitting at her desk, surrounded by papers, tax encyclopaedias, half-empty coffee cups, and overflowing ashtrays, more than ever resembling in appearance some particularly dishevelled heroine of Greek tragedy. I concluded that she was working on a matter of some importance.

"Yes," said Julia, waving hospitably towards an armchair. "Yes, I am. I'm writing a letter to my aunt Regina. She is in urgent need of my advice." She spoke a trifle defensively, no doubt aware that I would find the claim improbable.

Julia's aunt Regina, having spent several periods of her life in more distant parts of the world, had now chosen, as I recalled, to settle in Parsons Haver in West Sussex — a charming village on the banks of the Arun or the Adur, I forget which, of the kind that Londoners are usually thinking of when they dream of the pleasures of rusticity. Having at one time in the Middle Ages flourished as a seaport, it has long since been deprived by the changing coastline of any commercial importance; but its cobbled streets, its knapped flint cottages and its fine Norman church continue to attract the discerning tourist and those in quest of an idyllic retirement.

Regina Sheldon herself, whom I had once or twice had the pleasure of meeting, had also struck me as having something about her appearance which savoured of the medieval. As a girl, I suppose, she would rather have put one in mind of a good-looking pageboy at the court of one of the Plantagenets; now, though her figure was no longer boyish and the dark auburn of her hair must have owed less to nature than to her hairdresser, one could still imagine her as the same pageboy, grown up to be an ambassador or a rather worldly cardinal. Having married four husbands and brought up two sons, she professed to have retired from matrimony: the chief outlet for her talents and formidable energies was a small antique shop, adjoining the discreetly modernized cottage in which she lived.

There were few areas in which I could imagine her requiring the benefit of Julia's wisdom and experience.

"She has a tax problem," said Julia. "If you'd like to read about it, while I finish writing this —"

She offered for my perusal a letter running to several pages, written in distinctively elegant but perfectly legible manuscript.

24 High Street
Parsons Haver
West Sussex

Monday, 14th June

Dear Julia,

Now do please read this properly as soon as you open it, instead of putting it somewhere safe and forgetting about it. There's something I need your advice on — I think it's the kind of thing you're supposed to know about — and it's much too complicated to explain by telephone.

It all started in February last year, when Maurice and Griselda and I were sitting in the Newt and Ninepence. And don't be tiresome, Julia, you know perfectly well who Maurice and Griselda are, or if you don't it's quite disgraceful of you.

Maurice Dulcimer is the vicar at St Ethel's. Well, in a manner of speaking — the Church Commissioners decided that St Ethel's was too small to have a full-time vicar to itself, so he's been rationalized into an assistant curate — but they let him go on living at the Vicarage and everyone still calls him "Vicar". I always invite him to dinner when you're down here and you usually seem to amuse each other.

And you certainly ought to remember Griselda — Griselda Carstairs, my neighbour, who does people's gardens and has cats. The first time you met her she was weeding my rose bed and you spent ten minutes flirting with her before you realized she was a woman, not a young man. And I do think, Julia, though of course I wouldn't like you to be the sort of girl who's obsessed with sex, that you ought to be able by now to tell the difference. Just because Griselda has short hair and was wearing trousers —

Well, as I say, there we were in the Newt, as we usually are on a Saturday morning, helping each other to finish our crosswords and talking of this and that. And it turned out that we were all a little bit richer than usual, to the tune of four or five hundred pounds each. Maurice had written an article on Virgil for one of the up-market papers, and been quite well paid for it. Griselda had been left a small legacy by someone whose garden she used to look after. And a charming American tourist had walked into my antique shop and bought some things I'd quite despaired of selling.

So we had an extra round of drinks to celebrate and talked about how to spend the money. By and by, though, we began to realize that it wasn't actually quite enough. Not enough, I mean, to do anything exciting with. When Maurice and I were your age, five hundred pounds was a very large sum of money — it could almost have changed one's life. And even when Griselda was your age, which isn't nearly so long ago, it would still have been pretty substantial. But nowadays — and yet it seemed a shame just to put it in the bank, and let it trickle away in everyday expenses.

"It would be awfully nice," said Griselda, "if it were about twice as much." Which summed up our feelings in a nutshell.

Maurice thought we might put it on deposit, and leave the interest to accumulate for a while. We were working out how long it would take for us to double our money in that way, and getting a bit depressed about the answer, when Rick Farnham came in.

Do you remember Ricky? Square-shouldered and brick-coloured, with a handlebar moustache to show he was once in the RAF, and a rather lively taste in ties? He came to dinner once when you were down here, and took a great fancy to you — I think not reciprocated. Not your type at all, poor Ricky, even if he weren't thirty years too old — you like them willowy, don't you, and he definitely isn't that. (I dare say Maurice would have been your type when he was younger — he must have been very willowy.) Still, Ricky's not a bad chap, as long as one's firm with him. I'm quite fond of him really, though over the past few months —

But that's neither here nor there. The point is that until he retired he'd spent most of his life looking after pension funds and investment trusts and things like that, so he seemed like the very man to advise us about our problem. He wasn't at all keen on the deposit idea.

"Booze," he said, "I can understand. Expensive restaurants I can understand. Fast women and slow horses, God knows I can understand. But throwing your money away on bankers — that's what I call sheer senseless waste."

What we wanted, said Ricky, was equities, by which he seemed to mean shares in companies. And as what we were talking about wasn't our life savings, but a little windfall that wouldn't do us any good anyway unless we could make it grow a bit, not shares in the big companies that everyone's heard of, but in what he called "double or quits" companies. By which he seemed to mean that they either do very well very soon or go bust. And he happened to have just heard of one which might be the very thing for us.

It was pure chance that I was the one who actually bought the shares. Ricky had told us, you see, that one of the disadvantages of investing small sums was the high cost of dealing, so we'd decided to pool our resources and invest all the money as a lump sum. And as I had some banking business to deal with anyway on Monday morning, I said I'd arrange about the shares at the same time.

We looked in the paper every morning to see how they were doing, and for a week or two nothing happened at all. Then suddenly the price began to go up quite quickly — something to do with a takeover, I think. When they were worth nearly twice what we'd paid for them, Ricky said it was time to sell, but if we wanted to reinvest the proceeds he knew of another company which looked rather promising. So we did, and more or less the same thing happened — the second company didn't do quite as well as the first, but well enough to encourage us to go on investing.

After we'd reinvested three or four times, Maurice began to have scruples — I suppose it comes of being a clergyman. Giving all those sermons about not laying up treasure on earth is bound to have an effect on one, isn't it? He seemed to feel the whole thing was becoming too important to him, and distracting his mind from higher things.

"When I find I'm reading the financial page before I've even looked at the crossword," he said, "I think it's time to stop."

Griselda and I didn't feel quite the same about it. I paid Maurice his share of the money, and reinvested ours in a company called Giddly Gadgets, which was Ricky's latest tip. It didn't do nearly as well as the others, though, and we hardly made any profit at all. We began to wonder whether it might be some kind of warning that we were being too greedy, or a sign that Ricky was losing his touch, and we were still trying to make our minds up what to do when I found out that Ricky —

But that, as I say, is neither here nor there. The point is that we decided to stop. We just took the money and — well, spent it.

Maurice had already spent his. He has a weakness for old books and manuscripts, and he'd gone up to London for the day and fallen into temptation. An illuminated frontispiece for a copy of some poems of Virgil — Venetian, fifteenth or sixteenth century, illustrating a scene he says is from one of the Eclogues — it really is quite lovely. (He's longing to show it to you, by the way — he says it's just your sort of thing.) But then he had a bad conscience about spending so much on purely personal pleasure and made a large donation to the fund for maintaining St Ethel's. And then he realized that St Ethel's also gives him personal pleasure, so he gave the rest to a charity for the homeless — poor Maurice!

Griselda spent most of hers on a rather splendid greenhouse and new baskets for the cats, and I had new central heating put in. After that, and a few presents and celebrations, I had just enough left to go to Paris and stay with your aunt Ariadne for a week — which, as you know, is about as long as we can spend together before we quarrel about politics.

And if that were the end of the story it would be an extremely satisfactory one from everyone's point of view. But it isn't.

I had a wonderful time in Paris, eating and drinking too much and seeing old friends from art school, and came back feeling ready for anything. I thought that I ought to make the most of it, so I sat down straight away and did my accounts, so that I could put in my tax return. (No, Julia, it would *not* be better if I had a professional accountant — the accounts of the antique shop are childishly simple, and I'm damned if I'm going to pay someone to do something I can do perfectly well myself.)

When I'd finished, I took the accounts along to the income tax people in Worthing — it's always better to do it in person, so that one can explain anything they don't quite understand — and just to be helpful I took my bank statements as well. I handed everything over to a young man in horn-rimmed glasses, who seemed at first to be perfectly sensible and obliging, and he noticed an entry in my statement arising from one of the share sales. And when I explained what it was, he asked me to send him a list of all the shares I'd bought and sold during the past year. Which I did, that same afternoon.

And now he wants three thousand pounds.

When I first got his letter I thought it was just a mistake. I rang up and explained to him that shares are capital, not income, and I shouldn't have to pay income tax on them. But he said it made no difference, and he was very sorry if it came as a shock to me.

It's all very well for him to say he's sorry — which I don't believe he is at all — where does he think I'm going to get three thousand pounds from?

Well, I know, of course, that when I tell Maurice and Griselda they'll raise their share of it somehow, and so shall I. But we're all going to find it a bit difficult — it's twice as much as we had in the first place, and, as I say, we've spent all the money, mostly on things we can't get it back for. I dare say Maurice could sell the Virgil frontispiece, but I think it would break his heart.

So before I spread alarm and despondency, I'd very much like to know whether you agree with me, or with the beastly young man in horn-rimmed glasses. I enclose a copy of the list I sent him and of his beastly letter. I'm almost bound to see Maurice and Griselda in the Newt on Saturday, so I'd be most grateful if you could let me know by then what you think.

What makes me so furious is that if I hadn't been trying so hard to be helpful the beastly young man would never have known anything about it.

With very much love,
Reg

♣   ♣   ♣

I felt a trifle anxious on Julia's behalf: knowing that she would wish to take that view of the question becoming to the duty and devotion of a niece, I feared that some provision or other of the Taxes Acts might prevent her doing so. Little as I know of such matters, I had the distinct impression that there was a tax called capital gains tax: it seemed all too likely that it was chargeable on capital gains.

"Yes," said Julia, leaning back and drawing deeply on a Gauloise. "Yes, you're quite right, Hilary, there is such a tax as you mention, and by some oversight on the part of the legislature my aunt Regina is not exempt from it. I am happy to say, however —"

Her remarks were interrupted by the arrival of Selena, who had noted my brief appearance next door and guessed that she would now find me with Julia. Having handed me the keys to Timothy's flat, she sank with perceptible weariness into the remaining armchair. Her pale blond hair, normally brushed to polished smoothness, was rather engagingly tousled and there was a smudge of dust on her nose: she had the expression of a Persian cat which has been having a difficult afternoon.

In response to Julia's sympathetic enquiry, she described the incident which I had lately witnessed in the Clerks' Room: the young man who had fallen from the ladder was the carpenter recently engaged by her Chambers to install new cupboards and bookcases — he had experienced, it seemed, a sudden impulse to measure something; the gentleman on whom he had fallen was her most valued client.

"The carpenter?" Julia looked anxious. "Do you mean the young man with the eyelashes and the Renaissance mouth? Oh dear, I do hope he didn't hurt himself."

"The carpenter," said Selena, "is a fit and agile young man who spends half his time climbing up ladders, and the other half, I dare say, falling off them again. A more suitable object of your concern would be my unfortunate client, who is a merchant banker in his mid-sixties, with very limited experience of being fallen on."

It was plainly regrettable that such a person, no doubt frequently in need of the advice of Chancery Counsel and no doubt with ample resources to pay for it, should incur the smallest inconvenience in the precincts of 62 New Square. Still, he did not appear to have suffered any serious harm: neither Julia nor I could believe that he would deprive himself, on account of so trifling a misadventure, of the benefit of Selena's advice.

"Hmm," said Selena, wrinkling her nose, seeming to draw little comfort from our encouraging remarks.

It soon became clear that the true cause of her dissatisfaction with the afternoon was not the incident with the carpenter and the ladder, which had merely, as it were, added a final flourish to its vexations. Her conference with her client had gone badly: that is to say, she had been unable to assist him with the problem on which he had sought her advice. She felt that he was disappointed in her.

"What kind of problem was it?" asked Julia, preparing to be indignant on her friend's behalf.

"He wants to retire from the chairmanship of his bank, and doesn't know whom to nominate as his successor."

"Oh, but that's absurd — it's obviously not a legal question. How can he expect you to advise him about that?"

"Well, there's slightly more to it than that. He has reason to believe that one of the two potential candidates — this is all, I need hardly say, in the strictest confidence." She paused to settle herself more comfortably in the armchair and looked, for some reason, rather severely in my direction. "Well, I shall name no names. My client, whom I shall refer to as 'my client', is the Chairman of a small but highly respected merchant bank, which I shall refer to as 'the Bank'. On his retirement, his voice will be decisive in the appointment of his successor. There are two possible candidates, both already members of the board of directors, whom I shall refer to as 'A' and 'B,' though those are not their real names. My client has reason to believe that one of them has been guilty of . . . rather serious misconduct."

She again fell silent — the details were apparently almost too shocking to be spoken of. Julia raised an eyebrow, inviting her to continue.

"The business of the Bank, as you'd expect, includes advising on takeovers — if one company's thinking of taking over another, it goes to the Bank for advice on how to go about it and how much to offer. In theory the client company makes the final decision, but in practice the Bank's advice is almost always acted on. And, as of course you know, the announcement of a takeover bid is usually followed by an increase in the price of the shares of the target company — sometimes quite a dramatic increase. So you see, Hilary, one way for you to get very rich would be to find out in advance what the Bank was going to recommend."

"My dear Selena," I said, "it's most kind of you to think of it. I suppose there's a snag of some kind?"

"Well, the snag is that the Bank goes to a good deal of trouble to make sure you don't. It operates, as my client likes to put it, on the basis of a need-to-know system. So buying ice cream for the office boy or chocolates for somebody's secretary, or even dinner at the Savoy for a senior executive, won't do you any good, because they won't have the information you need. My client, until a week ago, believed these

16

systems to be entirely effective, and lived, in that belief, a happy and contented man. But then . . ."

"But then?" said Julia, perceiving some further encouragement to be expected.

"But then one of the Bank's computer people, having nothing better to do and some exciting new software to play with, decided to do an analysis of the takeovers which the Bank had been involved in over the past two years. And the results were rather disturbing, because they showed that in at least eight cases there had been a significant increase, immediately before the bid was announced, in the buying of shares in the target company."

"Phew," said Julia. "And no one had noticed? Not the Stock Exchange or the Department of Trade or anyone?"

"Well, not so far. It's really rather a lesson in the value of moderation. You see, if you look at each case separately, the amounts involved weren't enough to set any alarm bells ringing — never more than one hundred thousand pounds. It's only when you notice that it's happened several times to the same bank —"

"Once may be a misfortune, twice looks like carelessness, and eight times —"

"Really must be insider dealing — which of course is not only most improper but a criminal offence. And the only people who knew about all eight takeovers, apart from my client himself and his personal assistant, who has been with him for twenty years and can be trusted he says, absolutely, are his two potential successors. That is to say — A and B."

The discovery placed her client in the most painful dilemma. Could he leave the Bank, at the conclusion of a long and honourable career, in hands which might be guilty of such a crime against the laws of England and commercial honour? Unthinkable. Equally so to instigate any official inquiry by the Stock Exchange, which might well of itself prove ruinous to the Bank's reputation and interests. The only solution to his problem was to identify the person responsible; but in this Selena had been unable to assist him.

"And I suppose one might say that it's unreasonable of him to expect me to. But you see, he first came to me about a fairly minor matter that I happened to be able to help with and he was evidently rather impressed. Since then he's behaved as if asking my advice is an infallible solution to every problem, which is the sort of attitude one likes to see in one's clients and has had a very invigorating effect on my bank balance. So I don't want him to be disillusioned with me.

"So far as I recall," said Julia, "the specialities mentioned under your name in the Law List do not include clairvoyance. You are, it is generally agreed, unrivalled in our generation in your knowledge of the Companies Acts, but you are not Madame Louisa."

"No," said Selena. "Who is Madame Louisa?"

"Madame Louisa writes the astrology column in the *Daily Scuttle* and has amazing gifts. She predicted this morning, I remember, that you might have frustrations in the workplace."

"I would say," said Selena, "that her gift is for understatement. What did she say about you?"

18

"That I might feel anxious about a business transaction, perhaps involving a relative, and that legal advice would be helpful. That too turns out to be an amazingly accurate prediction, though I'm hoping that in this case the advice in question will be my own." Julia related the disagreement between her aunt and the unhelpful young man from the Revenue.

"But Julia," said Selena, looking puzzled, and with the diffidence of one perhaps trespassing on a friend's area of expertise, "what about the individual exemption? Aren't the first six thousand pounds of capital gains in a fiscal year exempt from tax?"

"Yes, of course," said Julia. "That's why people so often forget that capital gains tax exists — the gains of the small private investor are usually covered by the exemption."

"But then —"

"The claim to tax is on the gains over six thousand pounds. Unfortunately, all the gains were realized in the same financial year."

"On an initial investment of fifteen hundred pounds?"

"Yes, about that."

"But Julia, that means that the gains over the year must have been of the order of one thousand per cent."

"Yes," said Julia. "Yes, when you look at it like that, it's rather impressive, isn't it?"

"Over the same period," said Selena, "the most successful of the investment trusts made gains of just under thirty per cent. How on earth did she do it?"

19

"Just a minute, I'll show you the list of the shares she bought." After a relatively brief search among the papers on her desk, Julia found what she seemed to be looking for and handed it to Selena. "But she obviously didn't tell the man from the Revenue that she was investing on behalf of herself and two other people. If she'd told him that, I don't see how he could dispute that they're entitled to three exemptions. So as long as Maurice and Griselda haven't incurred any other chargeable gains, and as long as the chap from the Revenue doesn't try to say —"

Selena was looking at the sheet of paper in her hand with an expression of perplexity, one would almost have said of dismay.

"Julia, are you quite sure this is the list your aunt sent you?"

"Yes," said Julia. "Why shouldn't it be?"

"Earlier this afternoon, my client handed me a list of the companies which appeared to have been the subject of insider dealing. And all the names on her list are also on his."

CHAPTER
TWO

In the café where I breakfasted on the following Tuesday, on my way to the Public Record Office, someone had left a copy of that day's edition of the *Daily Scuttle*, open at the City page. A photograph at once caught my eye: I could not fail to recognize the cherubic features of the gentleman I had last seen on the floor of the Clerks' Room, in the involuntary embrace of the young carpenter. I made haste to read the accompanying text.

> Sir Robert Renfrew, the Chairman of Renfrews' Bank, is pictured here making his speech of thanks at a dinner held last night in the Guildhall by the Worshipful Company of Thimble and Buttonhook Makers at which he was the guest of honour.
>
> Sir Robert, who is sixty-seven, had been widely expected to use the occasion to drop a broad hint or two as to the identity of his probable successor, a subject on which there has been considerable speculation in the City. Instead, however, he seemed at pains to make it clear that such speculation is premature: he mentioned that he

was in excellent health and emphasized that he was enjoying his job more than ever.

Renfrews' is still a family bank, something of an anachronism in the era of multinational giants. Since its foundation early in the nineteenth century the chairman has always been either a Renfrew or an Albany, the two families being closely linked by marriage. Traditionalists, who include some of the bank's most valued and prestigious clients, hope that Sir Robert's successor will be the present deputy chairman Edgar Albany, fifty-one, educated at Eton and Cambridge and a direct descendant of the bank's founder.

It is thought, however, that most institutional investors would prefer to see Renfrews' facing the twenty-first century under the chairmanship of Geoffrey Bolton, the very able forty-eight-year-old director of corporate finance. Born and brought up in Lancashire, Bolton was wooed back to London five years ago from the Leibnitz Bank of New York to revitalize an investment department which had frankly ceased to sparkle. His success in this area is a personal triumph for Sir Robert, who was directly responsible for his recruitment.

It was thus, entirely by chance, that I first learned the identity of Selena's client and something of the two men whom he suspected.

The remarkable coincidence that the names of the same companies appeared on both their lists had at once seemed to Selena and Julia too remarkable to be a coincidence: they thought it virtually certain that Ricky Farnham had obtained his information from someone who was in some way involved in the insider dealing.

This had placed them in something of a dilemma. They had reached their conclusion on the basis of evidence obtained from two separate and confidential sources: what use, if any, could properly be made of it in connection with the problem troubling Selena's client? None, it went without saying, which might cause Mrs Sheldon the slightest embarrassment; but there could be no harm, thought Julia, in adding a tactfully worded paragraph to her letter, asking if her aunt by any chance happened to know the source of Ricky Farnham's information.

I wondered, as I walked along Chancery Lane towards the Public Record Office, whether she might by now have received an answer. The report in the *Scuttle* had awakened in me a greater degree of curiosity about the insider-dealing affair than I had felt when the two suspects were merely letters of the alphabet. I looked forward with interest to learning whether Mrs Sheldon could shed any light on it.

Selena had kindly invited me to a meeting of the 62 New Square Chambers Restoration Committee, which was to be held at lunchtime in the Corkscrew. The committee, I gathered, consisted of the three most junior members of Chambers — Selena herself, Desmond Ragwort and Michael Cantrip — and was responsible for the overall organization of certain building works intended to be carried out in Chambers during the long vacation. The meeting was also to be attended by a representative of their neighbours in 63 New Square — that is to say, Julia. The proceedings were to include lunch: it was in this aspect of them that I was invited to participate.

The architect of the Corkscrew, as I believe I have mentioned elsewhere, does not seem to have cared much for daylight or windows. Arriving there shortly after midday, I paused for a moment in the doorway to accustom myself to the dimness of the interior after the midsummer sunlight outside.

Selena was sitting at one of the round oak tables between two young men in some respects similar — both thin, and of pale complexion — but at the same time presenting a pleasing contrast, as if created by two different artists: Ragwort by one working in watercolours to convey the subtle tints of autumn; Cantrip by some no less skilled but more impatient draughtsman, using a few strokes of charcoal on a background of white paper. A bottle of Nierstein had already been purchased, and a glass had been filled for me by the time I reached the table.

"Tell me," I said, not wishing to be accused of distracting them from the business for which they were gathered, "what exactly is the purpose of this building work for which you are responsible?"

"We're going to be modernized," said Cantrip triumphantly. "Hot-and-cold running everything and state-of-the-art communication systems. When the twenty-first century hits us, we'll be there waiting to hit back."

"We intend," said Ragwort, "to restore Chambers to the simple yet dignified elegance which prevailed in Lincoln's Inn during, let us say, the reign of the later Stuarts."

These objectives seemed to me to be not identical. I wondered if it might have been prudent, before engaging builders, to make a choice between them.

"Not at all," said Selena. "It's simply a question, you see, of how you look at it. On the one hand, as I hope you know, Hilary, we yield to no one in our respect for the great traditions of the English Bar. On the other hand, it has sometimes occurred to us that it might be possible, without gravely compromising those traditions, to make certain minor improvements to our working environment."

"Such as central heating that actually works," said Ragwort.

"And a proper computer system," said Cantrip, "instead of a couple of laptops that our junior clerk got cheap because they'd been obsolete for ten years."

"And even," said Selena rather wistfully, "somewhere to have a shower before one goes out for the evening. But whenever we suggest anything of that kind — I don't know, Hilary, whether you've ever heard Basil Ptarmigan pronounce the word 'modernization'?"

"Seldom," I said, "and only in accents of the utmost distaste, as if picking up some unpleasant object with his fingertips and holding it as far away as possible." I could imagine that Basil Ptarmigan, QC, the most silken of Chancery Silks, would have little sympathy for any proposal requiring the use of the word.

25

"Basil takes the view," said Ragwort, "that modernization goes hand in hand with reform, and we all know what that leads to. Some of the older members of our Chambers do tend to be a little conservative in their thinking."

"The way they see it," said Cantrip, "everything's been pretty much going to pot since someone went and abolished the rule in Shelley's Case. And that was in 1925."

"And naturally," said Ragwort, "we've always felt that we must defer to their wisdom and experience."

"Because they'd have to put up most of the cash," said Cantrip.

It had seemed that there was an impasse and that dreams of showers and computer systems must remain mere dreams. The possibility of a solution revealed itself unexpectedly, when Ragwort was invited to a small drinks party by Benjamin Dobble —

"Whom, of course, you know," said Ragwort, for Benjamin is a fellow scholar and, I hope I may say, a friend of mine. I have described him elsewhere: he plays too small a part in my present narrative to justify my repeating the description.

The party was intended to celebrate the recent refurbishment of his flat in Grafton Street. His guests had been called upon to admire in particular the oak-panelled cupboards and bookcases, Jacobean in style, which concealed the collection of filing cabinets, computers, printers, fax machines and other impedimenta nowadays considered indispensable to the pursuit of learning. The craftsman responsible for designing and building them, a young man by the name of Terry Carver, had naturally been the guest of honour.

Congratulating Terry Carver on his achievement, Ragwort had been inspired to ask whether he might be interested in carrying out a similar scheme of refurbishment at 62 New Square.

"So Terry came round to Lincoln's Inn," said Selena, "and measured things and took photographs and so on and seemed rather excited at the idea — he said he was thinking Inigo Jones."

"Inigo Jones?" I said. "Isn't that rather early for New Square?"

This comment, however, being thought unconstructive, I hastily withdrew it.

"And in due course he sent us some drawings, showing how we could have as many showers and computer terminals as we liked and at the same time look like a set of Chambers where Lord Nottingham's just invented the Rule against Perpetuities. We showed them to Basil and the others, and they were even more impressed than we'd hoped."

"Absolutely knocked sideways," said Cantrip. "And couldn't wait to get started."

"So they did us the great honour," said Ragwort, looking at the ceiling, "of entrusting us with the organization of the project."

"Well, yes," said Selena. "Because it was clear, of course, that someone was going to have to do a good deal of work to make it all happen, and whatever anyone says about the senior members of our Chambers, no one's ever said they were stupid. So we've had a rather exhausting few months, drawing up specifications and getting permission from the Inn and inviting tenders and so on. But we've finally got it all sorted out, and the builders are starting work at the end of next month."

"My dear Selena," I said, "you sound as if you thought that once the builders arrive your troubles will be over. That is not the universal experience."

"Well, there'll obviously be a certain amount of noise and mess while they're actually there. But they've promised to finish by the end of the long vacation, so it shouldn't be too disruptive."

She leant back and drank her wine, with the serene contentment of a young woman who has agreed on a satisfactory estimate and a convenient timetable, and has never had builders in before.

"It sounds," I said, "as if this young man Terry Carver were very much the lynch pin of your enterprise. Are you sure he's reliable?"

"He does have one or two little failings," said Selena. "His tendency, for example, to flutter his eyelashes in a way that distracts Julia from her Finance Act. And of course his habit of falling on one's clients from the top of ladders. What one has to remember is that he's good at making bookcases."

"According to Benjamin," said Ragwort, "he is not only one of the finest craftsmen in London but extremely dependable."

Knowing that Benjamin, in the matter of eyelashes, is almost as susceptible as Julia, I feared that his judgement might not be entirely objective; but I felt that this too might be thought an unconstructive comment.

Julia joined us soon afterwards, with apologies for her lateness. She had received another letter from her aunt, evidently posted on the way to a further interview with the young man from the Revenue: she had been trying to telephone to learn the outcome, but had found Mrs Sheldon's number constantly engaged.

"I don't suppose," said Selena, "that her letter happens to say anything about those shares?"

"A certain amount," said Julia. "Would you like me to read it to you over lunch?"

"Well . . ." said Selena, looking doubtfully in my direction. She has the curious notion that no one but a fellow member of the Bar can be trusted with a confidence.

I explained to her, as I have already to my readers, that by the purest chance the identity of her client was no longer a secret from me. She gave me a rather sideways look; but with various admonitions unnecessary to repeat she resigned herself to relying on my discretion.

24 High Street
Parsons Haver
West Sussex

Monday, 21st June

Dear Julia,

There is something rather odd, if I may say so, about the tone of your letter — almost as if you

29

thought I'd been doing something wrong. All I've done is buy some shares and sell them again — are you going through one of your Socialist phases? If so, do write and tell Ariadne — she'll be so pleased.

But I'm very glad, of course, that you don't think I have to pay the beastly young man three thousand pounds. I've made an appointment to see him this afternoon, to explain about the shares belonging partly to Maurice and Griselda, and they're both coming round to supper afterwards to hear what he says. We all think you've been most helpful, and we're planning to take you to lunch at the best restaurant in West Sussex next time you're down here.

So I hope you won't think it too ungrateful of me to say that if you don't mind I'd much rather not ask Ricky where he got his information from about the shares. The thing is, you see, that I'm not at all pleased with Ricky at the moment, and I don't want to do anything to make him think that I've stopped not being pleased.

You may say, I suppose, that it's unreasonable of me to be not pleased with him. I know he was only advising us as a friend, in exchange for a few drinks, and perhaps one couldn't expect it all to be confidential in the same way as if one got advice from a solicitor or someone like that. Well, Julia, I don't care what you say, I still don't think it's right for him to go babbling about our affairs to all and sundry.

When I say all and sundry, I mean Isabella del Comino, as she calls herself, though I doubt if that's the name on her birth certificate, or on her marriage certificate, if she has such a thing. Which I dare say she has — men can be complete idiots sometimes.

So far as I know, you've never met Isabella. If you have, it certainly wasn't at my house. She lives at the Old Rectory, on the other side of the churchyard, which she bought two or three years ago from rather good friends of mine. They didn't find it an easy house to sell — it's one of those rambling Victorian places that cost a fortune to heat and maintain properly. The Church Commissioners very sensibly sold it a long time ago, and kept the little house opposite as the Vicarage. And though it's quite a handsome building in its way, I always feel there's something rather cold and forbidding about it — an estate agent would say that there's a fine view of the church, but one can't help thinking of it as a view of the graveyard.

My friends had made all kinds of improvements to it. They'd turned the ground-floor rooms at the back into one long drawing room, with French windows all the way along opening into a big conservatory, and a colour scheme of honeys and apricots. And from there one went into the garden — oh, Julia, it's a shame if you never saw the garden. Griselda had laid it out in an Elizabethan sort of style, using a design in an old book Maurice had given her, and gone to endless trouble to get the right plants for it. I found some antique statues and urns and things, and we all felt we'd made it into something rather special. Griselda looked after it practically as if it were her own — she has quite a good view of it from the roof of her potting shed, so she could always see when something needed doing.

My friends sold the house without ever actually meeting the purchaser. I suppose she must have come down and looked over it before she bought it, but no one seemed to have seen her. Even after she'd bought it, she didn't move in straight away, and there were signs that she was having a good deal of building work done — plumbers' and electricians' vans outside the house, and sounds of hammering and drilling. So everyone was beginning to be rather curious about her.

And then, one morning when I was sitting in the antique shop, Griselda came running in, as white as a sheet, and said there were men at the Rectory levelling the garden.

I could hardly believe it at first, but of course I went back with her to see what was happening, and it was true, they were — just taking a bulldozer across it, destroying everything.

I managed to discourage her from climbing over the wall and lying down in front of the bulldozer — Griselda can be rather physical sometimes — and called out to the man in charge to ask him what he thought they were doing. His answer wasn't at all polite, but I explained to him that we simply didn't want him to get into trouble for destroying plants which might turn out to be valuable. Anyway, I offered him thirty pounds for the ones that were left and he ended by agreeing to fifty, on the understanding that we'd have to remove them that day.

So we spent the day frantically digging up plants in the Rectory garden and running back with them to Griselda's potting shed. Fortunately, it was one of the days when Mrs Tyrrell comes to clean for me, so there were three of us to do it, and by midnight we'd rescued pretty well everything that we minded most about — all the rose trees, and the plants from the physic garden. We shared them out between the three of us and gave some to Maurice. At fifty pounds they were really rather a bargain — some of them were quite valuable — but of course it didn't make up for the garden being destroyed.

The next day they flattened it completely, and began to put up something that involved concrete posts and a lot of wire mesh. We couldn't work out what it was — Griselda said it looked like a cage.

Two or three weeks later there were signs of someone being in occupation, though no one had actually seen her arrive — not even Maurice, whose study looks straight out on to the front drive of the Rectory. But there were lights on in the evening, and the postman said he'd started to deliver letters there.

We're very informal down here in Haver — we don't go in for visiting cards and so forth — but when someone new moves in we usually put a note through the door, introducing ourselves and inviting them to ring us if they need help with anything. So I wrote a short letter along those lines — no, Julia, it was *not* mere curiosity — and walked across to the Rectory to deliver it. And just as I was putting it in the letter box, the door suddenly opened and I found myself facing a fat, pale woman with fat, black ringlets.

When I say that she was fat, I don't so much mean that she was of enormous size but that she gave the impression of being made of fat, all the way through, with no underlying framework of bone or muscle — which, of course, isn't actually possible. She had a rather ugly, squashed button sort of nose — I suppose when she was young people would have called it retroussé — and very small black eyes, like currants in a suet pudding. She was wearing a long black velvet kaftan, of the kind one can buy cheaply in Tangier or expensively in Knightsbridge — it might have been rather elegant, if it hadn't shown so many signs of her being a rather careless eater.

"Good morning, Mrs Sheldon, how nice of you to call," she said. "Won't you come in and have a glass of sherry?"

That looks, when one writes it down, like quite a normal and pleasant thing to say, but it didn't sound like that. There was something gloating, almost sinister, about the way she said it — as if my name were a secret she's been very clever to find out and could use against me in some way.

I accepted, naturally, and she led me through to the conservatory. As we went in, she said, "I hope you don't mind birds?"

Well, as it happens, I do rather. When they're flying about in the open air, I don't mind them at all, but in a confined space with them I get an absurd sense of panic, like you with spiders. I know it's completely irrational, but that doesn't stop me feeling it.

But of course I said, "Not in the least," and followed her into the drawing room.

She had had it entirely redecorated, no doubt at great expense. The walls were covered with a heavily embossed wallpaper — black. The ceiling and woodwork had been repainted — black. There were thick black velvet curtains, and the floor was tiled in black marble. Poor woman, I suppose she'd expected it to look very dramatic, but of course with nothing there to provide contrast, the effect was simply dreary.

I saw at once that Griselda had been perfectly right about the cage. The conservatory and the area beyond it had been turned into an aviary, now occupied by a flock of ravens — I don't know how many exactly, but there must have been at least a dozen. It wouldn't have been so bad if the French windows had been closed, with the ravens safely on the far side — but they were open, and the horrible creatures were flapping and hopping about the drawing room as if they owned the place. The worst of it was, though, that when they weren't moving they were more or less invisible against the black background — I thought that at any moment I might accidentally brush against one. I began, I'm afraid, to feel rather sick, and almost to wish I hadn't come.

She poured me a tumblerful of sherry — such an excessive amount that I couldn't think of it as generous, but more as a device to make me stay longer than I might have chosen — and invited me to sit down. Which I did, with considerable caution, on one of three chaises longues — I need hardly say, upholstered in black — which provided the seating accommodation.

The room was quite sparsely furnished — I couldn't tell whether from choice, or because she hadn't finished unpacking. There were no pictures or ornaments or books. Or, rather, just one book — it looked like one of those old family Bibles, so big you can hardly lift them. Isabella seemed to regard it as an object of interest, or even veneration — she'd put it on its own in a display cabinet at the far end of the room from where we were sitting. I resisted the temptation to ask for a closer look at it — the rest of that end of the room was in deep shadow, which I suspected of harbouring still more of the beastly ravens.

She asked me what I thought of her colour scheme. I said that it was interesting.

"Ah," she said, "I didn't think it would be quite to your taste." She said it with a smile which suggested that her taste was bold and adventurous, while mine was timidly conventional.

"Black's such a difficult colour," I said, "if one isn't an experienced designer."

"Ah, yes," she said, "I know you're the village expert on design."

"That's a far too flattering description," I said. "I haven't worked seriously as a designer since I lived in Paris."

Our conversation might have been more memorable if my attention hadn't been distracted all the time by the flappings and cawings of the birds. Not much more memorable, though, because Isabella is one of those tiresome people who enjoy being mysterious about themselves. Trying to show a polite degree of interest in her, I asked if she had any special reason for choosing Parsons Haver for her retirement — she seemed of the sort of age to have recently retired, though from what profession one wouldn't have cared to speculate.

"Oh," she said, "I haven't exactly retired." And she gave a wouldn't-you-like-to-know little smile, as if knowing her occupation were my dearest wish and I would beg her to tell me.

In case you happen to be tormented by curiosity on the subject, I found out later that the profession from which she had "not exactly retired" was what I would call fortune-telling, but I gather is nowadays called psychic counselling. On this occasion, though, I didn't ask her any more questions about herself but simply invited her to ask me anything she'd like to know about shops and buses and so forth. I did also mention that if she wanted anyone to clean for her, I could thoroughly recommend Mrs Tyrrell — Mrs Tyrrell is a single mother, and I thought she might be pleased to do a few extra hours.

"Oh no, thank you," she said. "Women of that class are such gossips, aren't they?" Women of that class indeed — some people are enough to turn anyone Socialist. "Anyway, I have my niece to do that sort of thing."

"Oh really?" I said, rather surprised to hear that there was another member of the household, and wondering where she was. "How nice for you to have such a devoted niece. I'm afraid mine's far too busy with her practice at the Bar to come and do my housework for me."

"Oh yes, I'd heard you had a clever niece," said Isabella. "Daphne's not clever. She isn't really my niece, she's my cousin's daughter. Still, her mother was more like a sister to me than my damn sister's ever been, so when she died I had to take over Daphne." She talked as if the girl were a servant — not that anyone has servants nowadays and even when they did no well-bred person would have talked about them like that — as if she were some kind of object which Isabella owned.

I said that, whatever the relationship, I looked forward to meeting her.

"Oh, you can see her now, if you like," said Isabella, and shouted "Daphne, come here," like a man calling a dog. A man one wouldn't much like, to a dog he enjoyed ill-treating.

There was a noise of something breaking in the kitchen, and a girl came in — an awkward, skinny little thing, all knees and elbows, somewhere in her early twenties. Not, I have to say, at all a pretty girl — lank brown hair, a poor complexion, a rather receding chin and overprominent front teeth. She had quite large brown eyes, which should have been her best feature, but very listless and watery looking — do always remember, Julia, that the expression "bright with unshed tears" is a most misleading one. Still, I've seen women with fewer natural advantages persuade half London that they were irresistible — a little make-up and a little animation can do wonders.

"Daphne," said Isabella, "this is Mrs Sheldon, who's kindly come to see how we're getting on — say 'How do you do' to her."

The poor girl obediently stammered the words out and then stood jiggling about from one foot to the other, pushing down her skirt with the palms of her hands as if she were hoping to make it cover her knees. It was certainly far too short — I mean, the sort of length one should only wear if one has very nice legs and is wearing pretty underwear — and looked like something she had had in her teens and grown out of. As her hands were moist and not very clean, all she achieved was to make the skirt even grubbier than it already was.

I was trying to think of something kind and encouraging to say to her when something moved in the shadows at the far end of the room. And screeched. And flapped its wings. Something much larger than a raven.

I do strongly advise you, Julia, to try to conquer your feelings about spiders — one really never knows what embarrassments these ridiculous phobias can get one into. As you'll have gathered, I was already more disconcerted than I would have liked by finding myself in the same room as a dozen or so ravens. When I realized that I was also sharing it with a vulture, I came closer to screaming than I care to admit.

"Oh," said Isabella, "this is my friend Roderigo. I do hope he didn't startle you?"

It was all I could do to say "What a handsome creature" and remember an urgent appointment at the Vicarage. And I wouldn't want you, Julia, to find yourself at a similar disadvantage in a situation involving a tarantula.

CHAPTER
THREE

It was Cantrip, misguidedly in my view, who chose at this juncture to refer to the spider episode. I have always refrained, and I hope shall always refrain, from offending the sensibility of my readers with the details of that regrettable incident: I mention merely that it conclusively marked the end of what some would term the more intimate relationship formerly existing between Cantrip and Julia.

"I bet your aunt Reg's thing about birds isn't really as bad as your thing about spiders. I mean, if she'd ever woken up on April Fool's Day and found some witty chap she was chums with had put a stuffed parrot —"

"Cantrip," said Julia, "although the spider episode has left scars on my psyche for which a litigious woman could undoubtedly recover an enormous sum in damages, I have tried for friendship's sake to erase it from my memory. Do you really want to remind me of it?"

"There you are, you see it was simply ages ago, and you're still miffed about it. So what I'm saying is, your aunt Reg can't be anything like as bad about birds as you are about spiders. Because let's face it, if someone took you into a room crawling with spiders, you wouldn't hang about drinking sherry and making small talk, you'd be out in nought seconds flat, screaming like a banshee on bath night."

"I cannot imagine," said Ragwort, "that Mrs Sheldon would in any circumstances allow herself to leave the drawing room of a new acquaintance in the unladylike and precipitate manner you describe."

"No," said Julia, "I'm sure she wouldn't, but that's simply a question of character. I think, as a matter of fact, that she's just as frightened of birds as I am of spiders."

♣　♣　♣

Maurice, of course, also had to call on Isabella — apart from anything else, he's her nearest neighbour. He came round afterwards to tell me about it, shaking like a leaf and needing a stiff gin.

This wasn't because of the vulture, it was because she'd told him that he was a true priest and a man of great spiritual authority. Poor Maurice, he'd been terribly embarrassed — he kept saying "Oh, my God, what would the Bishop say?" and needing more gin every time he thought of it.

She'd also told him that he'd think her a very wicked person and perhaps denounce her as a heretic and blasphemer. He'd tried to explain that he didn't go in for that sort of thing, but she didn't take any notice. She seems to imagine herself as the high priestess of some kind of alternative religion — that's how she claims to have the gift of prophecy. Maurice thought she'd probably got the idea from reading something about the Albigensians.

"And I'm not saying a word against the Albigensians," said Maurice, "who I'm sure were very good people and extremely badly treated. And no one's sorrier than I am about it, so I don't see why I should be cast as some appalling character like St Dominic. Who was a ghastly man, Reg, really perfectly ghastly, and with all my faults I don't think anyone can say I'm like him."

Whatever religion it is, the big leather book seems to be a central feature of it. Maurice asked her if he could have a closer look at it, but she wouldn't let him — "I know, Father Dulcimer, that it is lawful for me to read in your Book, but it is forbidden for you to read in mine." He thinks it's probably part of her fortune-telling paraphernalia — there's a very old form of prophecy, he says, where you open a book and point to a line at random and it tells you what you want to know. It has to be a very important and serious book, of course — the Bible or Virgil's *Aeneid* or something of that sort. What Isabella's is there's no way of knowing — one thing we're pretty sure of is that it isn't the Bible.

She'd ended by saying that though she and Maurice were destined to be adversaries, they were adversaries who respected each other and could perhaps be friends. Poor man, no wonder he needed gin.

♣   ♣   ♣

"Ragwort," said Julia, pausing in her reading, "we look to you for enlightenment on questions of a religious nature. Why should a clergyman object to being called a true priest and told he had great spiritual authority?"

"He would have felt, I imagine," said Ragwort, "that such expressions savoured of the charismatic — happy-clappy music and the Toronto Blessing. People don't much care for that sort of thing in Sussex — not in West Sussex, at any rate."

"And would that also be his objection to the comparison with St Dominic?"

"Not exactly. St Dominic, one would have to say, went to rather different extremes."

♣ ♣ ♣

You'll have gathered, I expect, that neither Maurice nor I was much taken with Isabella, and even if she'd been a perfect angel Griselda wouldn't have forgiven her for destroying the garden. So we were all a little surprised when Ricky began to be quite friendly with her. They'd apparently known each other in London some years ago — she invited him round for drinks soon after she moved in and since then he's been a regular visitor.

Well, of course, Ricky's old enough to choose his friends for himself, and if he enjoys Isabella's company that's no one's business but his own — one just finds it slightly odd, that's all. Apart from anything else, he's always been rather an enthusiast for comfort and good cooking, and I wouldn't imagine there's much of either to be had at the Rectory these days. So presumably there's some other attraction — there are men, I know, who like women who don't wash much.

Still, as I say, that's no one else's business. The only tiresome thing, as far as I'm concerned, is that he put her up for membership of our little boating and tennis club, and she seems to spend half her time there. It's just a small clubhouse and bar overlooking the river, with a couple of tennis courts, but it used to be a convenient place to meet friends if none of us felt like entertaining at home. Now one can only go there if one's in the mood for running into Isabella, which in my case isn't often.

But I suppose it's rather unkind of me to resent her being there so much — without it, so far as I can see, she'd have no social life at all. Since neither she nor Daphne can drive a car, and public transport is beneath her dignity, she doesn't get about much outside the village. She hasn't made many friends since she arrived here, and if she had any before then, they evidently aren't close enough to come and visit her. The fortune-telling business seems to be done mostly by correspondence — Mrs Makepeace at the Post Office says she gets quite a lot of letters.

There is one exception, which I have to admit we're all very curious about. Every four or five weeks or so, at about seven in the evening, a large black Mercedes car with tinted windows drives rather fast into Parsons Haver and straight to the Rectory, where it parks in the part of the drive that is hidden from view by the shrubbery — this could be pure chance, but no one in the village believes that. The man who gets out of it rings at the front door and is let in. After two or three hours, he comes out and drives off again equally fast, heading towards London.

And what everyone wants to know is — who is he? We all agree he must be rich or he wouldn't have a Mercedes. And famous, or he wouldn't need tinted windows. But is he a famous footballer? Or a television personality? Or a member of the Royal Family? These are the main possibilities put forward in the bar of the Newt and Ninepencc — in some circles he's thought to be something far more sinister.

The only person who's actually seen him is Maurice. His study window is the one place in Haver with a clear view of the Rectory doorway, and he's seen the man quite plainly several times. But that's no use to anyone, because Maurice is almost as unobservant as you are — is it something that happens to people who read Classics at Oxford? All he can find to say about the man is that he's an ordinary, middle-aged man, in a City suit.

The visits of the black Mercedes are at irregular intervals, but one can always tell when it's expected. Poor Daphne is banished from the

Rectory at about six o'clock, with just enough money to buy herself a sandwich and a glass of wine, and sits hunched up all evening in a corner of the Newt and Ninepence, looking like a puppy that's been turned outdoors in disgrace and doesn't understand why.

If I see her in there, of course, I say "Good evening" and buy her another glass of wine. She used to be very hesitant about accepting — she was obviously embarrassed, poor girl, that she couldn't buy me one back — but now she seems used to the idea. And she always tells me that she has to stay out all evening, because Aunt Isabella is giving a Personal Reading — one can hear the capital letters — and anyone else in the house would disturb the vibrations. So it looks as if the visits are professional, rather than personal.

It's really too mean of Isabella — if she wants the girl out of the house, she might at least give her enough to go into Brighton to enjoy herself a bit. She doesn't seem even to give her pocket money, let alone any proper wages. I suppose one would say that she pays for Daphne's keep, but she certainly doesn't buy her any clothes — or if she does, it must be at jumble sales. I've never seen Daphne in a pretty dress — really, some of her things look as if she'd got them from someone's dustbin, and not a very clean one either.

I don't say Isabella physically ill treats her — though Griselda's sure she does — but her feet are always rubbed sore from going without stockings in badly fitting shoes, and she often has quite painful-looking peck marks on her face.

Griselda gets very upset and indignant about it all, and says that we ought to do something. But what? One can't ring the RSPCA or the cruelty-to-children people — Daphne's not a child or an animal, she's a grown-up human being, not all that much younger than you are.

And she's not a prisoner — she could leave Isabella tomorrow if she chose. But if she did, where would she go, and what would she do? She isn't qualified for anything — Isabella's brought her up to think that "what they teach you in school isn't true knowledge" and exams aren't important, so of course she's never passed any. And she certainly wouldn't get a job on the strength of her looks or personality.

In any case, she doesn't want to leave. If one asks her what she wants to do with her life, she looks very round-eyed and earnest and says, "I just want to feel I'm caring for someone who needs me." And she seems to believe that Isabella does. Why a grown woman in the prime of life and possession of all her faculties should need a full-time personal attendant I can't very well imagine, but she's somehow persuaded Daphne — "brainwashed" says Griselda — that she's not merely an invalid but practically a saint, who's sacrificed her health in the cause of helping others, and it's an honour and privilege to serve her.

Personally, I don't think there's anything wrong with Isabella's health that a little fresh air and exercise wouldn't put right, and I feel there are probably more effective ways of helping people than telling them to avoid travel when the sun's in Capricorn and distrust dark-haired strangers when Mercury's in the ascendant or whatever it is she does. One can't say that to Daphne though — any criticism of Isabella almost reduces her to tears.

Which does make talking to her rather a strain on one's patience. Her conversation consists almost entirely of quotes from the same source — "Aunt Isabella always says this" and "Aunt Isabella always says that" — as solemnly pronounced as if she were citing scripture. Someone has evidently told her that it's polite to talk to people about things they're interested in, but she hasn't quite grasped how it works in practice. So her idea of conversing politely with me is to tell me Isabella's views about art — "Aunt Isabella says real artists don't need to go to art school, they're born knowing how to paint" — and with Griselda Isabella's views about gardens — "Aunt Isabella says it's cruel to shut flowers up in flower beds, they ought to be allowed to grow naturally." Even if I liked Isabella I'd be getting heartily sick of her.

Blast the woman — I've talked as much about her as if I found her almost as interesting as she thinks she is, and still not explained why I'm not pleased with Ricky.

Well, as I think I told you, the last company that Ricky advised us to invest in was one called Giddly Gadgets. Just after we sold our shares in it, and while we were wondering whether or not to reinvest the proceeds, I happened to be in the wine merchant's, being tempted by a rather delicious claret they had in, much more expensive than I usually buy. I was trying to make up my mind if I could afford half a case of it when Isabella came in, attended by Daphne to do the carrying. She doesn't usually do her own shopping, of course, but the wine merchant counts as grand enough to deserve a personal visit.

I didn't want to stay and make conversation, so when we'd exchanged good-mornings I gave my usual order and told the young man serving me that the claret was really too expensive. And Isabella smiled at me, in that infuriating way she has, as if she knew something you didn't want her to know, and said, "Ah — what a pity Giddly Gadgets didn't do better."

"Yes, isn't it?" I said, and walked out of the shop feeling absolutely furious.

As I say, if Ricky chooses to be friends with Isabella that's entirely his own business, but he must have known that she's the last person on earth whom Griselda or Maurice or I would want to know any details of our financial affairs. And he was absolutely the only person who could possibly have told her about us investing in Giddly Gadgets

— anyway, I rang him to say how surprised I was, and he didn't deny it.

So you'll understand, if you don't mind very much, and think it too ungrateful of me, that I'd rather not ask him where he got his information from.

Yours with much love,
Reg

♣   ♣   ♣

Few of the tables in the Corkscrew were still occupied: it was thought time for the proceedings of the Restoration Committee to be adjourned. Even Julia could not be persuaded to linger for another glass of wine: fearing that the interview with the young man from the Revenue might for some reason have proceeded less smoothly than it should have done, she was anxious to telephone again to find out what had happened.

When she finally succeeded, however, in speaking to her aunt, she found her too preoccupied to discuss income tax: Mrs Sheldon had a funeral to arrange.

CHAPTER
FOUR

My duty to historical truth does not, I think, require me to bewilder my readers with the version of the day's events in Parsons Haver which we received from Julia on the basis of her telephone conversation. A more complete and orderly account is contained in the letter which she read to us when we gathered once more in the Corkscrew on the Thursday evening.

24 High Street
Parsons Haver
West Sussex

Tuesday, 22nd June

Dear Julia,

Do forgive me if I was slightly distrait when you rang earlier — I'd had a rather trying day. I suppose, if I'm going to tell you properly about it, that I ought to start with yesterday evening.

I'd had a most satisfactory interview with the income tax man and it occurred to me, as I was beginning to get supper ready for Maurice and Griselda, that we had a first-rate excuse for champagne. So I ran down to the wine merchant's and bought a couple of bottles, and on my way back I saw poor Daphne, sitting all by herself on a bench outside the Newt and Ninepence.

I was rather surprised to see her there. The black Mercedes had been seen here less than a week ago, and there's usually at least a month between its visits. I didn't feel I had time, though, to stop and talk to her, so I waved and went on my way.

But a moment or two later she came running after me and seized hold of my shopping basket, saying it looked much too heavy for me and I must let her carry it. I could hardly take it back from her by physical force — which it almost seemed I'd have to, she was so determined — so I let her go on carrying it, and she came trotting home beside me.

It seemed churlish, when we got back, simply to say thank you and shut the door in her face, so I invited her in for a sherry. It struck me, as I was giving it to her, that she looked even more miserable than usual — I mean, not just as if she might be going to cry, but as if she'd been crying a good deal already. So I asked her whether anything was the matter.

"Nothing — I don't know — everything," said Daphne, and did indeed burst into tears.

It wasn't easy, between the sobs and the stammers, to make out exactly what she was upset about. In the end, it seemed simply to come down to this — that Isabella was giving her second

"Personal Reading" in the space of a week, and Daphne thought she was dangerously overtaxing her strength. I'm afraid I may have looked rather sceptical.

With more sobs and stammers, Daphne said that I didn't understand. No one understood. No one understood what Isabella put into a Personal Reading. No one knew how exhausted she was for days afterwards. She ought to be still resting after the last one. And Isabella wouldn't admit to physical weakness, and said she just had a cold, but Daphne knew there was something badly wrong with her. She didn't know how, she just knew. And something awful was going to happen, and she didn't know what to do about it. More tears.

Well, what could I do? I thought she was talking nonsense, of course, but I didn't have the heart to pack her off to sit on her own in the Newt. So I told her that if she'd stop crying, I'd lend her a comb and facecloth to tidy herself up with, and she was welcome to stay for supper. I didn't think Maurice or Griselda would mind — I had quite enough food for four, and I knew they both felt sorry for her.

It was a beautiful evening, and the garden's at its best at the moment, so we ate out of doors. It was a very simple meal, just a salmon mousse with salad and new potatoes, and some strawberries afterwards, but it went quite well with the champagne, and everyone seemed to enjoy it.

Daphne had two helpings of everything, and said it was the best meal she'd ever had. Which, without unduly flattering myself, I could all too easily believe, poor girl.

The conversation, I have to admit, didn't exactly sparkle, though I'm sure that Daphne was doing her best — like a little girl at a grown-up party, trying hard to do the proper thing but not quite knowing what it is. She didn't seem to realize that people don't always mean exactly what they say, not because they're insincere but because they're making a joke about something. And she evidently expected Maurice to keep talking about religion, which of course he wouldn't dream of doing over dinner.

A minute or two after ten she said she had to go home, in case Isabella needed her for anything before she went to bed. Maurice said that he ought to be leaving too — he had to be up early to take morning service at a church ten miles away — and suggested that they should keep each other company across the churchyard. Dear Maurice — he'd normally have stayed much later, morning service or no morning service, but he wouldn't have liked to let Daphne go home in the dark by herself.

He rang a few minutes later, to say they were both safely home — he'd waited at the gate of the Rectory to make sure she got in all right, and he'd heard Isabella shout out to Daphne that she wasn't needed and telling her to go to bed. The visitor had evidently left — Maurice said he'd seen no sign of the black Mercedes.

So it sounded as if Daphne's anxieties had been as misplaced as I thought.

I usually wake up at about seven, but this morning I was woken earlier than that by the sound of someone ringing my doorbell. Not just ringing and stopping and going away again, like the postman leaving a parcel, but going on ringing, as if they didn't mean to stop until I'd answered. I looked out of my bedroom window and saw that it was Daphne, so I put on my dressing gown and slippers and went down to let her in.

She was in such a state of agitation, and stammering so badly, poor girl, that I could make no sense at all of what she was trying to say. All I could gather was that something was seriously wrong — or at least that she thought there was — and she wanted me to come straight back with her to the Rectory. So without being sure there was any real urgency, but not liking to take a chance on it, I put on my raincoat over my dressing gown and ran back with her across the churchyard.

She'd left the front door open. We went straight in, and through the hallway to the black drawing room.

The first thing I noticed was the smell — it was the first thing anyone would have noticed. A perfectly disgusting smell, acrid and sweet at the same time, mainly, I suppose, of bird droppings, but as if someone had tried to sweeten it with something else — incense or camphor or something like that. The second thing I noticed was the vulture, perched on the back of one of the chaises longues. The third was Isabella, lolling on another of them, dressed in the kaftan she'd worn on my first visit, with her little black eyes staring at me without blinking, out of her white pudding face. I almost apologized for my intrusion.

"She's been sitting there like that since I came down this morning," said Daphne. "She doesn't seem to hear what I say to her. There's something wrong with her."

I knew straight away what was wrong with her, and I could hardly believe that Daphne still hadn't realized. I tried taking her pulse, and the other things they tell one to do in first-aid classes, but I already knew she was dead. The vulture knew it too, and was looking at Isabella in a way I didn't much care for.

I didn't think I was the right person to break the news — I asked Daphne who her aunt's doctor was.

"Aunt Isabella doesn't believe in doctors," she said, looking more frightened than ever. "She says that Nature has a cure for everything if you know how to look for it."

I said that nonetheless her aunt must have professional attention, and sent her off in the end to fetch Dr Selkirk. He's not the doctor I'd normally call — a bad-tempered little Scotsman, semi-retired, with a bee in his bonnet about keeping fit, and not much in the way of a bedside manner — but he was the one who lived nearest. I knew at that hour of the morning he was more likely to answer the doorbell than the telephone, and I thought that with any luck she could bring him back to the Rectory in ten minutes or so.

If I'd gone myself, I could have probably persuaded him more quickly, but I couldn't leave poor Daphne on her own with a corpse, and we couldn't both go. I've lived in Egypt and Syria, and I've seen what buzzards can do. So someone had to stay and discourage the vulture.

I don't know quite how long I waited for them — it seemed a good deal more than the *mauvais quart d'heure* I'd bargained for. Isabella still seemed to be staring at me with her little black-currant eyes, and from time to time the horrible Roderigo spread his wings and screeched at me. Having only my nightclothes on under my raincoat made me feel ridiculously defenceless, and I wished I'd something more effective than my bare hands to ward him off with if he tried to challenge me for his breakfast.

The worst thing of all, though, was still the smell — it wasn't simply disgusting but somehow narcotic, so that I felt dizzy as well as sick from it. I wondered if Isabella and her visitor had been smoking marijuana — I suppose it would be quite an effective way to heighten the atmosphere for a séance, or whatever one's supposed to call it. It's some years since I smoked any, and I don't remember the effects being so unpleasant — but that was in Paris and in better company.

There were no ashtrays, though, and no traces of smoke in the room, so perhaps I was wrong about that. There weren't any dirty glasses, either, which struck me as rather odd. Whatever else one might say about Isabella, I wouldn't have thought she'd have sat all evening with a visitor without offering him a drink, and having one herself. Anyway, there were two empty champagne bottles in the wastepaper basket.

And Daphne had been sent straight to bed when she got home the night before, so she couldn't have washed them then, and she certainly wouldn't have stopped to do it after she found Isabella in the morning.

Well, of course, it wasn't really at all odd — it simply meant that Isabella had washed the glasses herself, and then come back and sat down again on the chaise longue. That's not at all an odd thing to do — it's what I'd have done myself. Just not what I'd have expected Isabella to do — I'd have bet almost any sum you like to mention that she'd have left them for Daphne. Which shows how one can misjudge people. Or perhaps she'd just taken them through to the kitchen, and left them there to be washed.

It occurred to me, thinking of the kitchen, that I might find something there that I could use to ward off Roderigo. So I went quickly in there, leaving the door open so that I could keep an eye on him, and found just what I wanted — a long-handled broom, which made me feel much braver. But no dirty glasses anywhere, so Isabella must have washed them up after all. And yet somehow I still just couldn't imagine her doing it, so I decided that it must have been her visitor — the man in the black Mercedes.

Dr Selkirk, when he at last arrived, declined to examine the patient in the presence of the vulture. At the cost of several savage pecks, Daphne managed to remove the bird to the conservatory. After that, we waited at the far end of the room while the doctor carried out his examination.

"Heart," he said, when he'd finished. "What did she expect, carrying all that weight?" He seldom misses a chance to point out the dangers of obesity.

"Will she have to go to hospital?" asked poor Daphne.

"It's not the hospital she's needing," said Selkirk, with his usual tact. "It's the undertaker's. She's dead, lassie — been dead for hours."

And poor Daphne threw herself down on the floor and howled.

You'll understand by this time why it's been a trying day. It's now nearly midnight, and I thought when I came to bed that I'd go straight to sleep. But I found I couldn't, and decided to write to you instead.

The funeral's on Friday, and with Daphne having no close family I somehow feel responsible for seeing that it all goes properly. There are all sorts of things that I could quite reasonably be lying awake and worrying about — like how to make Daphne presentable for it, and what to give people to eat, and whether we can find anyone to say a few words about how nice Isabella was.

What seems to be stopping me from sleeping, though, isn't any of those things but a perfectly idiotic question of no importance at all, which is nagging away at me like a clue in the crossword that one hasn't managed to get the answer to. As soon as I close my eyes, the absurd question which comes into my head and starts buzzing round there is, "Do men with Mercedes cars usually wash their own glasses?"

Yours with very much love,

Reg

♣   ♣   ♣

"Dear me," said Selena, turning her wineglass between her fingers, "it almost sounds as if she thought —"

"She can't really be suggesting —" said Ragwort.

"She thinks there's something fishy about it," said Cantrip, his eyes brightening with innocent enthusiasm at the thought of homicide. "The way she sees it, when you're rich enough to have a Mercedes, you leave the dirty work to someone else. So if you suddenly start offering to help with the washing up, it's a definite sign of fishiness. Bet you anything she's right."

61

"On the other hand," said Selena, "isn't it just possible that it was simply an act of politeness?"

"Though perhaps," said Ragwort, "a rather officious one. One doesn't normally offer to do the washing up if one's simply been having drinks with someone — one would think they might feel embarrassed if they hadn't tidied the kitchen. It's different, of course, if they're family, or if one's staying the night."

"Right," said Cantrip. "So he didn't do it to be polite, he did it because Isabella's had cyanide in the bottom."

"Surely not cyanide?" said Julia. "According to all that I have read on the subject — which I may say includes the complete works of the late Dame Agatha Christie and other almost equally distinguished authorities — the effect of cyanide is virtually instantaneous. When Maurice took Daphne home, the black Mercedes had already gone and Isabella was still well enough to shout out to Daphne that she didn't want her for anything."

"Oh, all right then," said Cantrip, "arsenic or something — there are lots of poisons that take an hour or two to work. So at some stage in his chat with Isabella he slips whatever it is into her glass and sticks around until she's finished drinking it. Then he does his new man bit and washes up the glasses before he goes. He drives off, and Daphne and the Reverend get back ten minutes later, before whatever it is has started to work."

"I defer," said Selena, "to those who have read more widely than I have on the subject, but isn't it considered usual for murderers to have some sort of motive?"

"Certainly," said Julia. "But Isabella sounds like the sort of woman practically everyone wants to murder."

"But not the man in the black Mercedes. He was a regular client and presumably valued her advice. Why should a satisfied client want to murder his fortune-teller?"

"Lots of reasons," said Cantrip. "I expect she told him it was a good day for travel and romance and he'd got stuck in traffic on the M21 and had a blazing row with his bird. So he got miffed and poisoned her. Which is good, because now you can do your ace detective bit, Hilary, and unmask the villain and put it all in a book. 'The Case of the Vulture, the Vicar and the Virgin' is what you want to call it, and you'd better make this Daphne bird a gorgeous-looking blonde. Then you'll make pots of money out of it and you can take us out to dinner."

"My dear Cantrip," I said, "alluring though these prospects are, I fear I must disappoint you. Julia's aunt Regina is without question a shrewd and observant woman, but I think that in the present case she is being unduly fanciful. There are many possible explanations, all more commonplace and therefore more probable than murder, for the absence of unwashed glasses. I see no reason to doubt that Isabella died, as most people do, from perfectly natural causes."

As I have already admitted to my readers, during my investigation of these events I was on several occasions entirely mistaken.

CHAPTER
FIVE

DEL COMINO — Isabella, suddenly on 22nd June at her home in Sussex. A wonderful and caring person whose great gifts as a healer and teacher were devoted to helping others. Her wisdom and guidance will be missed above all by her niece, Daphne, who will humbly but proudly strive to continue her work. Funeral 12 noon on Friday, 25th June, at St Ethel's Church, Parsons Haver.

[Deaths column of *The Times*]

It was a Friday suitable to funerals, the sky sombre with the threat of unseasonable rain and an unpleasant clamminess in the air. Rather earlier than usual — a document crucial to my researches had been capriciously removed to Kew — I left the Public Record Office and made my way to the coffeehouse at the top of Chancery Lane, expecting it to be some time before I was joined there by any of my friends.

Soon afterwards, however, Selena appeared and began to talk about men, expressing herself on that subject with unusual bitterness. Thinking that this must signify some unhappy rift in her relationship with my young friend and colleague Sebastian Verity, the customary companion of her idler moments, I enquired with some concern what he had done to displease her.

"When I speak of men," said Selena, "I do not mean Sebastian. Sebastian is not a man in the sense in which I am at present using that term — that is to say, he is not a man who undertakes any kind of building work. Three weeks ago I arranged to have a site meeting at nine-thirty this morning with the carpenter, the plumber and the electrician, to work out exactly what was going to be done when and how they were all going to fit in together. Since when, rather than cancel it, I've turned down a very nice little brief in the Companies Court. And now the plumber's rung up to say that his van's broken down and he can't be here before midday. And the electrician's rung up to say that he has an emergency in High Barnet and can't be here until the afternoon. And the carpenter's rung up to say that he has a family bereavement and can't be here at all. Hilary, do you think men in the building trade always behave like this?"

"No, no," I said soothingly. "I'm sure it's most unusual." What was unusual, from all I had ever heard of such matters, was not their failure to arrive but their telephoning to give notice of it; I did not think it constructive to mention this.

"Still, I suppose there's a bright side. Sir Robert Renfrew's suddenly decided he wants another conference — he's coming round at eleven-thirty. At least I don't have to worry about him being showered with carpenters." She gave a small sigh, as if nonetheless expecting the conference to present her with further troubles.

I asked if Sir Robert was still expecting her to advise him on the choice of his successor.

"I'm afraid so. His latest idea is that if I meet the two directors concerned I'll somehow be able to tell which of them is the insider dealer. He's bringing them along so that I can have a look at them. They don't know that's why, of course — ostensibly I'm advising on the documents for the next takeover."

"It's gratifying, at least, that he has such faith in your judgement."

"Well, it would be if it weren't utterly absurd — I'm beginning to feel like the girl in the fairy story who was expected to spin straw into gold."

Julia arrived: she had received a further letter from her aunt.

24 High Street
Parsons Haver
West Sussex

Thursday, 24th June

Dear Julia,

I had a rather strange conversation with Ricky yesterday, and he told me why he advised us to buy those shares you were interested in — this is the first chance I've had to sit down and write to you about it. I seem to have spent as much time on Isabella's funeral as if she'd been my dearest friend — which, as you know, she wasn't.

Maurice is in rather the same position — he's been spending as much time on it as if she'd been his most devout parishioner, which she also wasn't. Still, it does make things a bit easier that he's going to conduct the service, and that it's going to be at St Ethel's. I'd have expected her to want Stonehenge, with the Archdruid presiding, but Daphne seems quite sure she'd have wanted Maurice to do it — "She always said you were her adversary, Father Dulcimer, but an honourable adversary and a true priest." Oh dear, poor Maurice.

He seems at the moment to be the only person who can deal with Daphne — she's still very upset, poor girl. Understandably, of course, as Isabella was all she had, even if — well, never mind. I brought her back here with me on Tuesday morning and Mrs Tyrrell fed her on tea and chocolate cake while I rang the undertakers and so on, but it was only when Maurice arrived that she began to calm down at all. I dare say Isabella would have seen this as a sign of his "great spiritual authority".

He asked Daphne the name of her aunt's solicitor — a Mr Godwin, living in London — and rang him up and told him what had happened. It seems that Isabella made a will about two years ago, soon after she moved here, and Mr Godwin is appointed the executor — it doesn't say anything about funeral arrangements, except that she wanted to be buried rather than cremated. Mr Godwin said he couldn't come down for the funeral, but he'd be getting in touch with Daphne in due course.

He was rather cagey about the provisions of the will, but Maurice thought it sounded as if Daphne didn't have much to worry about financially — it sets up some kind of trust and she'll get the income from the whole estate. She doesn't have much for immediate living expenses — just sixty pounds or so that Isabella had in her handbag — but Maurice has had a word with Mr Iqbal at the supermarket, and she can go on using Isabella's account there for the next three or four weeks, until it's all sorted out.

There didn't seem to be anyone else to be personally notified of Isabella's death — she'd apparently never been married, though the name she was born with turns out to have been Isabel Cummings. Her only sister died a year or two ago. But Daphne was very anxious to have it announced in all the newspapers, national as well as local, and wanted Maurice to help her with getting the wording right.

So he told her to write out what she wanted to say and said he'd come back later and look it over. I settled her down in the garden, with a notepad and a couple of ballpoint pens, and left her to work on it.

After three hours or so she came back into the house, with ink all over her face from chewing on the ballpoint, and showed me what she'd written. It ran to about a dozen foolscap pages — at a guess, roughly twice what *The Times* would allow for a senior statesman or Nobel Prize winner. There wasn't much in the way of factual detail — when Isabella was born, or where she'd lived, or what she'd actually done that was at all remarkable — but a great deal about what a wonderful, caring person she'd been, and a wide selection of her views on life, death, and the nature of the universe.

I felt I had to say that it was on the long side.

Tears of indignation. Daphne said that Aunt Isabella had been a wonderful person, and she ought to have a proper obituary — meaning, I gather, a full page in *The Times*. Aunt Isabella would have *wanted* a proper obituary, not a stupid little two-line notice, as if she were just anybody, and if she couldn't have one it wasn't fair.

At this stage, luckily, Maurice came back. I must say, he coped splendidly. Truly gifted and remarkable people, he said, very seldom get the recognition they deserve in their own time. Some of the greatest thinkers and prophets, including Socrates and the founder of the Christian Church, would quite possibly not have been given a full-page obituary in *The Times*. *The Times* — and all the other newspapers, even the *Guardian* — were essentially establishment minded and conservative in their thinking, and couldn't be expected to appreciate someone whose ideas leapt over the traditional boundaries. After about an hour of this, Daphne agreed to cut down what she'd written to a length which could be inserted at reasonable cost in the deaths column.

She stayed here all day and Griselda joined us for supper and to offer condolences. I'm afraid that by the time we'd finished I was rather longing to have the house to myself again, but it seemed wretched for Daphne to have to go back and spend the night on her own at the Rectory. The undertakers had removed the body, of course, but even so — I felt I had to ask if she'd like to sleep in the spare bedroom.

"Oh no," she said, "I have to stay at the Rectory. If Aunt Isabella's dead, I'm the Custodian."

"You could go and put out food for the birds," I said, "and then come back here."

"Not of the birds," she said, looking very anxious and solemn. "Of the Book. I'm the Custodian of the Book."

So I didn't feel I had to argue any more about it. Griselda very kindly walked back to the Rectory with her, and I went off to bed expecting to go straight to sleep.

But as you know I didn't, and instead sat up writing you a ridiculous letter all about dirty glasses — please take no notice, it was simply because I was tired.

I woke up next morning worrying about something completely different — who was going to give the eulogy at Isabella's funeral? You know the kind of thing I mean — a little speech about nice things she'd done and how everyone would miss her.

What really worried me was that if there was no one else Daphne might expect me to do it, and I'd have to say no. It's all very well for Maurice — clergymen have to get used to saying things they don't mean, just like lawyers — but I simply didn't think I could do it.

And then I thought of Ricky. It seemed like rather a brainwave, because he'd known her longer than anyone else in Haver and was actually a friend of hers. So I rang Maurice and asked him to sound out Ricky to make sure he'd say yes if Daphne asked him to do it. Maurice said it would be better if I did the sounding out — he'd already talked to Ricky and felt that he'd like it if I got in touch.

So I rang Ricky and explained that I was helping Daphne with the funeral arrangements and there were one or two things it would be nice to discuss with him. I was really rather glad to have a reason for ringing him — I thought he might be feeling upset about Isabella and want someone to talk to, and I wouldn't have liked him to feel he couldn't come round and see me just because I'd been a bit cross with him. On the other hand, not being sure exactly what terms he'd been on with her, I couldn't very well offer anything like formal condolences.

He came round bringing a bottle of Sancerre, and we sat out in the garden drinking it. I still didn't quite know what to say about Isabella. In the end, I thought that the best thing was simply to begin by talking about the funeral arrangements, and leave it to him to say how sad he was she was dead, or whatever he wanted to say. Instead of that, he suddenly interrupted me, and said, "Reg — about those shares you thought I told her about."

Of course I told him not to be silly — it was all water under the bridge and there was no need to mention it.

"No," he said. "No, I want to explain — I didn't tell Isabella about those shares."

"Now really, Ricky," I said, almost beginning to feel a bit impatient, because after all no one else could have done.

"I didn't tell her about them," said Ricky. "She told me."

Not long after she moved here, and she and Ricky renewed their acquaintance, she'd said that she'd like to give him a present — he was a friend, and she liked to give presents to her friends. The present was simply a free prediction — the shareholders in a particular company were going to have something to celebrate within the next month — he could make as much or as little of it as he liked.

Well, Ricky couldn't see any reason for the shares to go up, but so that she wouldn't be offended he bought a few. A couple of weeks later there was a takeover bid, and they doubled in value almost overnight. By the time Maurice and Griselda and I asked him for his advice, this had happened three or four times and he thought that the best thing he could do for us was to give us the benefit of Isabella's predictions.

"But look here," I said. "You don't actually believe that Isabella could foretell the future?" From the way he'd told me the story, it seemed to be the only explanation.

"Oh," said Ricky, "anyone can foretell the future, if their information's good enough."

According to Ricky, Isabella hadn't always been a fortune-teller. In her younger days, she was a hostess at a London nightclub which was popular at that time with businessmen and stockbrokers and so on. In the course of her conversations with customers — well yes, Julia, I think that probably is a slightly expurgated version — she learnt a great deal about what was going on in financial circles, including a lot of things that no one was supposed to know were going on and some things that weren't supposed to be going on at all. That, in Ricky's view, was the basis of her success as a fortune-teller.

I was surprised, if her information was as reliable as that, that she hadn't simply used it to make money on the stock market, instead of bothering with the fortunetelling business. But she seems to have had some kind of superstition about that — she thought it would be unlucky for her to invest in shares herself, and she never did.

"But Ricky," I said, "all this must have been at least twenty or thirty years ago. How could she still go on getting information?"

"Information's like money," said Ricky. "Once you've got it, you can use it to get more. You can buy one secret by keeping another. 'I'm keeping your secret because you're my friend — prove you're my friend by telling me —' Well, whatever it is you want."

I thought this was all beginning to sound rather unpleasant — almost as if Isabella had been a professional blackmailer.

"Yes," said Ricky. "That's right. That's what she was. There must be quite a number of people who aren't sorry she's dead — as a matter of fact, I'm one of them. I've had a pretty rotten two years of it, Reg."

I didn't really feel, after this, that I could ask him to deliver the eulogy.

♣   ♣   ♣

Selena had allowed her first cup of coffee to grow cold. She ordered another and sat gazing at it with a look of judicial severity, as if it were a witness she suspected of being evasive.

"According to Madame Louisa," said Julia, "this ought to be a good day for me to solve problems. But she doesn't seem to mean that I can be any help with yours — knowing that Ricky Farnham's information came from Isabella doesn't really take you any further."

74

"Oh," said Selena, "I wouldn't say that exactly. At least it means I know what question I'm trying to answer. I thought what I had to guess was which of the directors wanted money enough to take the risk of insider dealing. Whereas what I actually have to guess is which of them was being blackmailed by Isabella into giving her confidential information."

"You sound quite sure that that's what was happening."

"How else could she have known about the shares? Unless she really did have prophetic powers, of course — but it would be rather odd, wouldn't it, if they only applied to takeovers involving one particular investment bank?"

"But how could she make use of the information if she never invested in the stock market?"

"Oh, by selling it — that's to say, by passing it on to one or two favoured clients in the form of a psychic prediction. But the fee, I imagine, would have been considerably larger than people usually get for crystal gazing or reading tea leaves. It's really rather clever — it would be almost impossible to prove that any offence had been committed."

"Well," said Julia, "if you'd like to tell your client about Isabella, I don't see any reason why you shouldn't — it can't cause any embarrassment to my aunt."

"No," said Selena, frowning slightly. "No, I suppose not, but — all the same, I don't think I'll tell him. What he knows at present is that one of his co-directors is guilty of insider dealing. He doesn't know which and it's making him very unhappy. If I tell him about Isabella, he'll know that one or the other of them must also be guilty of something else — something serious enough to be blackmailed for — and he still won't know which. I don't think that's going to make him feel any happier. And since it's the duty of Counsel, so far as humanly possible, to keep the client happy, I'm not going to tell him."

Her decision was taken, as my readers will have observed, with full and proper regard to the interests of her client. If I say that it might have been better had she decided otherwise, I speak with the benefit of hindsight.

♣　♣　♣

Anyway, as it turned out, I needn't have worried at all about the eulogy — Daphne wants to do it herself. There's no reason why she shouldn't, of course — we all just assumed that she'd be too upset, and nervous of speaking in public.

The only problem now is making her look presentable — we really can't let her go to the funeral looking like some sort of vagrant, especially if all Isabella's friends from London are going to be there. So I'm giving her my grey silk Chanel dress, with the little jacket — I'd have to lose half a stone to wear it again and I'm quite resigned to never doing that.

I've told her to come round here to change into it, in good time for me to see that it fits properly — it needed a bit of taking in — so I'll be able to make sure she's properly washed and brushed and doesn't have a chance to get it dirty before the funeral.

She had some idea at first that this wasn't a suitable time to be worrying about her appearance, but I told her that it would be disrespectful to Isabella not to try to look her best. I said that if my niece didn't wash her hair and wear a nice dress for my funeral I'd be so cross I'd jump out of my coffin — and I would, so don't dare forget it when the time comes. Anyway, Maurice said he agreed with me and since, in Daphne's eyes, he is now the fount of all wisdom, there was no further argument.

We've also persuaded her to invite people here, rather than the Rectory, for something to eat and drink afterwards. The only room for entertaining guests at the Rectory is the drawing room, where Isabella died — it really would be too macabre. It's absolutely typical of Isabella — oh dear, I know the poor woman didn't do it on purpose, but it's quite the most inconvenient room for anyone to die in.

I've no idea how many there'll be. Daphne seems to be expecting hundreds — "all the people Aunt Isabella helped so much" — though after what Ricky's told me I'm not at all sure how many that means. I'm simply going to assume that I'm catering for about three dozen — if it's a hopeless underestimate, she'll just have to be selective about who she asks back.

Anyway, I'm not doing anything elaborate — mostly sandwiches, with a choice between ham and chicken and prawns and so on. And some stuffed eggs and some cheese puffs and odds and ends like that. And some little éclairs, in case they want something sweet. And Daphne says she's bringing some sponge cakes, made from a recipe Isabella taught her.

Mrs Tyrrell's coming in to help, though it isn't one of her mornings, and won't let me pay her for it — something to do with Daphne being an orphan. And Griselda's doing all the flowers, of course.

I must admit, I'm very curious to see all these friends of Isabella's. I'll let you know in due course how it all goes.

Yours with much love,
Reg

♣   ♣   ♣

"I remember your aunt's little éclairs," said Selena dreamily. "Do you think we could get ourselves invited?"

"Too late," said Julia. "The service starts at twelve and it's already twenty past eleven. Even if you drove —"

"Twenty past — ? Oh Lord," said Selena, and left in haste for her conference.

Julia and I finished our coffee and returned to Lincoln's Inn at a more leisurely pace. We were in time to see a large black Mercedes motor car draw up opposite the entrance to 62 New Square.

CHAPTER
SIX

It looked like a funeral procession: four dark-suited men emerged from the long black motor car and walked silently, in single file, towards the steps leading up to the main doorway.

From the doorway of 63 New Square, Julia and I had no difficulty in observing them. They were led by an elderly gentleman, whom I recognized as the senior partner in a firm of City solicitors — his name, as I recalled, was Mr Vavasour — and who was, I assumed, the solicitor instructing Selena on behalf of Sir Robert Renfrew. He was followed by Sir Robert Renfrew himself. I concluded that the other two were Sir Robert's co-directors and potential successors — Edgar Albany and Geoffrey Bolton.

They might have been chosen to illustrate the characteristic differences between those of Saxon and those of Celtic descent. The one I thought of as Saxon was a little over six feet in height, heavily built and of florid complexion, his face egg-shaped under thinning fair hair, with blue eyes as round as marbles and a small rosebud mouth curiously inappropriate in the face of a middle-aged man. He walked rather stiffly, always looking straight ahead, as if not wishing to appear in any way impressed by his surroundings. Sir Robert, turning at the top of the steps to make some remark to him, addressed him as Edgar.

By a process of elimination, then, the other must be Geoffrey Bolton. He was several inches shorter than his rival and lighter boned, but giving the impression of a certain muscularity. His complexion was rather pale, his hair and eyebrows very black by contrast. Though I had read in the *Scuttle* that he was only five years younger than Albany, the resilience of his step and the alertness of his expression made the difference appear greater — at a distance one might almost have taken him for an undergraduate, still eager and curious.

And yet, despite these differences, either of them might reasonably have been described as "a middle-aged man in a City suit"; neither had any physical characteristic so remarkable that some reference to it would necessarily be added to that description; either, in short, might be the man whom the Reverend Maurice had seen emerging from the black Mercedes on its visits to Isabella.

That the mysterious visitor had been one or the other of them I already had little doubt. One of the directors of Renfrews' had been supplying Isabella with confidential information: he must therefore have been in some form of regular communication with her. If one of them owned or habitually drove a black Mercedes, it would be perverse to imagine that her only regular visitor from outside Parsons Haver had been someone entirely different, driving by pure coincidence a black motor car of the same expensive and accordingly unusual make.

I had only to discover which of the directors was the owner of the car and I would at once know the answer to the problem which was so much troubling Selena.

There was one obstacle, however, to my reaching an immediate solution: neither Albany nor Bolton had on this occasion actually been driving the car. The driver was a young woman, who remained in the driving seat while the four men descended. Having set down her passengers, she manoeuvred the car into a parking space in the middle of Old Square and set off on foot in the direction of the gateway to Lincoln's Inn Fields. She walked briskly, as if with some definite objective.

Though there might have been other ways of learning who owned the Mercedes, the Scholar in pursuit of knowledge is impatient of any delay. Bidding a hasty good-bye to Julia, I set off at a similar pace in the same direction.

The young woman went through the gateway and was hidden from my view, but came in sight again when I reached the Fields — a tall, slim figure in a beige raincoat, her fair hair drawn back to the nape of her neck in some kind of knot or chignon. The athletic vigour of her stride began to suggest to me that she intended to walk some distance, perhaps, after all, despite the threatening sky, only for the sake of exercise. It was with some relief that I saw her enter the small museum on the north side of the Fields founded by the late Sir John Soane.

There is a book, in the entrance hall of the museum, in which visitors are invited to inscribe their names. I noticed, as I signed, that the name above mine, neatly written, with a fountain pen rather than a ballpoint, was Katharine Tavistock, with an address in Islington.

Not seeing her in any of the ground-floor rooms, I climbed the winding staircase to the first floor, my progress a little impeded by enthusiastic groups of tourists and school-children. I eventually caught up with her in the Picture Room, where she appeared absorbed in the series of paintings by Hogarth known collectively as the *Rake's Progress*. Concealing myself behind a conveniently placed statue of Apollo, I was able to study her unobserved while considering how I should approach her.

She was older than I had at first imagined — not less, though perhaps not much more than forty — and too large boned and large featured to be, or ever have been considered, beautiful. She was wearing a severely tailored trouser suit — no doubt expensive, but seeming designed to convey competence and professional standing rather than any interest in allurement. Some quality about her made me dismiss the idea of a matrimonial connection with any of her former passengers; and yet she did not quite look like a person employed solely as a driver. I decided that she must be the personal assistant of whom Selena had spoken and in whom Sir Robert had expressed such absolute trust.

When finally she turned away from the misadventures of Tom Rakewell, I stepped forward, so that for the first time we were face to face. "Miss Tavistock," I cried. "What an unexpected pleasure — are you playing truant from your office?"

Few people have the self-possession, when warmly greeted by name, to disclaim all acquaintance with the person addressing them: Miss Tavistock did not prove to be one of them. To have forgotten merely my name would have been enough to embarrass her; to have forgotten me entirely, when I so clearly remembered her, was a discourtesy unthinkable to admit. With a blush and an anxious smile, she entered on an explanation for her presence in the museum.

"Oh no, not really — I had to bring Sir Robert to a meeting in Lincoln's Inn, and two of the directors, and of course I have to pick them up again afterwards, so I thought I'd look in here and see how poor Tom Rakewell was getting on. I usually do that when we're in this part of the world."

"Are you hoping for a happy ending? One day you'll come in and find a picture showing him reformed, and married to Sarah, and living comfortably and respectably ever after?"

"Well, not quite that. Though as a matter of fact, you know, I think it would be a more realistic ending. Tom's quite an ordinary sort of person — he's not really wicked, not wicked on principle like Lovelace or the Vicomte de Valmont. He's just selfish and greedy and — well, not terribly bright. I've never actually met anyone like the Vicomte de Valmont," she said, sounding as if it were something she rather regretted, "but of course I've met lots of people like Tom. And they usually end up being respectable, unless they're very unlucky."

Though she seemed to accept it as natural that I should remain in her company, I judged it prudent to approach the subject I wished to speak of by a slightly circuitous route. I began, since it was clearly an interest of hers, by talking of the eighteenth-century novel; from there it was an easy step to the drama of the same period; this allowed me to refer to the celebrated performance of David Garrick in the role of King Lear; having mentioned Lear, I felt able to enquire, as I hoped apparently *en passant*, whether Sir Robert had said anything further of his plans for retirement.

She smiled, evidently not doubting that my question showed merely a friendly interest in a subject of which she had spoken to me in some previous conversation, now unaccountably forgotten.

"Poor Sir Robert, I suppose he does feel rather like that about it — having to give up his kingdom and not knowing which of his daughters deserves to get it. But it wouldn't really be fair, you know, to think of Mr Albany and Mr Bolton as anything like Goneril and Regan."

I had no difficulty, after this, in encouraging her to go on talking about them — more freely, perhaps, than she would have done if she had not still felt embarrassed by her inability to remember who I was.

It appeared that Edgar Albany was related to Sir Robert both by blood and by marriage. His great-grandmother had been a Renfrew who had married an Albany: I gathered from Miss Tavistock's

84

discreet summary of the circumstances that she had done so to improve her social position. His aunt, the Chairman's wife, was an Albany who had married a Renfrew: I gathered from an even more discreet summary that she had done so to improve her financial position.

Geoffrey Bolton's background was less distinguished — indeed, Edgar Albany sometimes said that he had no background. He had been born, as one could tell from his accent, in Lancashire, and his parents had not been the sort of people that one expected to have heard of.

"Which of course," said Miss Tavistock with sudden asperity, "may reflect rather well on them, because the things one hears of people for aren't always things to be proud of, are they?"

Albany had been educated at Eton and Cambridge, where he had obtained a third-class degree in History. Bolton had not enjoyed the same educational advantages: he had attended a state school and then, Miss Tavistock thought, some kind of adult education college — he never said much about his time there and she was uncertain about the details.

"So it's all the more to his credit, of course, that since then he's done so well."

Albany had been with Renfrews' since leaving Cambridge. Bolton, for much of his life, had worked abroad. Sir Robert had met him about five years before in the course of some negotiations with an investment bank in New York and been so impressed by his abilities that he at once offered him a senior position.

Their talents were also entirely different. It was universally agreed that Bolton was brilliant at the technicalities of investment management. Albany specialized more in interpersonal skills, which of course were also very important in investment banking.

"I don't mean," said Miss Tavistock, "that Mr Bolton doesn't get on well with people. Sir Robert says that he's a bit of a rough diamond, and he speaks his mind, of course — northcountrymen do, don't they? — but almost everyone likes him."

Though she disparaged neither, I observed when she spoke of Albany that almost imperceptible tightening of the facial muscles and vocal cords which indicates dislike, or at best irritation: I suspected that she thought him an example of the failings that she had attributed to Tom Rakewell. When she mentioned Bolton, on the other hand, her voice softened and she smiled slightly; but it seemed fanciful to infer that the blunt Lancastrian had any quality which she found reminiscent of the subtle and sophisticated Vicomte de Valmont.

None of this, however, shed any light on which of them owned the black Mercedes. I cautiously ventured to enquire further about their personal circumstances.

It appeared that Albany had been married to a very charming woman, entirely suitable in every way, and had two children, but to Sir Robert's great disappointment the marriage had ended in divorce. His wife and children now occupied the house in Norfolk which he had inherited from his grandmother, while he himself lived in a flat in central London.

Bolton had a wife, to whom he was still married, but whether she was charming or not neither Miss Tavistock nor anyone else at Renfrews' was in any position to say. He insisted on keeping his personal and his professional life entirely separate and accordingly had never introduced her to any of his colleagues, not even to Sir Robert. Though he had a flat close to the City, where he lived during the week, his wife, so far as Miss Tavistock knew, spent all her time at their house in Buckinghamshire, which no one from Renfrews' had ever been invited to visit. It was rather a pity, because it made people think that there must be something odd about her, something socially unacceptable.

"But probably she's just very shy and doesn't like meeting strangers, in which case it's really rather nice of Mr Bolton not to try to make her."

The indirectness of my approach had cost some little time: Miss Tavistock was looking at her watch. After all I had learnt about the two directors of Renfrews', I still could not think of any natural way of asking what kind of cars they owned. Not being greatly interested in motor vehicles, I could imagine no convincing reason for wishing to know such a thing. I resigned myself to disappointment.

She was a pleasant sort of woman and it would have seemed unkind to leave her in perplexity: saying that if she were at any time in Oxford she must be sure to get in touch, I wrote down for her the telephone number of St George's on the back of an envelope bearing my name. Her relief was perceptible: I no longer represented a nightmare of embarrassment.

We left the museum together and I walked back with her to Lincoln's Inn. When we reached Old Square, where she had parked the car, I saw that I had been singularly obtuse.

"What a splendid car," I said. "A Mercedes, I believe. Does it belong to Sir Robert or to one of his co-directors?"

"Oh no, Professor Tamar, it's a company car. We have a fleet of four of them, actually — so even when one of them's being serviced, there's always one available for the Chairman and each of the directors."

"But I suppose there are differences between them?" I said a little desperately, seeing that the solution was after all about to elude me. "Surely the Chairman's car must be grander than the others?"

"Oh no, Professor Tamar," she said, laughing, at ease with me now that she knew my name. "We're a very democratic organization — apart from the licence plates, they're all identical."

As is the way of the Scholar when Truth proves unexpectedly elusive, I was unable to dismiss from my mind the problem I had failed to solve. Finding no escape from it in my researches in the Public Record Office, I spent the afternoon walking restlessly in the gardens of the Inner Temple, pausing but seldom for refreshment or repose. I could hardly believe, having learnt so much, that I was no nearer to knowing whether it was Albany or Bolton whom Isabella had been blackmailing.

And yet it was so. Certainly, I had now no doubt that whichever one it was had been her visitor in the black

Mercedes: with four Mercedes motor cars provided by Renfrews' Bank, it would have been logically preposterous to invent a fifth. This information, however, now seemed to count for nothing: when it was put in the balance, the scales remained equally poised.

There was a further thought which I found slightly disturbing: the last visit of the Mercedes to Parsons Haver had been on the night of Isabella's sudden and unexpected death. I had dismissed rather lightly, as my readers may recall, the suggestion that she had been poisoned; but I had not known then that she was a blackmailer, or that the man in the black Mercedes was one of her victims.

Selena seemed not altogether grateful for my efforts to find the solution to her problem. Remark was made, when I told her of them in the Corkscrew that evening, on the readiness of Oxford academics, too idle to pursue their proper researches, to meddle instead with things that were none of their business.

"My dear Selena," I said, "do be careful — you're beginning to sound like the Bursar. Tell me, what happened at your conference? What opinion did you form of the suspects? Did you reach any conclusion?"

"Hmm," said Selena, with another of her sideways looks. She softened, however, under the benevolent influence of her wine. "Well, as a matter of fact, there isn't much to tell. So far as the insider-dealing problem is concerned, it was a complete waste of time — I had none of the miraculous insights that Sir Robert was evidently hoping for. He rang me later and I had to tell him I still couldn't help. Poor old chap, I'm afraid he was very disappointed."

"Which of them do you think he'd prefer it to be — Albany or Bolton?"

"I don't know. Albany's a sort of cousin of his, and Lady Renfrew's nephew into the bargain, so it would be fairly embarrassing if he turned out to be the insider dealer. On the other hand, recruiting Geoffrey Bolton was very much Sir Robert's personal decision, and so far it's been a great success and he's very proud of it. It would be quite painful for him to find that it was a misjudgement."

"Would it be unfair to suspect that Albany owes his position at Renfrews' rather to his family connections than to his personal qualities?"

"Well," said Selena, "I certainly wouldn't suspect him of owing it to his intellectual abilities. But then, he doesn't claim to be an expert on the technical side. They all agree that Bolton is the one with the technical expertise. Albany's the one who talks to clients and so on."

"Miss Tavistock said that he specialized in interpersonal skills. I understood her to mean that his chief asset was personal charm."

"Yes," said Selena, after some reflection. "Yes, I think that's how he would understand it, too. He has a way of treating one just like his social equal which one would find very charming, I expect, if one happened to think of oneself as his social inferior. On the other hand, you might understand it to mean that he went to the same school as a number of people who have money to invest and who like the idea of its being looked after by someone from their old school."

"While Bolton, having not been to a school of that kind, is considered to be something of a rough diamond?"

"That's how Sir Robert sometimes puts it, but all he really means is that Bolton has a Lancashire accent. As a matter of fact, I'd say that Bolton has infinitely more personal charm than Albany."

"Ah," I said.

"Not at all," said Selena, sounding a little vexed. "As you know, Hilary, I am devoted to Sebastian, and there can be no question of 'ah'."

I hastened to assure her that I had not used the word in any sense to which she could reasonably take objection.

"I was merely noting that you found Bolton a more attractive personality than Albany — it might follow that you thought Albany the more likely suspect. More likely, that is to say, to have done something sufficiently disgraceful to expose him to blackmail."

"Only if I thought that an attractive personality could be relied on as evidence of good character. As you may perhaps have noticed, that isn't always the case. No, I'm afraid I'd have to say that at the moment Geoffrey Bolton looks to me like the more likely suspect."

"Merely because he's the more attractive? My dear Selena, isn't that a rather prejudiced attitude?"

"No," said Selena, "not because of that. Because no one knows who he is."

She rose and went to the bar to replenish our glasses, leaving me in some perplexity. I gently suggested, on her return, that her previous observation was palpably untrue.

"Well, it depends on what you mean by knowing who someone is. My client met Bolton about five years ago, when he was working for a bank in New York, and offered him a job straight away, simply on the basis of personal impression. Exactly how long he'd been in New York and what he'd been doing before he got there Sir Robert has no idea — as far as I can see, he could have come from outer space."

"But surely he made enquiries of some kind about him before offering him a senior position at Renfrews'?"

"What sort of enquiries would you expect? If you meet a man in his forties, occupying a senior position in a bank of international standing, you don't ask him to prove that he's qualified to do it — you just assume he is. You don't mind if he started his career as an office boy — if he did, it's a sign of his ability that he's progressed so far. And you don't want to ask his present employers too many questions about him, in case they guess that you're trying to poach him."

"Didn't he even want to know about Bolton's educational background?" The fervent pursuit by the young of certificates, diplomas and degrees, of impressive curricula and favourable references — was it all mere wasted effort?

"Well, it was clear from his accent that he hadn't been to the kind of school Sir Robert had. He mentioned having been to a grammar school in Lancashire and then to some sort of college in some town in the Midlands. Sir Robert didn't see any point in pressing him for details — he was happy to accept him as more or less self-educated and rather admired him for it."

"But when he started work at Renfrews', weren't there forms to fill in? What about income tax and national insurance and pension schemes and all that sort of thing?"

"If he'd spent all his working life outside the United Kingdom, you wouldn't expect him to have been paying tax or insurance. When you come down to it, the only document one needs to prove that one exists is one's birth certificate. The bank's personnel department has a copy of Geoffrey Bolton's birth certificate and I dare say he was born when it says he was. But after that there's a period of over forty years unaccounted for."

He had been with Renfrews', however, for over five years: it seemed to me inconceivable that none of his colleagues should in that time have learnt any more about his previous career than had been known when he was first appointed. In the course of his ordinary day-to-day conversations, he must surely sometimes have said something, however trivial, which would give some hint of what he had done, whom he had known, where he had lived, during his twenties and thirties.

"Apparently not. He sometimes mentions things that he did in New York, but apart from that he simply never talks about his past. I suppose," said Selena, sounding, however, as if she thought otherwise, "that he may just think that people wouldn't be interested."

It seemed likely, I had to agree, that he had some more powerful motive for avoiding the subject.

"And I gather," I said, remembering what I had heard from Miss Tavistock, "that he's equally reticent about his private life — none of his colleagues has ever met his wife or visited his house?"

"Never once. You see, he insisted when Sir Robert offered him the post that he must be allowed to keep his business and private lives completely separate. Sir Robert rather assumed that it was actually his wife who'd insisted — that she didn't want to be a company wife and have to go to office cocktail parties and entertain clients at weekends and so on. So that was part of the deal, though I'm not sure my client expected to be held to it quite so strictly."

"If your client were determined to find out what Bolton did out of office hours, I imagine there would be ways of doing it."

"Private detectives? Well, I did suggest that possibility when he first asked me about the problem, but it didn't go down well — he thought it wouldn't be gentlemanly. That's to say, he thought he'd be found out and Bolton would be so angry he'd resign. And if after all it was Albany who turned out to be the insider dealer, that would be a rather major disaster for the bank. So you see what I mean, Hilary, when I say that no one knows who Geoffrey Bolton is. At Renfrews', he's a respectable banker. Outside Renfrews', he could be — anyone or anything."

I understood why she thought Bolton a likely subject for blackmail.

It was again in the Corkscrew, three or four evenings later, that Julia read to us her aunt's account of the funeral.

24 High Street
Parsons Haver
West Sussex

Saturday, 26th June

Dear Julia,

Oh dear, I always forget what a romantic sort of girl you are, probably because of all those Georgette Heyer novels I lent you when you had measles. I suppose I've led you to expect a Cinderella story and I'm afraid I have to disappoint you.

The Chanel dress didn't transform Daphne into a raving beauty. No charming man fell instantly in love with her. And no one came to the funeral.

No one, that is, of the sort that she seemed to have been expecting. Ricky and Griselda were both there, of course, and a handful of people from the village, either because they were sorry for Daphne or because they were curious about who else would come. Fewer than a dozen in the whole congregation, and only one that I didn't recognize — a rather good-looking young man in grey corduroy. Daphne said she'd never seen him before and had no idea who he was.

She delivered the eulogy without bursting into tears or stammering too much, so I suppose one ought to say that she did rather well. She spoke in a very portentous little voice, like an archbishop announcing the death of a senior statesman, and always referred to Isabella by her full name, as if she were one of the greatest figures of our time. It was along the same lines as the obituary she wrote — all about Isabella's great gifts for guidance and healing and how she'd been a caring and wonderful person who'd devoted her life to helping others. With many quotations, of course, from Isabella herself, and a bit about Daphne being sad but proud to be left to carry on her work.

She'd evidently written out what she wanted to say, and was reading from her notes, but they didn't seem to start or finish anywhere in particular — in fact, I began to wonder whether they'd finish at all. I had the distinct impression, after twenty minutes or so, that she'd got back to her starting point and was beginning all over again. Maurice must have thought the same, because he took advantage of what I suspect was only meant to be a pause to say, "Daphne, thank you — that was most moving" and make a signal to the organist.

Still, it seemed to make Daphne feel better, which I suppose is the main thing. Griselda and I stood beside her as the coffin was put in the grave, and she was calmer than we'd expected her to be.

Maurice stopped and had a word with the young man in grey corduroy and it turned out that he was there by mistake. He'd come into the churchyard to see if he could find the grave of his great-grandfather, who he thought was buried there — he was quite right, actually, and Maurice was able to show him the gravestone — and then been tempted inside by our beautiful stained-glass windows. He'd felt that it wouldn't be respectful to walk out again when he found there was a funeral going on, so he'd just stayed and listened. Poor Maurice, I could see he was longing to tell the young man all about our stained-glass windows — it's one of his favourite subjects — but he saw that Daphne was getting slightly fretful, and restrained himself.

As there were so few people, and I felt that the young man had behaved rather nicely about not leaving in the middle of the service, I suggested to Daphne on the way across the churchyard that I might run back and invite him to join us for the funeral breakfast. Daphne wouldn't hear of it, though. For some reason she'd taken an instant dislike to him — she said he had an untrustworthy aura.

Why she should have thought that I've no idea — perhaps she simply meant he was too good-looking. It's true, of course, as I suppose you know by now, that very good-looking men usually aren't to be trusted, but you must also remember that even quite ugly men often aren't to be trusted either. So in the end you might just as well enjoy yourself and be let down by the good-looking ones.

Now the only thing left to worry about is what to do with all the sandwiches. Not to speak of the éclairs and meringues. Not to speak of a couple of dozen little sponge cakes which Daphne made herself and are quite undoubtedly the worst sponge cakes I have ever eaten, or for the sake of politeness tried to eat — like slices of rubber cooked in rancid oil, but not so appetising. Daphne's convinced they're delicious, though — they're made from a recipe Isabella taught her.

Well, I don't know that one could call it a successful funeral exactly, but at least we've got Isabella safely buried.

Yours with very much love,
Reg

♣ ♣ ♣

A number of people, I imagined, would be hoping that Isabella's secrets were safely buried with her. I rather wished that Daphne had not announced so publicly as she had her intention to carry on Isabella's work: the phrase seemed to me to be open to misconstruction.

Long Vacation

CHAPTER
SEVEN

It would be an impertinence little becoming the modesty of the Scholar to trouble you, dear reader, with matters ungermane to my present narrative. I therefore refrain from any account of my own activities — though these, on some other occasion, might be not without interest — during the six or seven weeks which followed Isabella's funeral.

On the second Friday in August I again found myself in London, where I intended to spend the weekend before travelling by aeroplane to the United States of America. At the hour of the afternoon when tea is customarily taken I made my way to 62 New Square.

My first impression was that a small civil war had broken out, the result, possibly, of some unhappy disagreement between the Bar and the Law Society, and that 62 New Square had been chosen as a particular object of hostile bombardment. The air was heavy with the dust of shattered plaster; the walls and timbers shuddered at the pounding of hammers and the pitiless reverberation of electric drills; muscular men in string vests were attacking the building with blowtorches. In short, the builders were in.

In such conditions, an offer of tea seemed unlikely: I retreated to the Chambers next door. Even there, though tea was available in generous quantities, the level of noise remained too high for civilized discourse. Moreover, Julia had an urgent opinion to write on the provisions of the latest Finance Act. She proposed, therefore, that while drinking my tea I should read the most recent letters from her aunt Regina.

"Some rather odd things," said Julia, "seem to be going on in Parsons Haver. I'm beginning to feel slightly worried about it."

24 High Street
Parsons Haver
West Sussex

Friday, 16th July

Dear Julia,

I'm sorry I had to cancel our lunch. In London nowadays, I suppose, you're all quite used to people being burgled and wouldn't dream of letting it interfere with your social engagements. Down here, though, it's still something of an event.

It happened just before midnight last night. Daphne was asleep in bed, but she was woken up by the vulture screeching. It doesn't usually do that at night, she says, so she knew that something was wrong. She ran downstairs in her nightdress and into the drawing room and saw a man trying

102

to break open the display cabinet — the one that contains the Book.

She screamed and he turned around. He had a knife or a chisel or something like that in his hand and she was frightened that he was going to attack her. She ran out through the front door and across the road to the Vicarage, still screaming, and rang the doorbell until Maurice answered it.

Maurice rang the police and then me, so I was up most of the night soothing Daphne and making tea for people. Which is why I didn't feel at all like catching the train to London this morning.

The police came in the form of a young sergeant and an even younger woman police constable. They were quite pleasant and sympathetic, but they didn't seem very hopeful of catching the burglar. One can't really blame them — he had a black balaclava over his head and a long black raincoat over the rest of him, so Daphne wasn't able to give them much of a description. She said that she thought he was quite tall, but that seemed only to mean that he was taller than she is.

They're treating it as a fairly amateur sort of crime. They think that the burglar found the back door unlocked — it was open when they went round the house — and was simply making the most of his chances. Daphne, on the other hand, swears that it was locked when she went to bed and he must have used something quite sophisticated, like a skeleton key, to open it. She's convinced that he broke in on purpose to steal the Book.

But when the police asked if they could examine it she wouldn't let them — in fact she became almost hysterical at the idea. It isn't lawful for anyone except the Custodian to read the Book or even touch it, and if they do, something terrible will happen to them. The police didn't find this very helpful.

Even Maurice can't persuade her to explain sensibly what the Book is supposed to be or what's in it or why anyone might want to steal it. She simply says that the Book has its enemies and the enemies of the Book are the enemies of the Custodian, but it isn't lawful for her to try to explain who they are.

She's quite worryingly peculiar on the subject. If the idea of being the Custodian cheered her up and gave her a bit of confidence in herself one wouldn't mind, however silly it was, but in fact I think it rather frightens her. She talks about the Book as if it weren't a thing but a person — not a very nice person either, someone rather cruel and vindictive, who'll punish her if she doesn't do what it wants her to.

She also thinks she can read the future in it. She came round a couple of days ago, when Griselda was working in my garden, to warn her very earnestly that during August she should keep away from animals — not the most practical advice to a woman with three cats.

According to the Book, apparently, August is going to be the Month of the Animals. This means that animals are going to be very significant in all our lives and intensify the effect of all the other influences. For some reason August is a dangerous month for Griselda, so it'll be particularly dangerous for her to have anything to do with animals. For me, on the other hand, it's going to be rather prosperous, so something involving animals should be especially lucky for me.

I'm afraid we treated all this fairly light-heartedly, and poor Daphne became quite upset — she really seemed to believe that "something terrible" was going to happen to Griselda because of an animal. So Griselda had to promise to keep away from farms and zoos and wildlife parks, and be very careful of the bad-tempered Alsatian in the garden next door to the Vicarage.

Well, if that's the best the Book can do in the way of prophesying the future I don't think anyone's likely to go to the trouble of stealing it. I expect the police are right and the burglar was just a casual sneak thief, but the trouble is that Daphne doesn't think so and is frightened that he'll come back.

We're all hoping that when Isabella's estate is dealt with and the Rectory can be sold Daphne will forget all this nonsense about the Book and will get on with having a proper life in a sensible sort of way. The house alone must be worth between three and four hundred thousand, so she

105

should be able to manage pretty comfortably on the income from the proceeds. Griselda and I have all sorts of plans for her — we're going to transform her appearance and move her to a nice little flat in Brighton and enrol her in some not too demanding training course and make some nice friends for her of her own age. We haven't quite got round to finding her a suitable husband yet, but I dare say we will.

So her future, as you see, is in good hands, but none of it can actually happen until the solicitors have sorted out the estate. And lawyers, if you don't mind my saying so, don't seem to deal with things very quickly.

Yours with much love,
Reg

♣   ♣   ♣

I wondered whether Daphne might not be right in thinking that the burglar had had some specific objective. She was the heiress to a professional blackmailer: could he have been in search of some item of incriminating evidence, perhaps a document of some kind, which he believed to be now in her possession? Might he be in some way connected with — might he even be — the man in the black Mercedes? Was this the possibility that was worrying Julia?

Observing, however, that Julia was still diligently writing her opinion, I continued my reading without disturbing her.

106

Monday, 2nd August

Dear Julia,

Though one should not speak ill of the dead, I am prepared in Isabella's case to make an exception. She is managing — and it is, in her case, a considerable achievement — to make more trouble dead than alive. She has left poor Daphne in a quite impossible position, and Maurice thought you might know if there was anything to be done about it.

As I mentioned in my last letter, we've all been a little worried about the poor girl, but the one thing we didn't think we needed to worry about was her financial position — the solicitor had said that she was going to get the income from Isabella's estate, and we assumed that meant she'd be quite well provided for. It wasn't until yesterday that we found we were wrong.

Maurice and Griselda and I were sitting in the Newt and Ninepence, as usual on a Saturday morning, working hard at our crosswords. We'd polished off *The Times* and were getting on quite nicely with the *Guardian* when poor Daphne arrived, very moist and sticky and clearly on the point of tears. She was sorry to interrupt, she said, but she was in the most terrible trouble, and could she please talk to Maurice as soon as possible? So

107

Maurice downed his beer and went straight back with her to the Vicarage.

"When she says she's in trouble," said Griselda, "she surely doesn't mean —?"

I said I didn't think so.

"Men can be such pigs," said Griselda.

Which of course they can, but I still didn't think it was that kind of trouble. Later on Maurice came round and told me what kind it was.

It had taken him quite a while to find out what was upsetting her. What he gathered at first was that she'd been insulted by Mr Iqbal at the supermarket. He was very surprised about this, because Mr Iqbal is usually most polite and obliging, but when Maurice asked exactly what had happened Daphne just started crying and saying she hadn't known that people could be so beastly. It was some time before he realized that all Mr Iqbal had done was ask when she expected to be able to settle her account. And she can't, and has no prospect of being able to.

Yes, it's quite true that under Isabella's will Daphne gets the income from the estate — but only as long as she provides a home at the Rectory for the beastly Roderigo and the wretched ravens. At the Rectory, mind you — she isn't allowed to move anywhere else, even if she takes them with her. Either she stays here in Parsons Haver for the rest of her days with no chance of finding a job or making friends of her own age or doing anything with her life, or she gives up everything and is left homeless and penniless.

Well, as it turns out, she's penniless anyway. After taxes and legal expenses and so on the house is just about all that's left in the estate, and if it can't be sold there isn't any income. Or hardly any — Mr Godwin, the executor, says she can expect about twenty pounds a year. How could Isabella have expected her to live on that? And maintain the house? And feed the wretched birds?

And of course, the poor girl can't afford to get any legal advice, which might turn out to be no help anyway, but Maurice thought you might be able to tell us whether it's legal for anyone to make a will like that. I'm enclosing a copy of it, and I'd be most grateful if you could let me know what you think.

Can Isabella really go on controlling Daphne's life like this? Can she reach out of the grave to keep hold of her? It's monstrous — I can't believe it's allowed, and if it is it ought not to be.

Yours with much love,
Reg

♣ ♣ ♣

There was a lull in the noise of drilling and Julia had paused in her labours to pour further cups of tea. I enquired whether she had been able to assist with the problem of Isabella's will: it seemed to me to be one rather outside the area of her professional expertise.

"Yes, it is, but fortunately Selena and Ragwort had a similar case a few months ago, so they were well up on the authorities."

"A case about a vulture?"

"No, no, about a pet tortoise, which the testator had evidently held in high esteem and wished to make provision for. Ragwort represented the trustees of the will and Selena represented the residuary beneficiary."

"Who represented the tortoise?"

"No one — this placed it, I'm afraid, at something of a disadvantage. So with the benefit of their advice I was able to send my aunt a comprehensive account of the current law relating to testamentary dispositions for the benefit of animals, with particular reference to the provisions of Section 106 of the Settled Land Act. The gist of it was that if Daphne wanted to challenge the will she'd have to go to the Court of Appeal, if not the House of Lords, and the costs of the action would be prohibitive."

"And you were unable, I suppose, to suggest any other solution?"

"On the contrary," said Julia with some degree of indignation. "We suggested a perfectly sensible and practical alternative involving almost no expense at all. The will provided, you see, that Daphne was to have the income of the estate during her lifetime or until she ceased to live at the Rectory and provide a home there for Roderigo and the ravens."

"Yes," I said, "I gathered that."

"And subject to that, everything went to Isabella's sister, Marjorie, or if Marjorie predeceased Isabella, to

110

Marjorie's child or children. Which meant that Daphne and Marjorie, or Marjorie's children, were together absolutely entitled to the whole estate and if they agreed to divide it up between them there was nothing Isabella, or indeed the vulture, could do to stop them. So we suggested that Daphne should approach Marjorie or her children with a view to doing a deal — selling the house and sharing the proceeds and putting the vulture in the care of the community." She sighed. "But you know what beneficiaries are like."

The drilling began again with redoubled vigour; I resumed my reading.

24 High Street
Parsons Haver
West Sussex

Saturday, 7th August

Dear Julia,

Thank you for all those interesting stories about people leaving money to cats and donkeys — I'm afraid I must have put you to more trouble than I realized, and as it turns out completely wasted.

Maurice has explained your suggestion to Daphne, about coming to some sensible arrangement to divide up the estate, and Daphne says she'd rather starve. She'd rather beg. She'd rather go on the streets. (This isn't a very practical idea — there's not much scope for that sort of thing in Parsons Haver, and even if there were I frankly don't think it's something she'd have a talent for.)

Isabella's sister Marjorie died a year or two ago, leaving one son. Isabella's sister, according to Daphne, was an unkind and horrible person and hadn't been to Daphne's mother's funeral (so Daphne didn't go to hers) and hadn't spoken to Isabella for nearly fifteen years. So it obviously follows that her son is also an unkind and horrible person and Daphne doesn't want to have anything to do with him. And anyway, there can be no question of dividing up the estate, because Aunt Isabella wanted her to stay at the Rectory and keep the birds there and she could never even think of betraying Aunt Isabella's trust in her.

Naturally, Julia, I think it's very proper for a niece to regard her aunt's wishes as sacred, but in the present case it simply isn't practical. What is Daphne to live on?

She seems to imagine that everything will go on just as it did when Isabella was alive, and refuses to understand that it can't — they were living on the income from the fortune-telling business, which seems to have been quite profitable, and an annuity Isabella had bought which ended on her death. (How like Isabella!) But Daphne doesn't seem to understand that this means that she has to make some money — she just goes on blaming poor Mr Iqbal, and saying that he's insulted her.

"She says he ought to know," said Maurice, "that she isn't the kind of person who doesn't pay their debts."

112

"If she hasn't the money to pay them," I said, "what other kind can she be?"

"She's the Custodian," said Maurice. "The Custodian does not break faith. I wonder, Reg, if I could have a spot more gin?"

Poor Maurice, I'm afraid he's finding the whole thing rather wearing. You see, it isn't just her practical problems that she expects him to help her with, it's her great spiritual problem — can the Custodian go to church? She wants to go to church, so that she can listen to Maurice's sermons and help him with his important work, but the Custodian must keep faith with the Book, and she doesn't know if she can do both.

She apparently regards this as the most agonizing spiritual dilemma that anyone's ever had to face since the Temptation in the Wilderness, which makes it perfectly reasonable for her to expect Maurice to spend hours every day discussing it.

The fact is that Maurice isn't all that keen on having Daphne in his congregation — she's a little on the intense side for St Ethel's — but he feels rather conscience stricken about not wanting her.

"Because after all, Reg, one's supposed to believe that in the eyes of God every human soul is infinitely precious, and I suppose one's supposed to believe that He likes them all coming to church, though I've never quite understood why, so who am I to say that He wouldn't be pleased to see Daphne sitting in a pew in St Ethel's? I mean, for all I know He'd be thrilled to bits. Anyway, she thinks He would be and if I suggest He wouldn't she'll be terribly hurt. So I've simply told her that God is very broad-minded nowadays and if she feels it wouldn't be right for her to go to church He'll quite understand and do His best to manage without her. But of course that wasn't the end of it."

Which with Daphne it wouldn't be. She isn't the kind of girl, you see, who asks for one's advice and then either takes it or doesn't and leaves one to get on with something else. She's the kind who asks for one's advice and looks as if she's listening to it and comes back next morning to ask for it all over again.

One certainly can't accuse her of not being grateful to Maurice for the help he's given her — she's always saying how kind he's been and how lucky she is that he's there to give her spiritual guidance. And she's always trying, poor girl, to find ways to repay him — she goes round to the Vicarage every day to take his rubbish out to the dustbin and ask if he wants any shopping done and see if she can do anything to make herself useful. The trouble is, though, that Maurice doesn't really need anyone to do things for him — he has Griselda to help with the garden and Mrs Tyrrell to clean for him two mornings a week and otherwise he's quite good at looking after himself.

He came round for supper with me yesterday and we spent nearly the whole evening talking about Daphne's problems, drinking more gin than was good for us and not getting anywhere. With great difficulty — she evidently thought it beneath the dignity of the Custodian — he's persuaded her to ask for some money from the Social Security people. He helped her to fill in the forms and they're supposed to give her enough to keep her from starving. Apart from that, it's hard to know what to suggest.

I wondered for a while whether perhaps she could go on with the fortune-telling business — if she's going to go on claiming to be the guardian of some sort of sacred text I thought she might as well make some money out of it. But Maurice isn't sure it's something he could encourage — he feels it rather savours of witchcraft.

"And you might think, Reg, that in these ecumenical times that wouldn't matter much. But the Bishop's very down on witchcraft, almost as down as he is on ordaining women, and you know how he feels about that."

Besides, if it was the kind of business that Ricky says it was, it's out of the question — she couldn't get information by the same methods as Isabella, and even if she could, of course, it would be very wrong. It's rather a pity in a way, though, because she actually sometimes seems —

I don't mean I think that she can see into the future — that would be too ridiculous. But some quite sensible people do believe in telepathy, and she does sometimes say things —

Two or three weeks ago in the Newt and Ninepence, Ricky was buying a round of drinks and asked her what she would like. She hesitated a bit and then she said, "Oh well, as you're getting all that money next week, I'll have a glass of wine."

Ricky wasn't expecting any money, and asked her what she meant. She looked slightly bewildered, as if she didn't quite know why she'd said it, and said, "I just thought you were going to get some money — for some medicine you'd sold, or something."

Ricky was most amused by this — rather more noisily, in fact, than was quite kind or polite, and I told him so afterwards — and said he'd never sold medicine to anyone in his life.

But two days later, when he opened the post in the morning, he found he'd got quite a large dividend from a pharmaceutical company he had shares in. Poor Ricky, he was quite shaken — mind you, it serves him right for making fun of poor Daphne.

And then there was the day she came round to give me a box of chocolates, to thank me for helping her with the funeral and so on — very sweet, squishy chocolate creams, actually not at all what I like — it breaks my heart to think of her spending her money on them. Still, she ate several while she was here, so at least she did get some pleasure out of it. Just as she was leaving, she said, "Oh — give all my best to Mrs Tyrrell. I hope she finds whatever it is she's lost."

I said that I didn't think Mrs Tyrrell had lost anything — she'd been here that morning, and hadn't said anything about it. And again Daphne looked rather bewildered, and said, "Oh, I thought she'd lost something quite important — something to do with someone who's dead."

And half an hour later there was Mrs Tyrrell at the door, saying she couldn't find her ring and wondering if she'd left it here. It's a very pretty ring and rather valuable — late Victorian, turquoise set in silver — left to her by her grandmother, so naturally she was quite upset. We looked everywhere for it, and I'm glad to say we found it — she must have taken it off when she was cleaning the bathroom, and it had rolled behind the sink.

But the extraordinary thing is that the moment she discovered it was missing must have been almost exactly the same moment that Daphne told me she'd lost something.

Yes, Julia, I know it's all very trivial and I dare say it's only coincidence, but I can't help finding it slightly eerie. Which is why I'm feeling a little bit worried about Maurice, who seems to have disappeared.

♣   ♣   ♣

I experienced, on reading this, a sudden sharp sense of apprehension, which I could not at once account for. It was Daphne, if anyone, on whose behalf I had felt a

117

certain uneasiness; Daphne whom someone might suspect of being the heir to some still-dangerous secret. What cause had I for any disquiet regarding the Reverend Maurice?

I remembered, after a few moments, that he was the only person in Parsons Haver, indeed perhaps anywhere, who could identify the man in the black Mercedes.

The sound of drilling had been replaced by the thudding of gigantic hammers; Julia was still writing her opinion; I continued my reading.

♣   ♣   ♣

He wasn't in the Newt and Ninepence this morning, as he usually is on a Saturday, but at first I didn't even think of being worried about him. Griselda and I went and sat out in the garden, with our drinks and our crosswords, and grumbled a bit about not having anyone to tell us how to spell Sibylline. Or Sybilline, whichever it may be. Ricky turned up and bought another round of drinks, and we all just sat and talked about how hot it was, not worrying about Maurice or anything else.

Then Daphne arrived looking for him, and very agitated that he wasn't there. It wasn't clear why she wanted him so urgently — it seemed to have something to do with a lobster that she'd bought him for his lunch. We told her he'd probably turn up sooner or later and in the meanwhile she'd better sit down and have a glass of wine with us. Which she did, and sat quite quietly, apart from a few sighs and sniffles, while we went on with the crossword.

And then, completely out of the blue, there was a scene — ridiculous, but quite disagreeable — all on account of a clue in *The Times* crossword. Or perhaps the *Guardian*, I forget which.

Ricky is one of those people who never start a crossword on their own but always want to help when someone's halfway through. So we let him have *The Times* or the *Guardian*, whichever it was, and he was looking at the clues we hadn't done and sometimes reading them out — you know how one does.

In the course of this, he suddenly seemed to find something enormously amusing, and said, "Ah, here's one for you, Daphne." And he read out the clue for Sibylline, or Sybilline, whichever it is, which we only hadn't filled in because we didn't know how to spell it.

I don't know if you happened to see it? "Bein' silly, very silly, like prophetic book."

Instant rage from Daphne. She jumped up, knocking her chair over and spilling her wine, and started shouting that the Book wasn't silly, it was the crossword that was silly, and Ricky who was silly, and everyone in Parsons Haver who was silly. Apart from Maurice, who was a brilliant scholar and a true priest and could have been one of the great princes of the Church if he hadn't buried himself in a silly little tinpot village where no one could appreciate him. (No need to ask where she got that idea from.) And it was typical of us that we could just sit there doing our silly crossword and not caring where he was or what had happened to him. All this with floods of tears.

Ricky, having started it, simply walked out, saying he couldn't stand any more, leaving Griselda and me to mop up Daphne. I'm really feeling quite cross with Ricky — he's invited me to go to the races with him next week, but I'm feeling so cross that I've a good mind to say no.

We bought her a couple of ham sandwiches and another glass of wine and tried to explain about crosswords, and eventually she stopped crying. She was sorry, she said, she hadn't meant to be rude or upset anyone, it was just that she was so worried about Maurice. He'd told her he was going to be at home this morning, working on his sermon, and then come over to the Newt, but he hadn't been at home when she rang on his doorbell and he wasn't in the Newt, and she didn't know what could have happened to him.

We pointed out to her that he was a grown man in possession of all his faculties, and if he decided to go for a walk on a sunny Saturday morning he probably wouldn't feel that he had to notify all his friends in advance. But it was no use — she kept saying she was sure that he was in some kind of danger — in a dangerous place, or with a dangerous person, and she didn't know what to do.

When we asked what made her think so, she said that she'd read it in the Book. She'd seen his name there and it had a shadow over it.

Of course, I know really that it's all complete nonsense. But it's after six o'clock and he still isn't back, and I can't help feeling slightly anxious.

♣   ♣   ♣

There were several further pages of the letter. My perusal of them, however, was delayed: Cantrip arrived, carrying a pair of guns.

CHAPTER
EIGHT

It was, as I have mentioned, the second week of August: that season of the year when the warm days of summer draw luxuriantly towards their fruitful and abundant climax and there is an almost universal impulse to give thanks in some way for the richness and generosity of the earth; that is to say, in the case of an upper-class Englishman, to go out and kill something. Cantrip was on his way to the grouse moors of Perthshire, and had looked in to say good-bye to Julia.

"Cantrip," said Julia, looking nervously at the guns, "did you have to bring those horrible things in with you?"

"They're not horrible things, they're beautiful. They were a present for my twenty-first from my uncle Hereward. That reminds me, he sends you his love. He's always saying what a good sport you are."

For reasons of which some of my readers will be aware, the mention of the distinguished old soldier caused Julia to turn slightly pale; but she bravely instructed Cantrip to give his uncle her warm regards.

"Now, listen, Hilary," said Cantrip in a tone of accusation, "how are you getting on with the Isabella case?"

"My dear Cantrip," I said, perhaps a trifle defensively, "I am not getting on at all with the Isabella case, since I remain of the view that no such case exists."

"Come off it," said Cantrip. "The chap in the Mercedes was the chap she was blackmailing — Albany or Bolton, whichever of them it was. And he was the last person to see her alive. What more do you want — jam and custard on top?"

"The evidence is still entirely consistent with her having died of natural causes. And even if she did not, I hardly see why it should fall to me to investigate the matter further — it does not appear to be one on which the methods of Scholarship could shed particular light. There are other claims on my time and energies. I have responsibilities — to my pupils, to my College, to the whole University of Oxford. One is not appointed a Fellow of St George's merely in order to enjoy oneself, as the Bursar constantly reminds me."

"Oh well," said Cantrip, "if all you're interested in these days is cosying up to the Bursar —"

I shuddered at the thought.

"Moreover," I said, yielding to the impulse to justify my inaction, "I think that if there were anything sinister about Isabella's death we would by now have heard something more of the man in the black Mercedes. If he had had any hand in it, he would surely be desperately anxious to learn what had happened since — he would have made efforts to find out whether anyone suspected anything, whether the police were pursuing any inquiries, whether he had left any incriminating evidence. There has been no sign, so far as I am aware, of his having done so."

"Look here, Hilary," said Cantrip, "you can't expect him to go bowling into Parsons Haver in the Mercedes and ask the local fuzz if they happen to want him for murder. What he'd do is send a henchman."

"A henchman?" said Julia, as if unfamiliar with the word.

"A chap to do the dirty work," said Cantrip. "Like your aunt said about the glasses, if you're rich enough to have a Mercedes you get someone else to do it. So I expect that's what he's done — there's probably been a man in dark glasses and a false moustache snooping round Parsons Haver for weeks, pretending to read gas meters."

I perceived that Julia, for what reason I could not imagine, found this remark disturbing.

"Anyway, Hilary, if you're not in the mood for doing your Sherlock Holmes bit, that's all right with me, but you're going to feel pretty silly when I crack the case single-handed."

"I shall be happy, if you do so, to sit in admiration at your feet. What method of investigation are you proposing to adopt?"

"I'm going to interrogate Edgar Albany — he's one of the chaps I'm going shooting with this weekend. Which is what I was just going to tell you, but then you said you weren't interested in the Isabella case, so I thought I wouldn't bother."

"Cantrip," I said with some alarm, for with all his faults I am fond of the boy, "please do nothing rash.

Are you sure that the best time to question a murder suspect is when he has a gun in his hand?"

"I'll probably do it over dinner. Anyway, don't worry, I'm going to be tremendously subtle about it. You can't just go up to a chap you're shooting with and ask if he's poisoned any fortune-tellers lately, it would be bad form. I've worked out how I'm going to do it. What I'm going to do, first chance I get, is bring the conversation round to a point where I can just sort of casually mention Parsons Haver. And then I *will* mention Parsons Haver, just sort of casually, and if he looks guilty, that'll be jolly significant. And if he doesn't, that'll be jolly significant as well, because it'll mean it was probably the other chap that did in Isabella."

Only after Cantrip had left us, when I resumed my reading of her aunt's letters, did I begin to understand why Julia had seemed troubled by his reference to a mysterious stranger appearing in Parsons Haver.

Thursday, 12th August

Having left this unfinished and unposted in my bureau for nearly a week, I'm in two minds now about posting it at all. You'll probably say that I'm turning into a silly old woman, and I don't like to think of you being so impertinent — you used to be such a nice child.

Maurice came back, of course, perfectly safe and well, on Saturday evening. It was ridiculous to have thought of him as having disappeared — he'd simply been out for a drive.

I mentioned, didn't I, the young man called Derek Arkwright, who came to Isabella's funeral by mistake and showed such an interest in our stained-glass windows? Maurice invited him then to come down again and be given a proper tour of St Ethel's and some of the other Sussex churches, and he said he'd love to — well, people have to say that, of course, and one doesn't expect them to mean it. But on Saturday morning there he was on the doorstep of the Vicarage, saying that he'd driven down from London on the spur of the moment and wondered if Maurice might happen to be free.

So they spent the day driving all over West Sussex, looking at stained-glass windows and Norman fonts and medieval misericords. They arrived back in Haver at about seven and stopped here so that Derek and I could be properly introduced — we'd hardly spoken at the funeral. Maurice was in such high spirits that at first I thought he was tipsy — but he wasn't, he'd just been enjoying himself. They seemed to have eaten strawberries and cream in every café between here and Chichester, with Maurice telling all his favourite stories about Sussex saints who played jokes on the devil and pushed their mothers round the countryside in wheelbarrows.

"And since Maurice is a man of the cloth," said Derek, looking demure, "I had to believe every word."

He's really a most attractive young man. Very nice to look at, very willowy — just your sort of thing, so it's lucky you weren't here. I don't quite know what he does for a living. When I asked him, he said, "Oh, whatever I can get someone to pay me for, Mrs Sheldon."

Maurice is clearly extremely taken with him and hoping he'll come down again. He's even shown him the Virgil frontispiece, which is an exceptional privilege on such a short acquaintance. It isn't on display, you see — Maurice thinks some of his parishioners might find it slightly improper. So he keeps it in a drawer in the desk in his study and only shows it to people he's sure will like it. For example, he's never shown it to Daphne.

And do you think Daphne admits that her premonition or whatever one calls it was entirely wrong? Not a bit of it. Derek has a dark and untrustworthy psychic aura, and she knew right away that he was a treacherous and horrible person — it's dangerous for Maurice to spend any time with him, so she was absolutely right! She's getting quite silly and tiresome about it — she told Maurice all about the dangerous aura and tried to make him promise not to see Derek if he came down here again. When he refused, she came round here wanting me to try to persuade him.

I tried to explain to her that one simply can't ask one's friends for that sort of promise and she sat saying yes from time to time, as if I were making some kind of impression on her. After about half an hour of which, she said, "But I'm sure he'd promise if you asked him," and I saw that I might as well have been talking Swahili — there are times when I could shake her.

♣　♣　♣

Julia was no longer writing but gazing out of the window, her expression thoughtful: I had the impression that her mind was no longer on the Finance Act.

"Tell me," I said, "am I right in supposing that what you are worried about is this young man Derek Arkwright?"

"When I said I was worried," said Julia, lighting a Gauloise, "I didn't exactly mean that I was worried, only that I was — well, not worried exactly. But you must admit, Hilary, there's something rather mysterious about him. And he was, as you will no doubt remember, the only stranger at Isabella's funeral."

"Well, at least there's one thing you can be sure about — he isn't the man in the black Mercedes. From your aunt's description, he's far too young to be Albany or Bolton. Besides, the Reverend Maurice would have recognized him."

"Yes, I know — I was finding it a rather comforting thought. But now that Cantrip's suggested this henchman theory —"

I endeavoured to persuade her that her misgivings were unfounded. The young man had given a reasonable explanation of his presence at the funeral

128

and of his subsequent return: we had no grounds to suspect that his motives were in any way sinister.

"Daphne thinks they are," said Julia, drawing deeply on her Gauloise. "And it's almost beginning to look as if Daphne — well, as if she were right about things more often than one might expect."

"Julia," I said, "you're not seriously suggesting that Daphne has the power of prophecy?"

"I don't say prophecy exactly. But some sort of — some sort of something or other." Perhaps feeling that she had not expressed herself with that degree of precision usually expected of the Chancery Bar, she fell silent.

"My dear Julia," I said kindly, "you're talking absolute nonsense."

"You may not say so," said Julia, "when you've finished reading the letter."

♣ ♣ ♣

But I shouldn't be unkind about Daphne's prophesying — so far as I'm concerned, it's turned out rather well.

I told you, didn't I, that Ricky had invited me to go to the races with him? I didn't really feel cross enough to turn down a day at Goodwood, not in weather like this, so yesterday I put up the Closed sign in the antique shop and off we went.

We had a picnic lunch on the Downs of cold roast chicken and salad, washed down with a glass or two of Sancerre, and then went into the enclosure to try our luck.

For the first three races I didn't see anything that specially took my fancy — I just let Ricky put a couple of pounds on for me on whatever he was backing himself. He knows the form book pretty well, and we were a little bit ahead, but nothing spectacular.

But going round the paddock before the fourth race was a lovely little chestnut mare — a darling of a horse, the kind that makes one want to jump up and ride her oneself — and she winked at me. Not literally, of course, but you know what I mean.

I decided to put ten pounds each way on her. I didn't want to tell Ricky, though — he was backing a big grey horse, which on the form book was an almost certain winner, and he'd have tried to talk me out of it. I told him I was feeling lucky and I'd place my next bet myself to make sure the luck stayed with it.

And then, as I was standing beside the guichet filling in the slip, I suddenly remembered Daphne saying that I was going to have good luck with animals. And before I quite realized what I was doing I'd staked a hundred pounds — all on the chestnut mare and all to win.

I don't know whether to say I enjoyed the race. The hundred pounds was almost all the money I had with me, and I'd meant it to cover my living expenses for a week — the idea of losing it made me feel rather sick.

We were in the Richmond stand, right beside the finishing line, and even with binoculars I couldn't see exactly what was happening at the start — just a jumble of bright colours against the green of the Downs. When they turned for home, though, I could see my little chestnut was in the lead, pretty well ahead of the field but with the big grey about three lengths behind and beginning to gain on her — I almost couldn't watch. On heavier going or over a longer distance I dare say he'd have caught her, but my sweet darling chestnut found a bit of extra speed and came in a length ahead. Well, yes, of course I enjoyed it — it was simply perfect.

And I came home four hundred pounds richer, all thanks to poor Daphne.

Yours with much love,

Reg

♣ ♣ ♣

"Well?" said Julia as I put down the letter, as if supposing that in the face of such evidence my scepticism could not be maintained.

"My dear Julia," I said, "anyone who knew that your aunt was fond of racing could have guessed that sometime in the month of August she would make a successful bet on a horse."

"They couldn't be sure — suppose she'd lost?"

"Then they would say that the prediction had referred to something quite different. The art of

131

successful prophecy depends on ambiguity — it was, as you will remember, the distinguishing characteristic of the Delphic oracle."

"The fact remains that on at least three occasions Daphne has turned out to be right about things she couldn't have known about except by some sort of — some sort of whatever it is."

"And on innumerable others, I dare say, she's made equally vague predictions which turned out to be wrong and have therefore made no impression on anyone. Her prediction about Griselda, for example — if Griselda had had any trouble with animals we should no doubt have heard about it."

I was still trying in vain to reason with her when Selena arrived, tendering apologies for the noise the builders had been making.

"I'm very sorry — they've promised it won't last much longer, but I'm afraid that in the meantime there isn't much I can do about it." She had begun to have that slightly beleaguered look often to be observed in those dealing with builders.

"Oh," said Julia, "there's no need to apologize. It's in the nature of builders to make a noise — no one can say that it's your fault."

"Oh, can't they?" said Selena. "Everyone in 62 seems to have decided that the builders are entirely my responsibility. From the way Basil talks about it —"

"Even Basil Ptarmigan can't claim that you're solely responsible for engaging the builders."

"Not in so many words. He just goes round reminiscing nostalgically about when he was first at the

Bar and mentions, as if just in passing, that in those days there weren't any women in Chambers. And then goes on to add, also as if just in passing, that he doesn't remember there having been any builders in Chambers either. I've been wondering whether it counts as sexual harassment."

"Selena," said Julia, looking slightly puzzled, "what are you doing here? I don't mean that it isn't, as always, a pleasure to see you, but didn't you say you had a conference with your merchant-banking client?"

"I did, but I don't," said Selena with a touch of despondency. "It was arranged three weeks ago and sounded quite important, but Sir Robert's personal assistant rang up this morning and said that he had to cancel it. I'm afraid what it really means is that he's lost confidence in my advice, I suppose because I couldn't help him with the insider-dealer problem. I'm feeling rather put out about it, so I've decided to adjourn early to the Corkscrew. Can I persuade you both to join me?"

"Oh dear," said Julia. "I really ought to finish this opinion on the Finance Act."

"Of course," said Selena, "I wouldn't want to be a bad influence on you."

"On the other hand," said Julia, "Madame Louisa did say in my horoscope this morning that it would be a bad day for dealing with legal matters. And who am I to struggle against what the stars have ordained?"

We were on the point of leaving when Selena remembered that the Restoration Committee was in need of professional guidance on the choice of carpets and curtains. This they were hoping to obtain from Julia's aunt, when she next happened to be in London, in exchange for a reasonably generous lunch.

"Would you mind ringing her now to see if we can arrange a day? I'd like to feel that I'd made some progress with something."

Again, however, it proved an unfortunate moment for Julia to telephone her aunt. Mrs Sheldon had just returned from the hospital: Griselda had met with an accident — a serious accident, involving one of her cats.

CHAPTER
NINE

Scholarly considerations must yield on occasion to humane. Though my usual practise is to proceed chronologically, setting out the material events in the order in which I became aware of them, to follow it at this juncture would prolong an anxiety which will be painful to my readers and may well, while it continues, distract their minds from other aspects of my narrative. I hasten to say, therefore, that the cat was completely unhurt and remains, I am told, to this very day in the best of health.

I myself was obliged to leave for New York without such reassurance, or any details of the nature and cause of the accident. It was not until my return, a month later, that I received an account of it.

At 62 New Square I had found a pitiful scene of chaos and devastation: scarred ceilings and battered walls; piles of rubble in unexpected places; wires protruding from plaster; sundry items of sanitary equipment obstructing the corridors, as if ripped from their proper place to provide a last barricade against invasion — a scene, in short, such as was to be expected after the bombardment previously described. On the other hand, everything was very quiet: I concluded that the builders had departed, either for a rest or for some more lucrative project.

These not being the surroundings in which to recover from the rigours of a transatlantic journey, I had remained long enough only to assure myself of the continued well-being of my friends and to ascertain their arrangements for lunch. They intended, they said, to take that meal in the Corkscrew: if I cared to wait for them there, I could amuse myself in the meantime by reading the most recent correspondence from Parsons Haver.

24 High Street
Parsons Haver
West Sussex

Tuesday, 17th August

Dear Julia,

I really don't know what's happening to Parsons Haver — it seems to be turning into the crime capital of West Sussex. First Daphne's burglary, and now this. Perhaps I didn't explain properly, when you rang on Friday, that Griselda's accident had anything to do with a crime — the whole thing had been such a shock that I wasn't thinking clearly — but it quite certainly did.

And it all happened on such a lovely afternoon. Griselda and I were at the far end of her garden, which as you know is much larger than mine, so we were only a short distance from the back garden of the Rectory. We were just sitting there peacefully, admiring the clematis and enjoying the smell of honeysuckle, with Tabitha stretched out asleep in the sun on top of the potting shed, when all at once there was a tremendous crash, as if someone had dropped half a hundredweight of crockery. It sounded as if it came from the Rectory, or somewhere close by.

Tabitha is a very nervous cat, having come from a bad home, and always bolts from sudden noises — she leapt straight down from the potting shed, not into the garden but into the lane outside, and Griselda, of course, went running out after her.

There isn't any traffic in the lane, it's too narrow, but it leads into the High Street, which can be quite dangerous. It's part of the main road from London to the coast, and some drivers simply forget that they aren't on the motorway, especially on a Friday afternoon on their way to the seaside. By the time I reached the end of the lane, there was Griselda lying in a heap in the roadway, and the driver of the car that had hit her standing beside her looking very sick. Tabitha, of course, was quite unhurt.

The last thing that I had any time to worry about was what the noise had been that caused it all. I went with Griselda in the ambulance and rang Maurice as soon as I could from the hospital. That's when I found out what it had been.

Daphne had been in her kitchen, which is at the side of the Rectory facing towards the lane, and someone had thrown a stone at her.

A big stone — I've seen it — quite heavy, and rough at the edges, you could almost call it a rock. It had broken the kitchen window and brought the china cabinet crashing down — that's what made such a noise — just missing Daphne herself on the way. "Missing" isn't actually the word — it grazed the side of her head — but an inch or two away from being really dangerous.

As it was, there was a good deal of blood — you know what head wounds are like — and poor Daphne was absolutely terrified. She ran across to the Vicarage, crying and bleeding, and Maurice rang the police, still not knowing anything about Griselda's accident.

You could say that she and Griselda were both quite lucky, though I wouldn't advise you to say it to Griselda — she's simply furious about being in plaster for the next six weeks. But she doesn't have any permanent injuries and Daphne was more frightened than hurt, so the consequences of the stone-throwing weren't nearly as serious as they might have been.

Which is why, I suppose, the police clearly aren't treating it as the crime of the century. They make sympathetic tut-tutting noises about vandalism and juvenile delinquency, but as no one saw who threw the stone they say they haven't much chance of catching him, and I don't see signs that they're losing any sleep over it.

Well, that's all very well if one assumes he only meant to break the window, and didn't realize that

Daphne was behind it. It looks to me, though, as if the stone was aimed at her deliberately.

You see, it can't have been thrown by someone walking along the lane. Between the lane and the Rectory there's quite a high brick wall, which one would need a ladder to climb. If one managed to throw a stone over it from ground level it would hit the side of the house well above the top of the window frame. Whoever did it must have climbed up on to the wall of the churchyard, which is made of rough stone and quite easy to climb — I know, I tried it — and from there you can see quite clearly whether there's anyone in the kitchen. And it certainly wasn't a child who did it — the stone was far too heavy for a child to throw that distance.

So personally, I don't think it's at all trivial. Daphne could have been killed — and whoever threw it must have known that she could.

The worst of it is that Daphne also thinks it was deliberate, and is now completely convinced that she's the victim of some kind of religious persecution. All on account of the Book, of course — the enemies of the Book are the enemies of the Custodian. "If you seek for the knowledge that is hidden from others, they will persecute you as a blasphemer and heretic." Aunt Isabella always said so.

And naturally now she's frightened about what's going to happen next. It must be horrible for her, having to stay in that big house all on her own —

I'm sure she wouldn't stay there another night if she didn't have to.

Maurice has tried to persuade her that no one in Parsons Haver would do anything like this on religious grounds, but she simply doesn't believe him. "I know what it says in *your* Book," she says. "It says thou shalt not suffer a witch to live."

She thinks what people have against her, you see, is that she has the power of prophecy. And now she thinks it'll be even worse, because both her animal prophecies have come true — for Griselda and for me. I know, of course, that it must be pure coincidence, but one can't help finding it slightly eerie.

Please tell Selena that I'll be delighted to come and advise her about curtains, but with everything that's happening here it may be several weeks before I can get away to London.

Yours with much love,
Reg

♣   ♣   ♣

My first thought on the stone-throwing incident was that it could have nothing to do with the man in the black Mercedes. While admittedly showing no great concern for Daphne's welfare, it could hardly be regarded as a serious attempt on her life: a man determined on her perpetual silence would have chosen some more reliable method.

My second, however, was that a man who wished to search the Rectory undisturbed, let us say for some incriminating document, might well look about for means to frighten Daphne away.

Though the hour now seemed to me to be suitable for lunch, none of my friends had as yet arrived in the Corkscrew. I turned to the second letter, evidently written on the previous day and presumably received that morning.

24 High Street
Parsons Haver
West Sussex

8th September

Dear Julia,

Yet another thing I'd like your advice about — you'll think I'm becoming a perfect nuisance. Not exactly a legal problem — there's something I'd like to find out and I thought you might know if I could. It's because of the gravestone.

You see, Derek Arkwright, the young man I told you about, has become quite a regular visitor down here. He comes down on Friday evening and stays at the Vicarage until Sunday morning. He and Maurice spend Saturday driving round the countryside looking at churches and gardens and Roman pavements and so on.

And we all like him very much. Maurice in particular, of course, but not only Maurice — I like him, Griselda likes him, even Ricky likes him, though one wouldn't think that they had much in common.

Everyone except Daphne, who still has this extraordinary antagonism towards him. Whenever they meet — which we all do our best to avoid happening, but it sometimes does — she practically bristles, like a dog with someone it dislikes, and sits there glowering as if she were trying to put the evil eye on him. It's really quite embarrassing.

She goes on saying that he's a treacherous and dangerous person and whenever he's here there's a shadow over Maurice's name in the Book. That means that he's going to do Maurice some kind of terrible harm, though exactly what she never manages to specify. The worst she's been able to think of so far is that he encourages Maurice to drink too much — she makes dark comments on the number of empty wine bottles to be put in the dustbin after Derek's been staying.

What she really minds, I dare say, is that when Derek's here she can't go running over to the Vicarage to tell Maurice about her great spiritual dilemma. Which in my view is a very good thing — she's really been spending far too much time there. Some people are getting quite the wrong impression — I've been asked more than once whether invitations to Maurice ought to include Daphne. And Mrs Tyrrell has stopped going there to clean because she thinks Daphne's doing the housework, and she won't have Maurice paying her for work he doesn't need.

Ricky doesn't go round there any more either — he used to drop in quite often. "If you go round to see an old mate for a noggin or two and a chat about the Test Match," says Ricky, "you don't want to find bloody Daphne sitting there looking at him like a lovesick cow and behaving as if he was some kind of bloody saint and we all ought to kneel in his presence."

You may think, quite rightly, that that isn't a very nice way of putting it, but I'm afraid I do know what he means — it somehow just doesn't seem possible to have a normal conversation with Maurice while Daphne's there, and nowadays she almost always is. He's too soft-hearted to send her away, of course, but I'm sure he's more embarrassed than anyone about it — though I suppose any man, even one as nice as Maurice, can't help feeling a little bit flattered by such unquestioning devotion.

I don't at all mean that she's in love with him — certainly not in the sense of wanting anything physical. The fact is, I think, that she's rather frightened of sex — she's more unattractive physically than anyone could be without actually trying — and part of what she likes about Maurice is that she can feel safe with him without feeling rejected. She has this peculiar idea, you see, that he's taken some kind of vow of celibacy. She seems to think that's why he's never married — "Because for Maurice God would always come first, wouldn't He?"

But all the same, it was turning into a rather awkward situation, so I'm inclined to look on Derek as something of a godsend. At least, I would be if it weren't for the gravestone.

It's true that we still don't know very much about him — not even what he does for a living. Not rough work, certainly — one can tell by his hands. One can't quite imagine him working in an office, but he can't be unemployed — his car's less than two years old and although his clothes are mostly denim they look quite expensive. I suppose he might have a large private income, but he doesn't have quite the accent I'd associate with that — though young people have such extraordinary accents nowadays that one can never be quite sure.

When one asks him outright what he does, he just smiles engagingly and says he wants to go on being a man of mystery. I expect it only means that it's something he thinks is unglamorous — perhaps he's a travelling salesman or something like that — and doesn't want to tell us about. But Daphne, of course, thinks it means he does something shady.

We don't know exactly where he lives, either — he says he leads such a nomadic existence that it isn't worth giving anyone an address or telephone number. He *has* given Maurice the address of a friend, though, who he says will pass on messages in an emergency, so I don't think he's planning to defraud Maurice of his life savings and disappear without trace.

Which I gather is the sort of thing that Daphne is expecting. She keeps implying, at any rate, that he must have some kind of ulterior motive for coming down here. She doesn't believe, she says, that he's a bit interested in stained-glass windows.

I suppose it's a little surprising that Derek wants to spend his leisure time with someone so much older than himself, however charming and intelligent. But what ulterior motive *could* he have? After all, it isn't as if Maurice were rich — he has what he's paid by the Church and a modest private income from a family trust. If Derek were some sort of confidence trickster, what on earth could he hope to make out of Maurice that would be worth coming down here every weekend and pretending to be interested in things he isn't?

When one says that to Daphne, though, she just beats her little fists on the table, and says, "Oh, you're all so *trusting*."

Being the fount of all wisdom doesn't prevent Maurice from also being, in Daphne's eyes, as credulous and gullible as a four-year-old child. She sometimes talks as if he and I had both spent our entire lives wrapped up in tissue paper and never once had anything to do with anyone the least bit wicked. Which in fact is not the case.

She also keeps saying that she doesn't understand what Maurice likes about Derek. Well, if she really doesn't, then it's hardly for me to tell her — but she must be even more naive than she accuses me of being.

Anyway, now Maurice and Derek are going on holiday together. Derek has a friend, apparently, who has a flat in the south of France and has offered him the use of it for the next three weeks or so. He's invited Maurice to drive down there with him, with plenty of stops on the way to look at cathedrals and eat nice meals, and Maurice, as you'd expect, is enchanted at the idea. And they leave tomorrow.

Daphne, of course, doesn't know. Maurice has told her that he's going on retreat, and allowed her to imagine that this means he's going to stay in some kind of monastery and spend his time in prayer and meditation.

I don't want you to think that I'm worried about it, because I'm not. I'm quite sure everything Daphne says about Derek is complete piffle, and there's no reason to feel at all worried about Maurice going on holiday with him. Apart from the gravestone.

You see, I was walking through the churchyard yesterday, and for no particular reason I happened to stop and look at the gravestone of Derek's great-grandfather — the one he'd been looking for when we first met him, on the day of Isabella's funeral. It doesn't take much looking for, actually — it's quite close to the pathway up to the church door, and the inscription is very clear — Jeremiah Arkwright Died 26 February 1927 Aged 52 Years.

I found myself thinking it was a little odd that it didn't say anything about his children. Gravestones don't always, of course, but usually they do — Dearly Loved Father of Charles and Alice or something like that. Unless, of course, they're for someone who didn't have any children.

But if Jeremiah Arkwright didn't have any children, then he can't have had any grandchildren. And in that case, Derek can't be his great-grandson, can he? And if he isn't, why should he say he was?

It's ridiculous, but I'd somehow feel much happier if I could be sure that Jeremiah Arkwright had at least one son. Do you happen to know of any way of finding out?

Yours with much love,

Reg

♣　♣　♣

"So Julia's gone chasing off to the Probate Registry," said Cantrip, taking the chair beside me at the round oak table, "with a view to looking up this Jeremiah Arkwright character and seeing if there were any little Arkwrights. So she probably won't be here for a bit. And Selena's still telephoning the builders to try and find out when they're going to come back and finish. And Ragwort's just going to go to the bar to buy us a bottle of Nierstein, aren't you, Ragwort? Which all works out quite nicely, because what you want to hear about is how I got on in Scotland, and they've already heard about it."

Cantrip's host in Scotland had been Lord Invercrackett, the father of a young man who had been at Cambridge with Cantrip and the owner of several thousand acres of grouse moor in the beautiful county of Perthshire. He had arranged the shooting party chiefly for the purpose of securing the goodwill of Edgar Albany, in the hope of being offered a non-executive directorship of Renfrews' Bank; non-executive directorships, I gather, are nowadays the principal means whereby the impoverished aristocracy may supplement their meagre incomes.

It followed that the interrogation of Albany was a task of more than usual delicacy.

"Because at Invercrackett House they do the best breakfast I've ever had, with six different kinds of home-made marmalade, so I didn't want to do anything to stymie the old boy's directorship and not get asked back. So I had to be jolly subtle."

"As I recall," I said, "your intention was to bring the conversation with Edgar Albany round to a point where you could mention Parsons Haver."

"Just sort of casually. Yes, that's right."

"And if, at the mention of the place, he gave a guilty start, you could reasonably conclude that he had recently committed a murder there. It sounded, if I may say so, like a most discreet and subtle strategy."

"Yes," said Cantrip. "Yes, that's what I thought . . . Hilary, have you ever tried bringing a conversation

148

round to a point where you can just sort of casually mention Parsons Haver?"

I admitted that I had not.

"I went down to breakfast on the first morning and there was Albany tucking into kidneys and scrambled eggs and reading the *Telegraph*. So I said 'Good morning' and he said 'Good morning' and I said 'Anything interesting in the paper?' and he said 'Not much.' And after that I was a bit stuck. I mean, if I'd wanted to just sort of casually mention somewhere where there was a war or a revolution or a test match or something going on, it would have been easy. But saying 'What's the latest news from Parsons Haver?' didn't seem to make much sense.

"Still, the party was due to last three days, so I thought I'd still got plenty of time. The trouble was, though, that when you're actually out on the moors, you're not really close enough to anyone to have a conversation, so I didn't get another chance until teatime. But the only thing anyone was talking about at tea was what the shooting was like at Invercrackett compared with what it was like at other places, and it would have sounded a bit silly to start talking about what the shooting was like at Parsons Haver, because so far as I know there isn't any. And the only thing anyone was talking about at dinner was finance, and if you can think of anything that happens in Parsons Haver that has a special impact on interest rates, I'll buy the next three bottles.

"So I decided what I'd better do was think of something interesting to say about Parsons Haver and work out what sort of conversation I could say it in. But I stayed awake for hours trying to think of something interesting about Parsons Haver and I just couldn't think of anything."

"But my dear Cantrip," said Ragwort, having now returned from his errand at the bar, "there are any number of interesting things to be said about Parsons Haver. It has on several occasions played a significant part in our country's history, and the Norman tower of St Ethel's is described by Pevsner as one of the finest in the country."

"Well," said Cantrip, "if your mate Pevsner had been there, he could have said that, but he wasn't. The only thing I could think of that I knew about the place was that it was on the way to Brighton. So I decided what I'd better do was start talking to Albany about how we got from London to Invercrackett, and that could lead on to talking about how you could get from London to other places, and that could lead on to talking about how you got from London to Brighton. And then I could just sort of casually mention that I'd heard one of the best ways was through Parsons Haver."

I said that that sounded most ingenious.

"Well, it would have been, except that I couldn't get Albany to cooperate. Every time I started talking to him he'd sort of move away and start talking to someone else. The trouble was, you see, his List of People I Want To Be Friends With didn't exactly have my name at the top. On the first day I'd shot quite a lot more birds than he had and he'd been a bit miffed about it. After that old Invercrackett tipped me the wink to miss a few more, because the whole idea was to put Albany in a good mood.

"So on the second day I kept my bag down to six brace, which ought to have been safe, but Albany only got five. He started off by missing one or two shots that ought to have been easy and got shirty about it, and the shirtier he got the more he missed. He tried to make out it was his loader's fault — he kept shouting at the poor chap and calling him a bloody fool — but we could all see it wasn't. And the upshot was that by the end of the day we still weren't bosom pals.

"And that night I had this awful dream, where Albany was actually asking me the best way from London to Brighton, and I knew it was tremendously important to give the right answer and I simply couldn't remember what it was.

"By teatime on the third day I'd more or less given up. I wasn't even trying to chat him up any more, just wandering round the terrace eating a ham sandwich and admiring the rhododendrons. And then a chap I'd got quite matey with called out to ask me if I'd like a spot of fishing before dinner, and I saw that Albany was standing quite close to him. And quick as a flash, without even thinking about it, I shouted back, 'Sorry, I'd better stay in, I'm expecting a phone call from someone in Parsons Haver.'"

"And did this produce any reaction from Albany?"

"Oh, absolutely. He gave a sort of yell and jumped about three feet in the air, as if he was practising for some kind of Highland war dance."

"Dear me," I said, "that does certainly sound as if the name had some significance for him."

"Yes," said Cantrip, "that's what I thought. But it turned out he'd just been stung by a bee, so I suppose it's a bit inconclusive."

CHAPTER
TEN

There appeared in the doorway of the Corkscrew the dishevelled figure of a woman, that is to say Julia, who stumbled towards our table displaying various signs of agitation.

Her researches in the Probate Registry had not proved reassuring: the grant of representation to the estate of Jeremiah Arkwright showed that he had died intestate and a bachelor, leaving his sister as his only next of kin. It seemed unlikely, in these circumstances, that the young man who called himself Derek Arkwright was his great-grandson, or indeed that his name was Derek Arkwright.

"There are many persons," said Ragwort, "of the highest respectability, whose names are not Derek Arkwright."

"Absolutely," said Cantrip. "And the interesting thing is that most of them don't go round saying 'My name is Derek Arkwright.'"

I felt obliged to agree that the motives of those who seek to conceal their identities are not usually of the highest.

"You bet they're not," said Cantrip. "Jolly sinister is what they usually are. I'll tell you who this chap is who isn't Arkwright — he's the henchman — Bolton's or Albany's, whichever of them did in Isabella. And they sent him down to the funeral to nose around and see if there were any loose ends, just like you said they would, Hilary. And he's found out that the Reverend is the only person who could recognize the chap in the black Mercedes, so now he's lured him off somewhere to do him in as well."

Observing the effect of these remarks on Julia, who succumbs easily to panic, I endeavoured to persuade her that this was not the most probable explanation of the evidence before us: a man may be of dubious character without being a hired assassin. Though it did indeed appear that the Reverend Maurice might have been unwise or unfortunate in his choice of travelling companion, I thought it likely that his danger was financial rather than physical.

Selena, when she joined us, was in no mood to feel concern on behalf of those who went away on holiday. At a stage when the plumber claimed he could make no progress without the electrician, the electrician had been on holiday; by the time the electrician returned, the plumber was on holiday; by the time the plumber returned and agreed with the electrician that nothing more should be done without consulting the carpenter, the carpenter was on holiday. The only person, so far as Selena could see, who was not permitted to go on holiday, but was expected to remain in Lincoln's Inn throughout the long vacation and worry about the building works, was herself.

If, therefore, the Reverend Maurice had also chosen to go on holiday, neglecting, very probably, his duty to care for the souls of his parishioners, and if the project turned out badly for him, it was not to Selena that he should look for sympathy.

Having reported in the least alarming terms she could the result of her researches at the Probate Registry, Julia received her aunt's reply two or three days later.

24 High Street
Parsons Haver
West Sussex

Saturday, 11th September

Dear Julia,

Thank you for looking up Jeremiah Arkwright for me, even if I do now rather wish I hadn't asked you. I suppose, as you say, that there may be some quite innocent explanation, but it isn't likely, is it? The most likely explanation is that Derek's some kind of crook. I keep wondering how I'm going to tell Maurice, or whether I should tell him at all.

Well, one thing I'm not going to do is try to get in touch with him about it while he's on holiday. He did leave me a number to ring if there was an emergency — they're supposed to be staying at a place in the south of France that belongs to a friend of Derek's. If I rang it and found it didn't exist, or the person who answered had never heard of either of them, I'd be worried for the next fortnight without being able to do anything about it. And if I did manage to talk to Maurice, how could I possibly explain something like this over the telephone?

Daphne goes on being in her Cassandra mood, even though she doesn't know that he and Derek are together — Maurice's name in the Book still has a shadow over it, and she thinks it's getting darker. I don't take it seriously, of course, but it doesn't help to make me feel any happier about the situation.

Well, I suppose the worst that can happen is that he comes back minus his chequebook and credit cards — it won't be the end of the world.

Yours with much love,

Reg

♣ ♣ ♣

"Which is no doubt true," said Julia, continuing to look anxious, "if that really is the worst that can happen. But if Cantrip's henchman theory is right —"

"Julia," said Selena firmly, "Cantrip's henchman theory is complete moonshine. Albany and Bolton may have their faults, but they're not the sort of people who hire professional assassins to dispose of witnesses. Anyway, the henchman theory depends on the idea that one of them poisoned Isabella, which in my view is also moonshine."

"She was blackmailing one of them and he was there when she died — don't you find that a little worrying?

Or are you saying that the man in the black Mercedes wasn't Albany or Bolton after all?"

"No, I don't say that, but I do say that the man in the Mercedes wasn't the only person she was blackmailing. What about Ricky Farnham, for example? We know she was blackmailing him — not for money, but into doing favours for her and spending time with her that he'd obviously much rather have spent with your aunt. By his own admission, she'd been making his life hell for two years."

"Yes, but Ricky wasn't there when she died."

"How do you know? He was evidently quite a regular visitor — why shouldn't he have looked in for a nightcap after the man in the Mercedes had left and Daphne had gone to bed? And washed up all the glasses afterwards, including the one left by the previous visitor?"

"Selena," said Julia, disconcerted by this suggestion, "you don't seriously think that Ricky Farnham poisoned Isabella?"

"No, of course I don't. I think that she died of heart failure, just as the doctor said she did. But if anyone happened to dig her up and find she was full of arsenic, I'd expect the police to question Mr Farnham at least as closely as either of the directors of Renfrews'."

September is not the month for takeover bids: those whose profession it is to advise on such matters may safely withdraw from London to recoup their energies in the country or on the shores of the Mediterranean. A major client of Renfrews' Bank, however, unaware of

157

this convention or indifferent to it, had decided to proceed with an acquisition of sufficient magnitude to require the personal attention of the Chairman, who was spending the summer in his villa overlooking the Bay of Cannes, and of the two executive directors.

Sir Robert, it seemed, had not after all lost confidence in Selena's advice. On the second Monday of the month she received urgent instructions to fly immediately to the south of France to draft the documents required for the transaction. Undeterred by pitiful cries of "What shall we do about the builders?" from her fellow members of Chambers, she accepted instantly.

It was thus that she happened to be present when Sir Robert Renfrew was poisoned.

Of this, however, we knew nothing until the following Monday, when she was once more among those gathered in the Corkscrew. Having returned by way of Paris and spent the weekend there in the company of Sebastian, she had paid a merely fleeting visit to Chambers to enquire if there were anything which urgently required her attention.

Though there was by now an autumnal sharpness in the evening air, she was still dressed in sandals and cotton, with a look about her of summer and southern warmth. Her mood, however, seemed thoughtful, one might almost have said subdued. When asked whether she had enjoyed herself in Cannes, she reflected for some moments and gave an equivocal answer.

Her first complaint was about the weather.

158

"I was in Cannes for five days, and the sun shone on every one of them, from dawn until dusk. The sky was blue and the sea was even bluer. There were boats bobbing round in the bay that I was longing to sail in and restaurants all round it that I was longing to eat in. And I was cooped up in the villa, drafting offer documents from eight in the morning until nearly midnight and eating sandwiches because we didn't have time for proper meals. I admit that we were working outdoors, on a rather attractive roof terrace, and the sandwiches, as sandwiches go, were excellent. Even so —"

We agreed that in the circumstances it would have been more tactful of it to have rained continuously.

Her second complaint concerned what might be called the social aspect.

"If you're with two men who both want the same job and a third who's going to decide which gets it, the atmosphere tends to get rather strained. And you see, there wasn't anyone else there to dilute the tension. My instructing solicitor was on holiday in Cornwall and thought that as I was there to deal with the legal side it was quite enough if he kept in touch by telephone. Lady Renfrew doesn't enjoy business meetings and had gone to stay with friends in Switzerland until it was all over. Katharine Tavistock was there, of course, to deal with the word processing and communications and so forth — she's the only one of them who actually understands how to operate their computer system — but she hardly counts as an outsider. The only other

159

people at the villa were the housekeeper and her husband, who's the chauffeur and general handyman."

Her third complaint concerned the accommodation.

"It sounds ungrateful, but I found it a little awkward being a guest in my client's villa. It was very luxurious, of course, but in that situation it's difficult to tell where one's professional responsibilities end and one's social obligations begin. Sir Robert turned out to expect rather more of me than is generally required of Counsel in a professional capacity."

"My dear Selena," said Ragwort, preparing to be deeply shocked, "you surely don't mean —"

"No, no, of course not, Ragwort, nothing of that kind at all. What I mean is that he wanted me to act as a spy."

This was the first major takeover with which Renfrews' had been concerned since Sir Robert had become aware of the insider-dealing problem: it would represent, he believed, an irresistible temptation to the insider dealer and thus an ideal opportunity to identify him. Neither Albany nor Bolton had known before arriving at the villa which company was the target of the proposed takeover; by the time they left, the information would be public knowledge: in order to profit by it they would have to communicate with their brokers during the period of their stay there. Sir Robert was satisfied that any attempt to do so from the villa itself would be detected: Miss Tavistock was in charge of the communication systems and all telephone calls were automatically recorded.

"People have mobiles," said Cantrip.

160

"Not the directors of Renfrews' — Sir Robert thinks they're ungentlemanly."

Sir Robert was satisfied that if either Bolton or Albany wished to instruct a broker he would go outside the villa and telephone from elsewhere. This, he accepted, he could not prevent them from doing: not even the most high-handed of chairmen could place his co-directors under house arrest. They were in Cannes, however, for work, not pleasure, and therefore unlikely to go out often. When they did, he was relying on Selena and Miss Tavistock — the only people, he said, whom he could completely trust — to ensure that they would be accompanied or discreetly followed.

"Some people have all the luck," said Cantrip. "None of my clients ever ask me to spy on anyone."

"Cantrip means," said Ragwort, "that we all understand what an invidious and embarrassing position you were placed in."

Selena had not felt it possible to refuse. Quite apart from the fact that Sir Robert was her most valued client, she had felt sorry for him. It was clear that he had been greatly distressed by the whole insider-dealing business, to an extent which she thought was even affecting his health: he seemed to her to be looking far less fit than he had done a few months before.

She had considered again whether she should mention to him the part we believed Isabella to have played in the affair: if our conclusions were right, it seemed likely that there would be no more incidents of insider dealing and the surveillance of Albany and Bolton was doomed to failure. She still believed,

161

however, that to tell him about Isabella would aggravate rather than alleviate his distress.

"Besides, suppose we'd turned out to be completely wrong? Or suppose whichever one it was decided to do some insider dealing for his own benefit, instead of Isabella's? If I'd told him there couldn't be another insider-dealing incident, and then after all there had been, it would have been rather embarrassing. So I promised I'd do what I could to help with his surveillance plan."

For the first three days she had not been called on to give effect to her promise. They had all been fully occupied with the preparation of the documents relating to the takeover and no one had left the villa.

"You see, all the drafting took about three times as long as it needed to, because Edgar was trying to score points. As Geoffrey is the technical expert and all the documents were fairly technical, we'd begin with Geoffrey explaining what they wanted to do and then I'd draft a document that did it. And then Edgar would suggest amendments, just to show Sir Robert that he understood the technicalities after all. Which in fact he didn't, so then I had to explain tactfully why his amendments would make nonsense of the whole document. It was all rather time-consuming."

On Wednesday evening, however, when they had finished their labours relatively early, Geoffrey Bolton had said that he felt like going for a stroll along the Croisette, which he referred to as the Crozzit.

"Edgar said it was called the Kwuzzit, which I didn't think actually sounded much better, but Edgar was always trying to score points on the basis that he knew French and Geoffrey didn't."

Sir Robert had at once suggested that Selena should go too, saying that she had been shamefully overworked and he was sure she would enjoy a stroll around Cannes if she had someone to escort her. Even the bluntest of Lancastrians could hardly have said that he would prefer solitude; nor could Selena, under Sir Robert's pleading eye and remembering her promise to him, decline Geoffrey Bolton's invitation to keep him company. They had accordingly walked down towards the Casino and drunk liqueurs in a pavement café looking out across the bay.

"Right," said Cantrip. "So did you manage to get the conversation round to where you could just sort of casually mention Parsons Haver?"

"No, I'm afraid not. I remembered the difficulty you had had in introducing the subject convincingly, and I didn't feel that I would succeed any better. Besides, I wasn't really trying to find out anything from him — I was more worried that I might tell him something that he wasn't supposed to know. You see, he was obviously slightly puzzled about what had happened. He said — well, he said that Sir Robert had always been rather a Puritan and it wasn't like him to send one of his directors for a walk in the moonlight with an attractive woman. Or words to that effect."

By candlelight, it was difficult to be certain that she blushed; my impression was that she did.

"So he was wondering, he said, what the old boy was up to. I said that as Geoffrey was a simple innocent

163

Lancastrian in a wicked foreign city Sir Robert probably thought he needed someone to keep him out of trouble. And he laughed. And then he said something about the Chairman being 'proper mithered abaht summat' and that he wished he knew what it was. I said that a man in Sir Robert's position no doubt had a number of important matters to worry about. And he laughed again and said, 'Ah, well, lass, if tha knows nowt, tha knows nowt, and if tha knows owt, likely tha'll tell nowt, so I'll not vex thee wi' asking.' So we talked of other things."

It would somehow have seemed indiscreet to seek particulars. Whatever the subject of the conversation, she had learnt nothing more of Geoffrey Bolton's past or private life than she already knew. She could say with confidence, however, that while outside the villa he had made no attempt to communicate with his stockbroker.

In their absence, an unpleasant scene had taken place between the Chairman and Edgar Albany. Selena heard of it on the following day from Miss Tavistock, who was too angry with Edgar to be unduly discreet about it. Edgar, apparently, had tried to persuade Sir Robert that he ought not to delay any longer before announcing the date of his retirement and the appointment of his successor. It was bad for the bank, he said, for people not to know when the next Chairman was going to take office and whether he was going to be someone with a more or less suitable background or a jumped-up little bank clerk from nowhere. Sir Robert had replied that he was not yet ready to make a decision; Albany had lost his temper and become extremely offensive. His behaviour had so much distressed Sir Robert that he had become quite unwell.

None of the party left the villa again before midday on Friday, when the bid became public. There had been no significant alteration in the price of the shares. On Friday evening the Chairman took them all out to dinner to celebrate the successful completion of their task.

"We went to a Moroccan restaurant, quite near the villa. It was a very good restaurant — the *moules marinières* were simply delicious." Selena spoke wistfully, as if the excellence of the mussels were somehow a matter for regret. I assumed that she was merely wishing that she could have eaten more of them.

"Well," said Julia, "at least you had one evening devoted entirely to pleasure."

"I wouldn't," said Selena, "describe it quite like that."

"Oh dear," said Julia. "How *would* you describe it?"

"Well, at the beginning I'd have described it as rather sad. You see, I thought Sir Robert had been rather looking forward to having a celebration dinner — his dinner jacket smelt of mothballs, so it obviously wasn't the kind of thing he did very often when he was in Cannes. But he'd somehow caught one of those horrible summer colds that make one feel utterly miserable and he wasn't well enough to enjoy it. He'd completely lost his appetite and his sense of taste."

Julia, a notoriously sentimental woman, was visibly moved by the pathos of the old gentleman's disappointment.

"And then it also became embarrassing, because Edgar started making unpleasant remarks about Geoffrey never introducing his wife to anyone at Renfrews'. Remarks like 'I say, old boy, I hope you haven't made her think we're all frightful snobs and look down on anyone who isn't from the same social background? You know we're not like that, old boy, you must know, if anyone does.' I suppose he was hoping that Geoffrey would lose his temper. But Geoffrey just sat and smiled, and said 'Ah, she's a good lass, my wife, but she'd not feel at home in company like this.'"

"Dear me," said Ragwort. "Can it be that the relationship between the two directors is not one of friendly rivalry based on deep mutual respect?"

"No, it's one of bitter hostility based on deep mutual dislike. Or rather — Geoffrey deeply dislikes Edgar. Edgar, I think actually hates Geoffrey. Geoffrey's threatening to take something, you see, that Edgar's always looked on as his by right — that is to say, the chairmanship of Renfrews' after Sir Robert retires."

"It doesn't sound," said Julia, "as if having them at the same table would be conducive to an agreeable dinner party. One begins to see why you say that it wasn't an evening of unmixed pleasure."

"After that it got worse — quite considerably worse. Sir Robert suddenly seemed to get terribly angry about something — he went very red in the face and began shouting, talking about disloyalty and betrayal and not being able to trust anyone. He sounded as if he were drunk, but I knew he couldn't possibly be. We'd all had a glass of champagne on the roof terrace before we left the villa, but in the restaurant he'd hardly touched his wine — he was drinking mineral water. For a minute or two we all tried to pretend that nothing odd was happening, but then Katharine said, 'Sir Robert, you're not well — let me take you home.' And he stood up and then he collapsed — he seemed to be having some kind of convulsions."

At the hospital to which Sir Robert was taken he had been diagnosed as suffering from food poisoning. The doctors had at first had grave doubts of his survival and Lady Renfrew had been summoned urgently from Switzerland. Anxiety on his behalf had somewhat overshadowed Selena's enjoyment of her weekend in Paris. He had now, however, been pronounced out of danger.

"Poor old chap," said Cantrip. "What rotten luck — he must have got a dodgy mussel."

"Yes," said Selena, turning her wineglass between her fingers. "Yes, that's what everyone seems to assume. But the trouble is — it's true he ordered the *moules marinières* for his first course, we all did. But the trouble is — I was sitting next to him and I particularly noticed — he didn't actually eat any of them, or even a spoonful of the soup they were in. He took them out of their shells and then just put them back in the soup, so that the waiters wouldn't notice he wasn't eating. That's when he told me that he'd lost his appetite and I began to feel so sorry for him. And the second course hadn't been served by the time he was taken ill. So as far as I can see, he hadn't actually eaten anything since the lunchtime sandwiches at the villa. It does seem rather bad luck to get food poisoning when one hasn't eaten any food."

She fell silent, frowning slightly at her wineglass. It required little skill in telepathy to guess the thought that troubled her: Ricky Farnham had been some thousands of miles away from the scene of Sir Robert's mysterious attack; the man in the black Mercedes had been at the same dinner table.

Of the Reverend Maurice there was still no news. The only further communication received from Parsons Haver during the month of September was a letter from Griselda.

> 2 Churchyard Lane
> Parsons Haver

20th September

Dear Julia,

Thank you for the amusing get-well card and for pity's sake do stop trying to lure Reg off to London to have lunch with you. Don't you realize, you wretched woman, that I'm a poor helpless invalid and Maurice is away and Reg is all that stands between me and being ministered to by blasted Daphne?

Oh God, I shouldn't say that — the poor kid means well and she's had a rotten life and if I'm horrible about her I'll never get to heaven. I used to think heaven was just a place where everyone sang hymns the whole time and I wasn't too bothered whether I got there or not, but now I know it's a place where you can scratch your ankle whenever you want to for the rest of eternity and I really, really want to go there. So I've got to be nice to Daphne.

Daphne thinks that what she has a gift for is caring for people when they're not well. She's wrong about this, but if one told her so she'd be terribly hurt. She trots round here every day, laden with tinctures and embrocations concocted by her late aunt Isabella on the basis of traditional remedies from the mystic Orient, all smelling unutterably foul, and tries to make herself useful.

She started off by trying to make herself useful in the garden — she knew just what to do, she said, because Aunt Isabella had taught her all about plants — and she'd done quite a lot of work on it before I found out that what Isabella had taught her didn't include the difference between weeds and seedlings.

So I stopped her being useful in the garden and now she's trying to be useful indoors, by tidying up the house and cooking me things to eat. Tidying up means moving things from where I want them to be to where I don't want them to be, doing a certain amount of damage in the process. Cooking means taking a harmless, wholesome bit of food and doing something to it to make it inedible. (I don't quite know how she does it — she's got the idea that it's uncreative to stick to the exact recipe, so I suppose she just adds a bit here and leaves out a bit there until it can't get any worse.)

When she isn't being useful she's being sympathetic. This means that she sits looking at me with a sad and respectful expression, as if it might be the last time she sees me in this world, and keeps telling me in a mournful sort of voice how awful I must be feeling. After about half an hour of it I feel like asking her to ring the undertaker on her way out.

When Maurice was here, it wasn't so bad. There are lots of things she thinks he needs her to do for him, including weeding his garden — I warned him, but he was too soft-hearted to stop her — so she didn't have too much time to spend round here with me. But lucky old Maurice has now gone waltzing off to the south of France with a young chap called Derek Arkwright, who seems to have taken a shine to him.

Has Reg told you about Derek? Very easy on the eye, definitely the sort of thing I'd go in for if I went in for that sort of thing. Tabitha's besotted with him — he strokes her between the ears and flirts with her something outrageous and she laps it all up like best-quality cream. I've told her he probably does the same to every cat he meets and it'll all end in tears, but she doesn't take any notice.

But Daphne thinks he's bad news. She says he has a nasty aura and horrible things have been happening ever since he started coming here. She's even started hinting that he reminds her of the man who tried to burgle her a few weeks ago — which has to be pure make-believe, because her burglar was wrapped up in a balaclava and a long black raincoat and she said at the time she'd no idea what he looked like.

Anyway, the point is that now Maurice is away I'm the only person for Daphne to be caring to, and the only thing that gets me through a morning of it without throwing something hard and heavy at her is knowing that at lunchtime Reg will turn up and find a tactful way to get rid of her.

Oh God, I'm being horrible about her again and I won't get to heaven and Jenny Tyrrell won't think I'm a nice person. I'm not a nice person, but I want Jenny to think I am. Jenny thinks Daphne's problem is that she's never had enough love and we all ought to be specially nice to her to make up for it. So I'm trying, really I am, but it isn't easy pretending to be nice when one's not — it's all very well for Jenny, it comes naturally to her.

And you do understand, don't you, that I can't keep it up for a whole day?

Much love,
Griselda

♣ ♣ ♣

The suggestion that Derek Arkwright might be Daphne's burglar did nothing to allay poor Julia's anxiety on behalf of the Reverend Maurice. Indeed, as the days went by, I confess that I myself felt occasional pangs of uneasiness on the clergyman's behalf.

And yet, by the end of the long vacation, all these misgivings seemed to have proved groundless.

24 High Street
Parsons Haver

Saturday, 2nd October

Dear Julia,

I've decided to say nothing to Maurice about the Jeremiah Arkwright business, so please don't mention it to anyone when you're next down here. He came back three days ago, looking so well and in such high spirits that I couldn't bring myself to say anything to spoil things.

And Derek seems to have enjoyed the holiday just as much as Maurice. He drove down here yesterday evening and they both came round for drinks. He was looking more attractive than ever and bubbling over with stories about places they'd been to and things they'd seen. I simply don't believe there can be anything really wrong about someone I like so much, even if he is using a false name.

172

They've taken hundreds of photographs that they seem very excited about — they're hoping to collect them this afternoon from the place in Brighton where they're being developed and Maurice is going to show them to Ricky and me tomorrow evening. For some reason he's particularly keen to show them to Ricky, but refuses to explain why.

Daphne, of course, has now found out that Derek and Maurice were on holiday together and has been round here wailing about Maurice having "not been straight" with her. I've tried to explain to her that it really is none of her business who Maurice goes on holiday with, but it's no use. She just says, "I'd tell Maurice if I were going on holiday with someone, and if it was someone he thought was horrible I wouldn't go." She's still going on about Derek's untrustworthy aura, and making dark comments about how many wine bottles there were to put out in the dustbin this morning.

I'd better stop now — I've been writing this in the garden, trying to pretend it's still summer, when the fact is that it's far too cold now to sit out of doors. All the roses are finished, even the hardiest ones.

Yours with much love,
Reg

♣   ♣   ♣

Two days later, however, there was a further letter.

24 High Street
Parsons Haver

Sunday, 3rd October

Dear Julia,

Something rather beastly has happened — Derek has stolen the Virgil frontispiece. I'm afraid there can't be any doubt about it. There's no question, of course, of calling the police. Poor Maurice is dreadfully upset.

Vraiment sont finis les beaux jours.

Yours with very much love,

Reg

♣ ♣ ♣

Christmas

CHAPTER
ELEVEN

During the autumn term I gave but little thought to the affairs of Renfrews' Bank or to what might be happening in Parsons Haver. My time and attention were chiefly occupied by a childish and malicious vendetta being waged against me by the Bursar: the details, like everything connected with the man, are too tedious and trivial to be of the slightest interest to my readers.

On the few occasions when I was able to visit London, I found the building works at 62 New Square progressing normally: that is to say, more slowly than had been imagined possible. By an expenditure of energy which, if devoted to the practice of her profession, would have brought her, she said, success beyond her dreams, Selena had at last prevailed on the plumbers to finish the plumbing, the electricians to finish the wiring and the plasterers to finish the plastering. All was now ready for the installation of cupboards and bookcases; but the Christmas holiday approached and the carpenter continued to elude her.

"And as you once remarked, Hilary, long, long ago in the time before the builders came, when I was young and carefree and optimistic, Terry Carver is the lynch pin of the whole enterprise. If we can't have Terry's cupboards and bookcases, the whole enterprise is a catastrophe."

There appeared, however, to be a gleam of hope.

"It's possible," said Ragwort, "that I shall be seeing him over Christmas. It seems that we shall both be staying with Benjamin Dobble."

"I should prefer you," said Selena, "not to mention Benjamin Dobble in my presence. I regard him as the direct cause of all our troubles."

"That," said Ragwort, "is surely not quite fair."

"Fair?" said Selena, in a tone of astonishment. "What makes you think that I have any desire to be fair? What I want is someone to blame and I have chosen Benjamin. Why are you spending Christmas with him?"

"Benjamin, as you know, has a very sensitive social conscience. Last year he inherited a large flat in Cannes from a slightly eccentric great-aunt and ever since then he's been worrying about how unjust it is that he should own a flat in Cannes when so many other people don't. So he's invited all his less fortunate friends — that is to say, all those who do not have flats in Cannes — to come and stay there during the Christmas holidays. I've no idea how many have accepted — neither, I suspect, has Benjamin. But I'm one of them and so, I gather, is Terry — he's supposed to be advising on the refurbishment of the flat. So I hope I shall have a chance to talk to him, kindly but firmly, and remind him of his professional obligations."

The prospect of Terry Carver sitting in idleness by the Mediterranean while the bookcases were still

178

unfinished provoked comments from Selena which it would not be right for me to report: she had much to bear.

"I propose," she continued, when she grew calmer, "that you take with you to Cannes a pair of handcuffs. That you fasten them on his wrists. And that you refuse to release him until he comes back to London and finishes our bookcases."

"I fear," said Ragwort, "that that may not be entirely practical. I'm not sure that Terry would be able to do his best work if he were in handcuffs. But I will at least scold him severely and hope to bring him to a sense of his responsibilities."

"It sounds to me," said Julia, "as if Benjamin has arranged an extremely decorative little gathering for himself, if you and Terry are both going to be there. Isn't he at all concerned about the inequity of having two delightful profiles to gaze at while some people have none at all?"

"My dear Julia," said Ragwort, "if he has not invited you to join the party, I am sure it is an oversight. If you would like me to remind him that you also do not have a flat in Cannes —"

But Julia had made other arrangements: her aunt had invited her to spend the Christmas holidays in Parsons Haver and was counting on her to be there.

"Do you mean," said Ragwort, with a note of dubiety unflattering to Julia's domestic skills, "that she is relying on you to help her to stuff the turkey and make the mince pies? If so, of course, you must on no account fail her, but I would have rather thought —"

"No," said Julia. "No, I don't think that's quite what she wants me for. But she seems to be hoping that I can help to cheer up Maurice — she says he's ill and depressed and she's very anxious about him. Quite how one cheers up a depressed clergyman I don't know. I shall write to you for guidance, Ragwort, as an expert on all matters clerical."

It was not, however, until several weeks after Christmas that I read the correspondence which ensued. Visiting London in the first week in February, I found my friends much occupied; but Ragwort invited me, while waiting for them in the Corkscrew, to read the letters which he and Julia had exchanged during the period of the holidays.

24 High Street
Parsons Haver
West Sussex

Friday, 17th December

Dear Ragwort,

I write this, you will be pleased to hear, in performance rather than derogation of my duty to assist my aunt in her preparations for Christmas. I was told, having asked what I could do to help with these, that I could stay out of the way and keep myself harmlessly amused: I have accordingly withdrawn to the little sitting room which adjoins my bedroom and am applying myself to these tasks with the utmost diligence.

In the matter of cheering up Maurice, however, I fear I am not doing well: all that I seem to have achieved so far is an appalling scene with Daphne. If you ask me how a quiet, peace-loving woman such as myself could manage to have an appalling scene with anyone after so brief an acquaintance, I am rather at a loss to answer; but I will give you a full account of all that has happened since my arrival here yesterday evening.

My aunt had been hoping that Maurice would join us for supper, but Daphne telephoned from the Vicarage to say that he wasn't well enough to go out. Reg seemed not to find this unduly surprising: he had been, she said, in very poor health for the past three months — that is to say, since the Virgil frontispiece was stolen — and nowadays went out seldom.

"So as it turns out," she said, "it's rather a blessing that Daphne's available and willing to look after him."

It was the first chance I had had to ask in any detail about the theft of the frontispiece, and in particular why everyone was so sure that Derek Arkwright had stolen it; she said that there was no room for doubt.

"It was the day they collected their holiday photographs from the place in Brighton where they were being developed. They had dinner in Brighton and didn't get home until quite late. Then they sat in Maurice's study and had a nightcap, looking through the pictures to see how they'd come out — you know how one does. And then Maurice put the photographs and the negatives away in the drawer where he kept the frontispiece, and took that out so that they could admire it for a few minutes. Then he put it back in the drawer with the photographs. So you see, there's no chance that he's made a mistake about when he last saw it.

"Well, next morning they had breakfast together and after that Derek left to go back to London. Half an hour or so later Maurice went into his study, to fetch the notes for his sermon, and noticed that the drawer with the frontispiece in it was slightly open. And then he saw that it was empty — everything gone, the photographs as well as the frontispiece. And there'd been no one else in the house the whole time, apart from Derek and himself.

"So you see, it must have been Derek who took it. He doesn't seem to have cared that Maurice was bound to find out — I suppose he knew that Maurice wouldn't dream of going to the police."

I could understand his not going to the police; but I thought that in Maurice's position I would have made some attempt to trace the young man or at least communicate with him.

"He wrote to him at an address that Derek had once given him, of a friend who he said would pass on letters, but he never tried to find out whether it was a genuine address or whether Derek ever got the letter. We haven't seen Derek here since, but he'd obviously decided when he took the frontispiece that he wasn't coming back. And Maurice, I'm afraid, has never really got over it."

This morning she suggested that if I felt like going out I might call in at the Vicarage and see how he was. "And do see," she said, "if you can persuade him out for a walk — it isn't very cold and it can't really be good for him to stay cooped up indoors all day."

My ring at the Vicarage doorbell took so long to be answered that I began to think he was not receiving visitors. When the door at last opened, I was shocked to see how changed he was. He has become as thin as a skeleton, and similarly pale: if one met him walking in the churchyard of an evening one could all too readily mistake him for one of the permanent residents.

He seemed pleased to see me, however, and asked if it were too early to offer me a gin and tonic. On the point of accepting, I remembered my aunt's concluding instructions.

"In view," I said, "of the excesses I seem likely to commit during the next week in the way of eating and drinking, I had intended that my first gin and tonic of the day should be the reward for a health-giving walk as far as the George and Dragon. Can I persuade you to join me?" Rather to my surprise, he said that I could.

Few people would accuse me, I think, of any excessive enthusiasm for strenuous outdoor exercise in adverse weather conditions; but I found the walk rather enjoyable. The George and Dragon is in Little Haver on the other side of the river, only about a mile away, and the cold was brisk rather than biting. It seemed to me that Maurice also enjoyed it: it gave him, at any rate, sufficient appetite to order bacon and eggs, and eat them with more relish than one expects of a skeleton.

It had not occurred to me that we might be at a loss for a subject of conversation. Maurice, I assumed, would share my indignation at the outrageous clueing of 18 across in *The Times* this morning and this and related topics would take us companionably through most of the morning. He told me, however, that he had hardly looked at the crossword yet and that nowadays he seldom bothers to finish it. When I tried to think of some more fruitful topic, I realized that all the news I had had of him during the past few months had been in some way concerned with Derek Arkwright: this did not seem to be a subject likely to raise his spirits.

He suddenly began to apologize, however, for having neglected to thank me for my helpful advice — that is to say, the advice I gave my aunt on the capital gains tax position of her investment syndicate. Disclaiming, of course, any need for thanks or apology, I added some comment or other on the success of their investment policy.

"Yes," he said, but with a heavy sigh, as if taking no satisfaction from the thought. "Yes, we were successful, weren't we? Remarkably so. I'm glad it

184

turned out well for Reg and Griselda, of course. But I can't say it turned out well for me — it ended in my losing something I valued very much, I think more than anything in the world. I suppose some people would think it a suitable punishment."

"For what offence?" I asked, worried by his desolate tone and uncertain whether he wished to be questioned further.

"Oh, I suppose for allowing oneself to be blinded by greed. I always knew, you see, that it couldn't be quite right — so much money so easily. Reg says you thought straight away that there was something wrong about it."

And then he began to tell me, having evidently forgotten or perhaps never known that I had already heard about them from my aunt, of the visits made to Isabella by the man in the black Mercedes. He had reached the same conclusion that we had — that is to say, that the visitor was the source of her information about probable takeovers.

But Maurice, of course, knew nothing about the connection with Renfrews' Bank. This made the conversation slightly difficult: on the one hand, I was delighted to have come across a subject which seemed to stimulate his interest; on the other, I was rather worried that I might inadvertently mention something that I had learnt in confidence from Selena. In these circumstances I may not have reflected sufficiently on why the subject should be of such particular interest to him.

What he seemed to want to know was whether, in my opinion, the man in the Mercedes was guilty of any criminal offence and, if so, whether it was a serious crime or of a merely technical nature.

I told him that the question was outside the area in which I could claim any particular expertise; but from what I knew of the facts and understood of the law it seemed likely that Isabella's visitor, in disclosing to her confidential information about prospective takeovers, was guilty of the offence of insider dealing.

"You mean," said Maurice, "that if he were found out he would be sent to prison?"

I said that theoretically he could be sent to prison for a period of up to seven years; but that in practice convictions for insider dealing seldom led to imprisonment. The most serious consequence, for the sort of person that he seemed likely to be, would be the possibility of being disqualified from engaging in any investment business: a sentence of professional ruin might seem to such a man at least as bad as one of imprisonment.

Maurice at first appeared to think these penalties unduly harsh: it seemed to him that the man in the black Mercedes had not in fact done anyone any harm. I did my best to persuade him, however, that the severity of the law did not more than reflect the moral gravity of the offence. Though conceding that insider dealing was

186

sometimes spoken of as a crime without a victim, I said that it almost inevitably involved a betrayal of trust; and usually of the trust which had been placed by simple, inexperienced people, investing their hard-earned savings in the equity market, in those with greater knowledge and financial sophistication. In short, while not actually asserting that insider dealing was a worse crime than child abuse, I described it in terms which might reasonably have been seen as pointing to that conclusion.

I put the case, as you may think, rather high, not really because I have any strong views on the matter, but in the hope of lending a little colour and excitement to the subject and so distracting Maurice from whatever was depressing him. I now fear that this may have been a mistake; but I thought at the time that I was doing rather well and was pleased that he seemed impressed by the argument.

"And I suppose also," said Maurice, "that committing such a crime might make someone readier to commit another, perhaps far worse. *Facilis*, it is said, *descensus Averni*. One step on the road to hell leads almost inevitably to the next, or so people seem to think."

"I was under the impression," I said, "that the Church nowadays no longer believed in hell."

"We no longer believe in it as a geographical place, like Paris or Los Angeles. Not, of course, that one ever thought that it would be anything like Paris. But I think we still believe in it as a condition of the soul — something that follows from what I suppose one calls sin. Not a punishment, just an inevitable consequence, like darkness when you put the light out."

He spoke with great despondency: I saw that I had been unduly optimistic in thinking that I had raised his spirits.

"But I assume," I said, "that that is subject to the possibility of redemption?"

"Redemption? Oh yes, of course, one's supposed to believe in that." He did not say it, however, with the degree of conviction which I had thought might be expected from a man of his profession.

I must ask you to excuse me for a few moments: a warm and seductive smell of cinnamon and cloves has somehow found its way upstairs to my sitting room, and has inspired in me an irresistible impulse to neglect for a little while the duties previously mentioned and follow it back to the place from which it came.

♣   ♣   ♣

Up to this point, the handwriting of the letter had been, by Julia's standards, passably legible. The more erratic style of the succeeding paragraph would have led a graphologist to infer some change in circumstances — that the writer, perhaps, had consumed some quantity of wine, or instead of writing at a desk had adopted a semi-recumbent posture on a sofa or chaise longue.

♣ ♣ ♣

That is to say, the kitchen, where I found my aunt doing interesting and complicated things to various kinds of pastry. Though rigorously forbidden to assist directly in these activities, I was entrusted with a plateful of hot mince pies to take into the drawing room, where Griselda and Mrs Tyrrell were putting up the Christmas decorations, and told to make sure that they had enough wine to sustain them in their labours. I performed these tasks without misadventure, and lingered for a while to share the wine and mince pies and to exchange gossip.

Having no hope of equalling Mrs Tyrrell's dexterity with silver paper and drawing pins, or her agility on a stepladder, I did not offer to help with putting up the decorations: decorations which I put up never seem to hang with much symmetry or elegance, or indeed for very long at all. I did suggest that I could stand beside the stepladder and catch her if she happened to fall; but Griselda claimed that responsibility as hers, and would not by any means relinquish it. (I should mention that Mrs Tyrrell is rather attractive and has very prettily shaped legs.)

When I mentioned having seen Maurice, they both expressed anxiety about him. They seemed to think that he has financial problems, and that it is these that are affecting his health. I found this a rather surprising idea; but apparently Daphne made some remark to Mrs Tyrrell a few months ago about Maurice being very short of money and terribly worried about it. Then she realized she was being rather indiscreet, and asked Mrs Tyrrell not to repeat it to anyone; but if it's what's making him ill, Mrs Tyrrell feels it isn't right to keep it a secret from his friends.

I also told them, of course, about the appalling scene with Daphne, which I have already — or, no, I see that I haven't yet told you about it, and shall therefore proceed to do so forthwith.

By the time Maurice and I walked back from the George and Dragon, it was almost midday, and I was beginning to feel slightly hungry. Having told Reg that I would fend for myself as far as lunch was concerned, I decided that the time was ripe for a glass of wine and a toasted sandwich in the Newt and Ninepence. Maurice declined to join me, saying he must return to the Vicarage and deal with a number of things which he had neglected.

Having browsed for a few minutes in the High Street bookshop, I was soon afterwards comfortably settled in the saloon bar of the Newt and Ninepence with all that a reasonable woman could require for absolute contentment — that is to say, a glass of wine, a toasted sandwich, and a detective story I had never read before. This happy state continued for about ten minutes, at the end of which I suddenly realized that a small, indignant-looking person was leaning over me and accusing me of being Reg's niece, Julia.

Resisting a natural impulse to denial, I admitted that I was. "And I think," I said, "that you must be Daphne?"

I recognized her without difficulty from the description my aunt had given, though the expression "not at all a pretty girl" was something of an understatement: she was one of the most unattractive girls I have ever met, and I felt it optimistic to hope that lipstick or mascara could make a significant difference. Nor did it seem to me that what she lacked was animation, precisely, though what she was chiefly animated by was rage towards myself.

She stood with both hands planted firmly on my table, barring any possible escape route, and said that she wanted to talk to me.

"I just want you to know," she said, "that I've spent the whole morning looking for Maurice and not finding him and going simply frantic with worry about him. I rang and rang at his door and he didn't answer, and then I went round the back and looked through all the windows and I still couldn't see him, and I thought he must have been taken ill and be just lying there helpless. And he keeps forgetting to get a key made for me, so I couldn't get in to find out. I was nearly out of my mind with worry. And now he says he was just out for a walk. With you."

"I'm sorry," I said. "He didn't say anything about having an appointment."

"It wasn't an appointment, we don't need stupid appointments, he knew I'd be coming, I go round every morning to put his rubbish out for him and see if he wants any shopping done before I give him his lunch. He said you walked to the George and Dragon — is that true?"

"Yes," I said.

"To the George and Dragon?" she said again, with apparent incredulity.

"Yes," I said.

"You walked? To the George and Dragon?" Her incredulity appeared to increase.

"Yes," I said.

"To the George and Dragon? You walked?"

"Yes," I said again, wondering whether there was any limit to the number of times she could ask the question. "Do you have something against the George and Dragon? I've always thought it a rather agreeable place."

This answer seemed to enrage her further.

"Don't you know how far it is? Don't you know we're in the middle of winter? Don't you know how old Maurice is?"

"Well, not exactly," I said, "but —"

"Can't you see he's not a well person? Don't you care at all what happens to him? Don't you care if he gets pneumonia? No, I don't suppose you do, it won't be you who has to nurse him, you're much too clever and successful for anything like that — I've heard all about how clever and successful you are. Well, don't worry, I'll nurse him, he's a wonderful person and I'll be proud and honoured to nurse him, I'll stay with him day and night if he needs me. And you can just go on drinking wine and reading trashy paperbacks."

At this point she burst into tears and walked out of the pub, to the accompaniment of a certain amount of applause from several interested spectators, grateful for something to enliven what otherwise might have been an uneventful lunch hour. Shortly afterwards, finding myself now unable to give my detective story the attention it deserved, I also left, and returned to my aunt's house.

I feel that I must somehow have managed things extremely badly. It seems remarkably careless of me to have upset poor Daphne before even meeting her and at such an early stage in the season of peace and goodwill: we are bound to keep running into each other over the next ten days or so and not being on speaking terms is likely to prove a considerable embarrassment.

And I suppose she was right about my being irresponsible to have persuaded Maurice to walk so far; having always known him as notably fit and active, I never considered the possibility that in his present state of health a two-mile walk might be more than was good for him. I do hope that it hasn't really done him any harm.

What worries me most, however, is what I said to him about insider dealing. Can it be, do you think, that he regards himself, having profited by Isabella's predictions, as sharing in the guilt of the man in the black Mercedes? Does he believe that his subsequent misfortunes are a punishment for it? Is that why he wanted to know whether the crime was a serious one? If so, I have given him the worst possible answer.

I know nothing of the complexities of the clerical conscience — is there anything I can do to repair the damage? Would it be possible to persuade him that insider dealing, having been a criminal offence only since 1980, cannot in fact be a sin? Or, if it is, venial rather than mortal? Or, if mortal, still not beyond redemption?

In the hope of receiving your advice as soon as possible, I shall conclude and post this immediately. I am instructed by my aunt to add her Christmas greetings to my own. Please also give mine to Benjamin, and to the enchanting Terry.

I remain, as always, my dear Ragwort,
Your respectfully devoted
Julia

♣   ♣   ♣

CHAPTER
TWELVE

Résidence Belplaisir
Cannes

20th December

Dear Julia,

Painful as it is to be obliged to say such a thing, particularly to a dear and valued friend, I can see nothing at all to censure in your behaviour, either towards the Reverend Maurice or towards the girl Daphne.

Unless there is some very material omission in the account you have given me, you did not, when you called on the Vicar, take a pistol with you; or, if you did, you did not threaten to shoot him with it if he declined to accompany you to the hostelry of your choice. In short, his decision to do so was an exercise of what theologians call free will: the consequences are his responsibility, not yours. Moreover, it is not for you to advise him on whether insider dealing is a mortal or a venial sin: if he is troubled about the question, he should speak to his Bishop.

So please stop worrying about the Reverend Maurice and give me your undivided attention — I have things

195

to tell you which I think you will find of interest, relating, as it happens, to Selena's merchant bankers.

I have been here for two days and extremely busy, having promised Benjamin that I would arrive early and make sure everything was properly organized: it is several months since he was last here himself and, in spite of being a brilliant economist, he has no more idea of practical housekeeping than — well, than you have, if you will forgive my so expressing it. He seemed to have only a vague idea of how many people he had invited, when they were likely to get here and where they were all going to sleep: he said oh, that things would sort themselves out. Which things, in my experience, very seldom do without active encouragement from someone.

Still, I have now got the flat in reasonable order and feel entitled to relax a little. I am at present sitting on the drawing-room balcony, which has an exceptionally fine view across the bay. Immediately below there is a small *place*, with shops which include a good bakery, a passable delicatessen, and a disgracefully overpriced greengrocer, as well as two pleasant cafés and a slightly disreputable bar.

Beyond that, I can see the upper portion of a large and very grand-looking villa, built, I imagine, towards the end of the last century, in what would then have seemed an idyllically tranquil and private position. Its tranquillity must now be as sadly impaired by the noise of the traffic along the Corniche as its privacy has been by the subsequent building of residential blocks of flats, such as this one, on the hillside above.

196

For example, I have from here a clear view of the whole of the extensive roof terrace. And sitting on the roof terrace, even as I write, is Sir Robert Renfrew — I recognized him at once, having seen him several times on his visits to Chambers for conferences with Selena. Though I knew, of course, when she described his villa to us, that it must be in the same general area as Benjamin's flat, I had no idea that they were in such immediate proximity.

Sir Robert, I suspect, does not fully realize how open the terrace is to observation and regards himself as enjoying there the same degree of privacy as if he were indoors. I first saw him two days ago, the morning after I arrived here, when I was having my coffee and croissant on the balcony and he was performing his exercises, dressed only in shorts and a vest — an activity, I think, which an elderly gentleman with a tendency to plumpness would normally wish to engage in, if at all, without an audience.

He seems to spend a good deal of time on the terrace, not only doing exercises but also apparently working. He is from time to time attended on by three ladies, none, I am relieved to say, of scandalously youthful or seductive appearance: one in a black dress and apron, presumably the housekeeper, who brings him occasional refreshments; one in a well-tailored linen trouser suit, obviously Miss Tavistock, whom he summons by means of an old-fashioned handbell to take dictation; one of fairly advanced years and a somewhat equine countenance, no doubt his wife, who

197

favours him with her company for the customary aperitif before dinner.

Today, however, there has been an interruption in this tranquil mode of existence.

The first sign of it was just after midday, when the post and the English newspapers arrive here. I had collected your letter and a copy of today's *Times* from the concierge and settled down out here on the balcony to read them. Glancing at the terrace, I saw Sir Robert sitting peacefully in his chair and apparently similarly occupied. Your letter, I need hardly say, engaged my entire attention for several minutes, after which I again looked across at the terrace, just in time to observe a remarkable transformation in his demeanour. I thought at first that something in his newspaper or his correspondence had provoked him to a sudden rage, but decided after a few moments that his mood was one of excitement rather than anger.

He had leapt up from his chair and was brandishing his handbell with such vigour that I almost expected to hear the sound of it all the way across the *place*. Miss Tavistock came running and seemed to receive instructions, of a brisk and urgent nature, after which she disappeared again. Sir Robert did a few exercises, as if suddenly needing to work off surplus energy, and then also left the terrace.

I too went indoors, with the intention of making myself lunch — a task more difficult than I had envisaged. All the cooking appliances in the flat depend for their operation on a supply of gas, not from the mains but from a replaceable cylinder: I was halfway through cooking myself what might have been a rather delicious omelette with fines herbes when I discovered that the cylinder was empty, and must indeed have been nearly so when I arrived.

There was a note pinned up on the wall beside the stove giving directions on where to find the replacement cylinder: having followed them, I discovered that there was no replacement cylinder. I reminded myself with some effort that Benjamin was my friend and host and it would be unseemly to think unkind thoughts of him.

He had advised me, if I should have any unexpected problems, to seek the assistance of his next-door neighbour — a physiotherapist of some sort, who studied art in her spare time and painted quite interesting watercolours. She was, he said, a very helpful and competent sort of person, and he was on friendly terms with her. Feeling that the difficulty with the gas cylinder was one of the unexpected problems which Benjamin had been expecting me to encounter, I went out and rang on her doorbell.

The appearance of the young woman who answered was something of a surprise to me. For some reason I had pictured Mademoiselle Natasha as middle-aged and rather plain, wearing a sensible suit and perhaps a crisp white overall. In fact she was in her twenties and strikingly handsome, tall, dark-eyed, black-haired, with a splendidly aquiline profile — the product, one would guess, of a series of exotic alliances between different races and nationalities. She was dressed — well, her clothing is difficult to describe: it consisted largely of items of cream-coloured leather, including a pair of knee-high boots, which somehow left a number of areas uncovered — not at all the sort of garment which one associates with the medical profession.

But when I asked her, rather apprehensively, whether she was Mademoiselle Natasha, she confirmed that she was, albeit in a tone which somewhat suggested that her name was none of my business. On hearing, however, that I was a friend and guest of Benjamin's, she became quite cordial and proved extremely helpful in the matter of the cylinders. She was about to drive into town for lunch and intended to pass the garage from which replacements were obtained; she said that she would purchase two on my behalf and bring them back after lunch.

The least I could do was make sure of being at hand to unload them. I therefore decided to take lunch in the nearest café, which is only a few yards away from the entrance to our block of flats. Having consoled myself for my ruined omelette with a *croque-monsieur* and a chocolate ice cream, I remained there, reading my guidebook and glancing frequently out of the window to be sure of seeing her as soon as she returned.

And that was how I happened to see Miss Tavistock, driving through the *place* — a Bentley, as it happens, not a Mercedes — in the direction of Nice; she was alone in the car.

Natasha not only remembered to buy the cylinders but helped me to carry them up to the flat and to install one of them in its proper place beside the stove. After this, naturally, I offered her a drink, which she accepted, and we came and sat out here on the balcony.

Her English, like my French, is serviceable rather than fluent; but between the two we managed to have quite a pleasant and interesting conversation, mostly about painting. I did try asking her about her work as a physiotherapist — she tells me that she specializes in pains of the lower back; but she seemed to be far more interested in her artistic studies — she has promised to show me some of her watercolours. Her work has occasionally been exhibited in one of the small art galleries in the neighbourhood and sold sufficiently well to give her hopes of someday making her living by it.

As she was telling me this, she suddenly pointed towards the *place* and said, "Oh, there is one of my patrons. Madame Tavistock — she has bought several of my things. She is English, but very intelligent, very artistic — you should meet her, Desmond. Poor Madame Tavistock — she works for a bank and meets only imbeciles who talk about money and motor cars."

I looked in the direction she was pointing and saw the Bentley on its way back towards the villa. Miss Tavistock was still at the wheel, but no longer alone — she had two passengers. Her journey had taken about the time one would expect if she had been collecting someone from Nice airport: although I was too far away to see them clearly, I somehow at once felt sure that I knew who they were.

Natasha left soon afterwards, saying unenthusiastically that she had a patient arriving for treatment: "Another imbecile, but one must live." Her treatments are evidently on the vigorous side — she said that her patients sometimes became rather noisy, and she hoped I would not be disturbed.

Having become rather curious about what was going on at the villa, and hoping to confirm my speculation as to the identity of the two passengers, I remained on the balcony.

Just as I was beginning to write this letter, Sir Robert reappeared on the roof terrace, where he was joined soon afterwards by his wife and Miss Tavistock. And then, a few minutes ago, the party was further augmented by two men in City suits, as if they had come straight from their offices, who I have no doubt at all are Edgar Albany and Geoffrey Bolton. It's true I've only seen them once before, when Sir Robert brought them to see Selena in Chambers, but I'm quite sure I'm not mistaken.

I'm equally sure that their visit was not planned in advance — that they were summoned here by Sir Robert only a few hours ago, as a result of something he received in the post or read in the newspaper this morning. I suppose there may have been something in the financial pages which would provide a reason to convene an urgent directors' meeting. But is it the real reason or merely a pretext? I strongly suspect, given the similarity of the conditions, that he is trying again to set a trap for the insider dealer, in the same way that he did when Selena was here in the summer. I can't help feeling that this may be rather dangerous — another attack of food poisoning might have serious consequences.

Well, I shall keep as close an eye on the situation as circumstances permit. I have already, I'm afraid, spent more time on observing what is happening at the villa than is entirely consistent with my other obligations: Terry has rung to say that he is arriving this evening, and I haven't the faintest idea what to give him for supper — we shall probably have to go out somewhere. If he complains, I shall talk meaningfully of pots, kettles, and unfinished bookcases.

21st December

Do please forgive me if the rest of this letter is somewhat disjointed: there are some rather strange noises coming from the flat next door — if Natasha had not warned me, I should think them very strange indeed — which make it slightly difficult to concentrate.

Although it is after ten a.m., I have only just finished breakfast, having risen disgracefully late and with a slight hangover. For this I entirely blame Terry, of whose disgraceful behaviour I am about to give full particulars: really, I don't know what carpenters are coming to nowadays.

He arrived yesterday evening at about seven and readily agreed to go out to dinner rather than eat at the flat. What I had envisaged was a modest meal at one of the cafés in the *place*; but he persuaded me that we should go instead to a Moroccan restaurant, known to him from previous visits.

It was in a narrow side street a few minutes' walk away, behind the sort of unassuming frontage which in

France so often conceals a restaurant of some distinction. Inside, it was quite luxuriously furnished and decorated, in a quasi-Moorish style: thick carpets and silky draperies; divans round low circular tables in alcoves divided by carved wooden screens; brass lamps of the kind one might rub if one hoped to be given three wishes. At the end of the room, a piano and a small dais suggested that later in the evening some form of musical entertainment might be provided.

Rather to my alarm, the waiters all greeted Terry like a long-lost brother or nephew: the thing most likely to inspire such fond and enduring memories seemed to me to be a habit of reckless overtipping, which I feared I would be expected to emulate.

It also occurred to me that this might well be the same restaurant in which Sir Robert was taken ill in the summer. I decided not to risk the *moules marinièrcs*.

I refrained throughout the meal from any mention of bookcases. Terry was in an odd sort of mood, one moment excessively animated, the next despondent, so that I was reluctant to say anything which might depress his spirits. Besides, on the first evening of his holiday, I felt it would be unkind to reproach him. On the other hand, I thought it no more than polite to enquire about his plans for the refurbishment of Benjamin's flat.

"Oh," he said vaguely, "I'm thinking *fin de siècle*. Aubrey Beardsley and winters in Egypt and so on — you know the kind of thing."

But I was dismayed to observe that he spoke listlessly, with none of the enthusiasm which he used to show for such matters. I began to wonder if there were such a thing as carpenters' block, like writers' block, causing carpenters to be incapable of getting on with any work, and, if so, how long it might last.

So preoccupied was I with this question that I almost failed to notice the entry into the restaurant of the very people in whom I was so deeply interested — that is to say, Sir Robert Renfrew and his two co-directors, accompanied, of course, by Miss Tavistock.

For some reason — perhaps Lady Renfrew had objected to spending an evening hearing them talk business — they had evidently decided, like ourselves, to eat out. It was clear that Sir Robert was a known and valued customer: the head waiter greeted him by name and deferentially conducted him with his guests to the table in the alcove next to ours.

I now felt no doubt at all that this was indeed the restaurant where he had suffered his attack of food poisoning last summer. It seemed likely, however, from the fact of his returning there, that he did not hold the restaurant to blame for it — presumably he is well aware that on that occasion he had not actually eaten anything. I even began to wonder, indeed, whether he himself suspected that one of his co-directors had had some hand in the business and was staging one of those reenactments of the crime which I believe are popular in detective fiction. I thought that if so he was being extremely foolhardy.

The new arrivals took no particular notice of Terry and myself. There was no reason why they should — apart from Sir Robert's unfortunate collision with Terry a few months ago, which we all hope he has entirely forgotten, none of them had met either of us before. And since Terry was gossiping away with one of the waiters in fluent though ungrammatical French, they probably did not even realize that we were English.

In these circumstances I found that I was able — as of course you know, I would not dream of deliberate eavesdropping, but these carved screens do give an illusion of privacy and they were making no effort to lower their voices — that I was unable to avoid hearing a substantial part of their conversation. Moreover, when we had finished our main course Terry went off to the kitchen to say hello to the chef, who he said was an old friend of his, leaving me with nothing to distract me from it.

I gathered that Sir Robert had suddenly decided that morning that the time was ripe to proceed with a major acquisition which the bank had for some time been considering on behalf of a client; he had summoned his fellow directors to Cannes with a view to taking action before the Christmas holiday. If I had known which company they were talking about, I might have managed to persuade myself that there would be nothing improper in having a modest flutter on it: but they all discreetly referred to it as "the target company", rather than by name. Indeed, it appeared that before their arrival here neither Albany nor Bolton had known which company was to be the subject of discussion.

"If you don't mind my saying so, Chairman," said Albany, sounding decidedly peevish, "it's a pity you didn't feel able to tell us before we left London which target you had in mind. We'd have found it helpful to check what we had on file about it — at least, I know I would."

"Ah well," said Bolton, in his pronounced Lancashire accent, "I dare say we've looked at this one often enough to know pretty well what's what."

"It's a question of security," said Sir Robert. "Once you start mentioning names on the telephone, you might as well make a public broadcast and have done with it."

Still, it must have been a little disconcerting for them, like being at school and having an unexpected exam — particularly for Albany, who evidently remembered almost nothing about the company under discussion. His rival, on the other hand, despite the lack of preparation, seemed to have all the relevant details at his fingertips.

Becoming, as a result of this, increasingly ill-humoured, Albany rather forgot himself. He began making remarks to Bolton which were close to being openly offensive, most inadequately disguised as the kind of jovial banter acceptable between friends and colleagues. For example, after Bolton had asked some question about the meaning of something on the menu: "I say, Bolton, old chap, don't you find it a bit of a bore not knowing any French? Why don't you go on one of those courses?"

"Nowt wrong with plain, old-fashioned English, in my opinion. It were good enough for old Bill

Shakespeare, weren't it? And he were a great writer — or so they tell me."

"So most educated people seem to think. But I suppose they didn't go in for literature much at that college of yours at — where was it? Sorry, I always forget — Birmingham, was it?"

"It were Worcester — bit south-west of Birmingham. Oh aye, there were a few lads there that studied poetry and such, but I wanted summat that would help me make a bit of brass."

Even without the possibility of anyone being poisoned, I could hardly imagine, in such an atmosphere, that any of them was having a very agreeable evening. It must have been rather a relief to them when the lights, already low, were dimmed still further, the pianist took his place at the piano and the patron stepped forward to tell us that we were to have the inestimable privilege of hearing *la belle Zingara*, who had just returned to Cannes after her acclaimed tour of European capitals.

Whether Madame Zingara had any just claim to be described as beautiful it was impossible to tell: one had an impression merely of a tall, slim woman with a mass of dark hair and wearing more than enough make-up to conceal any defects of complexion. She was swathed in some kind of white, gauzy material, draped round her in the manner of a sari or toga. Inasmuch as it completely covered her from neck to ankle, one might have considered it a rather decorous garment; but the undulating movement of her hips and shoulders somehow made it look as if it were continuously in the

208

process of slithering to the ground, so that the actual effect was rather the reverse.

When she began to sing, however, her voice was unexpectedly attractive: a husky contralto with a touch of harshness, not of course in the class of Lenya or Mercouri but more than acceptable for delivering the same songs. So we had "Surabaya Johnny" and "Banal" and several others of that sort, mainly on the theme of overtrusting women deserted by heartless lovers. These were interspersed with songs of a rather different type, all unfamiliar to me and in the highest degree improper: from what I understood of them, which was rather less than half, I was extremely glad of my inability to understand the rest. The audience, however, seemed to find them amusing: they were greeted with much laughter and enthusiastic applause.

I felt a certain uneasiness, while all this was going on, about those in the adjoining alcove. The conditions were rather worryingly suitable, if one really believed Albany or Bolton to be capable of such a thing, for putting something unwholesome in someone's coffee cup. Still, there was nothing I could do about it. So far as I could tell, nothing untoward occurred save for Bolton suffering a fit of coughing and Albany, with manifestly insincere solicitude, thumping him on the back.

Madame Zingara concluded her performance with "Pirate Jenny" from *The Threepenny Opera*. She moved round the restaurant as she sang it, hips and shoulders still undulating, white muslin still apparently precarious, pausing at each table to hold out a large copper bowl. Having not quite expected this, I wondered anxiously what sort of sum it would be proper to contribute.

By chance, or so I imagined, my table was the last in her circuit, so that I had ample time to reflect on this question and to curse Terry for staying gossiping in the kitchen — I assumed that as an habitué he would have known how much was expected.

I finally settled on fifty francs as an amount which could be neither insultingly small nor ludicrously generous and by the time she reached my table had a note of that value ready to place in the copper bowl. She waved it away, however, saying, "*Ah, on ne prend pas de l'argent d'un joli garçon comme vous.*"

I looked at her in surprise and considerable embarrassment. She smiled and fluttered her long, mascaraed eyelashes. Under the heavy make-up I now recognized the features of our truant carpenter.

I was speechless. Fortunately, because anything I said would have been profane; it would also have been in English and audible at the next table.

"*Mais comment ça arrive que vous trouvez tout seul?*" the shameless creature continued.

I collected myself sufficiently to reply in the same language that I was with a friend: and that if he did not shortly rejoin me I should be extremely cross.

By the time he returned to our table, dressed in the rather more conventional garments he had arrived in, Sir Robert's party had left, apparently without mishap.

My intention had been, once we were back at the flat, to speak to him severely about his disgraceful conduct and then to retire early to bed. Somehow or other, this was not at all what happened. I had scarcely begun my lecture when he said, "Don't scold me, Desmond, I only did it to cheer myself up a bit. I'm feeling so miserable," and could not bring myself to go on.

He has a broken heart, poor boy, having formed a deep attachment which he believed reciprocal and found was not. "Cast aside," he said, "like the proverbial soiled glove. Too banal for words, isn't it?"

We sat up until nearly three in the morning, drinking Benjamin's brandy and playing Marlene Dietrich songs while I tried, unsuccessfully, to persuade him that from time to time in human history the same thing has happened to other people and they have sometimes managed to get over it. I even suggested the possibility of a reconciliation with the object of his attachment; but I was given to understand that things had been said which made this out of the question. If the object were to walk barefoot across France to beg for Terry's forgiveness and present him with a train of forty snow-white camels, laden with gold and diamonds and boxes of *marrons glacés*, such forgiveness would not now be forthcoming. I am not feeling optimistic about our bookcases.

The noises from the flat next door are becoming quite alarming — I can hardly imagine an ailment worth such an agonizing cure as Natasha seems to provide.

So far I have not seen anyone on the roof terrace this morning, nor much expected to, having gathered last night that the morning's work at the villa would consist mainly of Geoffrey Bolton making telephone calls. There has been, however, a certain amount of interesting activity in the *place*.

Shortly before ten o'clock, just as I was beginning my breakfast, Edgar Albany came into the *place* and walked across in the direction of the slightly disreputable bar I mentioned. Unfortunately, the bar itself is out of view from here, being on the same side of the *place* as this building: I am thus unable to tell you for certain whether he actually went into it and if so whether he stayed there.

My guess, though, is that he did, because almost immediately afterwards Miss Tavistock also came into the *place* and sat down in the café on the opposite side, from which she would certainly be able to see all the comings and goings through the door of the slightly disreputable bar.

Miss Tavistock does not strike me as the sort of woman who would normally fritter her time away in a café on a morning when there is work to be done. I am now as certain as can be that Sir Robert is repeating the experiment he tried when Selena was here: Miss Tavistock is acting on instructions to keep Albany under surveillance while he is outside the villa.

But if I am right about that, I also think that he has somehow eluded her — perhaps inadvertently, with no idea that she was keeping watch on him. A few minutes ago, after she had been in the café for about half an hour, she made a telephone call. After that she paid her bill and left, presumably to return to the villa. I think that Albany must have come out of the bar and done something, such as hailing a taxi, which prevented her from following. The telephone call would have been to Sir Robert to report and ask further instructions.

I am becoming quite seriously concerned about what is happening next door. I have just seen Natasha driving away in her car, and yet the cries of pain continue unabated — indeed, they almost sound like cries for help. I do not wish to do anything to offend her after she has been so kind, but it does seem irresponsible of her to have left her patient on his own in such a condition as he appears to be in.

I have decided to run down to the post box, so that this catches the eleven o'clock post and has some chance of reaching you before Christmas Day, and on my way back to knock discreetly at her door. If there is no answer and the cries are still continuing, I shall climb across on to her balcony, which adjoins this one, and find out what is going on.

In haste, therefore, and hoping that you and your aunt both have a splendid Christmas and an excellent New Year,

Yours,
Desmond

♣ ♣ ♣

CHAPTER
THIRTEEN

24 High Street
Parsons Haver
West Sussex

Christmas Eve

Dear Ragwort,

At least, I suppose that by now one should say it is Christmas Eve — the time is about two o'clock in the morning. A few minutes ago I was woken up by Daphne, tapping at my window and calling out to me to let her in. Since my window is about twenty feet above ground level, I found this disconcerting.

Having turned on my bedside lamp, I have decided that it was only the rowan tree that was tapping and only the wind in its branches that was wailing to be let in; but I see no immediate prospect of going back to sleep.

My room is at the back of the house and the window accordingly looks on to the graveyard; but I have slept here many times and never felt the slightest uneasiness about it. If I do now, it must be on account of the thought that Isabella is buried there: there was no one there before that I actually knew. Not, of course, that I actually knew Isabella. And not, of course, that I do feel any uneasiness about it: I am a rational, educated woman, brought up in the second half of the twentieth century — I do not imagine that the dead can climb up out of their graves.

I find myself becoming increasingly anxious about Maurice. This is partly because of something he said to me on the day that I last wrote to you. We met at the letter box, where he too was posting a letter, and he thanked me for the advice I had given him earlier in the day. He had found it, he said, most helpful and had acted on it. Since then I have spent many hours trying to work out what advice he thinks I have given him and what he may have done or not done in supposed pursuance of it.

But the real reason, I suppose, for my anxiety is that Daphne keeps saying that something terrible is going to happen to him: she says that in the Book his name still has a shadow over it. I do not for a moment believe, of course, in any of this superstitious nonsense — at least, not by daylight; but in the small hours of a winter night, with the wind howling and the rowan tree tapping so persistently against the window, one seems to see things rather differently.

I should explain — in view of my last letter, you may find it slightly surprising — that Daphne and I are now bosom friends. That is to say, she seems to think we are; and I do not feel that I know her well enough to dispute it.

Once more, I am at a loss to explain how this state of affairs has come about. Two days after our previous encounter, that is to say at lunchtime on Monday, I was again sitting in the Newt and Ninepence, assisting my aunt in the manner previously indicated and reflecting on the advice given me that morning by Madame Louisa: she had recommended the day as one for decisive action and I was trying to decide what to be decisive about. I observed the approach of Daphne too late to make my escape; but her motives proved to be peaceable.

"Look," she said, "I'm sorry if I went over the top a bit the other day, but I just felt I had to tell you how I felt. It's terribly important not to keep things bottled up, isn't it? Aunt Isabella always said you couldn't be friends with someone unless you were completely honest with each other."

It occurred to me that this might explain why her aunt had had few friends; but it was somehow the kind of sentiment with which it is difficult to express disagreement. I said that I was sure she was right, and offered to buy her a drink. After some urging, she accepted, and conversation ensued.

Chiefly concerned with Maurice: his saintly character, his towering intellect, his kindness to Daphne, Daphne's corresponding devotion and concern. He was now, she said, her only source of spiritual guidance.

"And the wonderful thing is, you see, that he's never tried to make me do anything I wasn't sure was right. He's never tried to persuade me to come to church or take communion or anything like that. Because he understands how terrible it would be for me if he wanted me to do that when I couldn't be sure it was right. I don't know if it would be a breach of faith. I'm the Custodian, you see — I'm the Custodian of the Book."

She spoke as of a position too eminent to require further explanation, as one might say "I am the Lord Chief Justice" or "I am the Governor of the Bank of England" if one happened to be either of those things. When I enquired what it entailed, however, she became wide-eyed and anxious.

"Oh," she said, "I can't tell you about that. People are always wanting me to explain it, and I can't — I can't tell anyone. Something terrible would happen — the Custodian must keep faith with the Book."

I assured her that I wished to know nothing which she thought it improper to tell me.

"Anyway, that's why sometimes I — I know things. About what's going to happen to people. And that's why I get so frightened of something terrible happening to Maurice."

It was at this stage that she told me about the shadow over his name in the Book, obviously portending some disaster. As to the nature of the catastrophe which threatens him, however — whether it is illness, or accident, or some act of human malice — she seemed to have no clear idea, and spoke as if envisaging sometimes one possibility, sometimes another.

"He doesn't take proper care of himself, you see. He's old and ill and needs looking after, and he just won't accept it. When I try to take care of him properly he gets cross with me, so I have to find ways of doing it without him knowing. And he trusts everyone — he doesn't realize that people can be evil and dangerous."

I said that I could imagine no reason for anyone to do him any deliberate harm.

"Oh, you don't know either, in spite of being such a clever lawyer and all that, you've no idea how wicked and horrible people can be. There was a horrible person who used to come down here in the summer, and I knew he was treacherous and dangerous, but Maurice just wouldn't believe me. And then he did something terrible that hurt Maurice very much, but he didn't come here any more and I thought the shadow would go away. But it hasn't, and I don't know what to do."

I could do no more than murmur sympathetically and buy her another drink. Our conversation concluded with her saying how glad she was we were friends and could be completely honest with each other.

The tapping on my window is more insistent than ever, and the wailing outside more pitiful, as if the rowan tree were trying to come in out of the cold to share the comfort of my bedroom. If it really is the rowan tree. Which it obviously is. If there were any doubt, I could go to the window and open it to make sure, but I somehow feel disinclined to do that. And since there can be no doubt, there is no point.

I know very well what's wrong with me — it's all because of what happened yesterday.

Yesterday was the day appointed by my aunt's investment syndicate, in token of their gratitude for my advice on capital gains tax, to take me out for lunch. The syndicate consists, as you may recall, of Maurice, Griselda and Reg herself; Ricky Farnham, having given the advice which led to the capital gains, was also considered entitled to be one of the party. The restaurant chosen for the honour of our patronage was in Bramber, some twenty minutes' drive away, reputed to be the most haunted village in England.

In the Middle Ages, I am told, Bramber was a place of some importance. It now consists chiefly of a single street of knapped flint cottages, with low doorways and diamond-paned windows, and the ruins of a medieval castle, whose one remaining wall rises into the sky above the village like a huge black tombstone.

Most notable among its ghosts are the two children of Walter de Braose, the lord of the manor in the thirteenth century, who were taken away by King John as hostages for their father's loyalty and never seen again. Having died, according to legend, of starvation, every St Thomas's Eve they go through the village, tapping on windows to ask for food. This was the account of events given to us by Maurice, who is a noted authority on Sussex folklore, and its truth is therefore beyond question.

I could not help regarding him, after what Daphne had said, with even greater anxiety than before; but he appeared to me to be looking a little better than when I first saw him, though he had the first signs of a cold and was rather worried that he might not be in good voice for the midnight service tonight. (I hope this is not my fault — it's nearly a week since the walk to the George and Dragon.) Still, he seemed to be enjoying himself, and to have an excellent appetite.

After we had eaten, and were sitting in the oakpanelled bar round a large open fire, drinking coffee and liqueurs, he told us further stories, all of unimpeachable veracity, about witches and ghosts and dragons and giants, now or formerly to be found in this part of the world. But even though it was St Thomas's Eve, and we lingered there until after darkness had fallen, we did not see any ghosts in Bramber.

On our return to my aunt's house, our entry through the front door was slightly impeded by a heap of little parcels which had been pushed through the letter box, somewhat to the detriment of their fancy wrapping. With them was a note addressed to Reg:

Dear Reg — didn't want to come round and interrupt while you were all enjoying yourselves, but I know Maurice needs to rest tomorrow to be ready for the midnight service, and I wasn't sure if I would see any of you in time to give you your presents. So I thought the best thing was to put them through the door while you were out at lunch — hope this is all right.
Love and greetings,
Daphne

There was a bottle of expensive scent for Reg; a pair of leather gardening gloves for Griselda; a half-bottle of whiskey for Ricky; a paperback guide to criminal procedure for me, given, according to the inscription on the flyleaf, in the hope of helping me to even greater success in my profession. Maurice's present was a cardigan, hand-knitted in Aran wool, which in the process had lost something of its attractive creamy colour. It is not for me to speak disparagingly of Daphne's skill at knitting, since it is undoubtedly greater than mine, but not much.

"Oh dear, poor Daphne," said Griselda.

My aunt suggested that she should telephone Daphne and invite her to join us for a mince pie and a glass of wine, so that we could all thank her for our presents. The suggestion seemed to be made, and was received, without overwhelming enthusiasm. To my surprise, however, it was Maurice who actually said, "Oh no, please don't do that, Reg — do let's have an afternoon without her. I'll call in at the Rectory on my way home and tell her how pleased we all were."

"Well," said Reg, evidently still suffering pangs of conscience, "she is coming to lunch here on Christmas Day, of course. I suppose —"

"If Daphne comes, we can't play Scrabble," said Maurice. "I haven't played Scrabble for ages."

The wistfulness of this last remark was allowed to prevail over my aunt's scruples. We laid out the Scrabble board on a table in the drawing room, dealt out the letters and settled down to argue amiably about such questions as whether *EM* is a permissible word. It seemed to me, however, that our enjoyment was slightly clouded by a feeling of having been less kind than we should have been to Daphne.

I happened to be facing the window which looks out on to the street. Although by now it was quite dark outside, we had left the curtains undrawn so that passers-by could enjoy our elegantly lit Christmas tree. After we had been playing for some time, I happened to look up from the board and saw a face, pale and large-eyed, pressed against the glass. Under the influence of the stories that Maurice had been telling, I took it at first for a ghost or hobgoblin at the very least; but after a moment or so I saw that it was Daphne.

None of the others had noticed her. The natural and friendly thing to do, I suppose, would have been to draw her presence to the attention of my aunt, who would no doubt have gone to the door and invited her in. For some reason, however, I hesitated about doing this; I looked away, uncertain whether she knew I had seen her. When I looked again she was no longer there, and it seemed too late to say anything.

All of which is plainly the explanation for my uneasy dreams and superstitious imaginings. Well, I have devised a plan of action to deal with them: I shall light a Gauloise; I shall gather up my courage; and then I shall go to the window and make sure it is only the rowan tree tapping.

I have lit a Gauloise.

I have gathered up my courage.

And I have been to the window.

And it is, as I have told you all along, only the rowan tree tapping on it; but it's bitterly cold outside and the wind is blowing something like a gale — one can't blame the poor rowan tree for wanting to come in. Well, she can't and that's all there is to it.

It looks as if Maurice is also unable to sleep — the downstairs lights were still on at the Vicarage and I could see him moving about in the kitchen. I wonder whether he did call on Daphne, as he said he would, on his way home last night, or whether by that time he would have thought it too late —

everyone stayed to supper, of course, but they all went home quite soon afterwards.

I shall now make a serious effort to go to sleep again, and resume this in the morning.

8:30a.m.

Your letter has arrived, causing considerable alarm. How far above the ground is this balcony which you speak so lightly of stepping across to? If it is anything more than three feet, I hope that on reflection you did nothing so imprudent. Surrounded as you appear to be by homicidal bankers and seductive physiotherapists, you surely have no need for any additional excitement.

I shall go out and post this at once, hoping to elicit a reassuring sequel. After that I must go and buy a present for Daphne, since she has given me one. What on earth am I to get her? There is a brand of chocolates which she is said to be fond of; but so many people seem to be adopting that solution that she may perhaps have an excess.

When I have done that, I suppose it would be prudent to have a restful day. Tonight I am going with my aunt to the midnight service at St Ethel's and tomorrow some one hundred or so persons of gargantuan appetite intend to descend upon us and feast continuously until Epiphany. That, at any rate, is the inference to be drawn from the quantities of ham, turkey, chicken, Brussels sprouts, roast potatoes, tarts, pies, brandy butter, bottled peaches and nuts of all varieties which

224

have been or are on the point of being prepared. My aunt, on the other hand, says that we are expecting only a dozen guests for Christmas lunch, and I do not like to express disbelief.

I am very sorry to hear of poor Terry's broken heart — please tell him that in my opinion anyone so fortunate as to be the object of his affections must be a monster of folly to disdain them.

I remain, my dear Ragwort,
your respectfully devoted
Julia

♣ ♣ ♣

I should at this juncture point out to my readers that the letter which follows, though written after the preceding letter was written and posted, was nonetheless written before that letter was received or read and cannot, therefore, be regarded as a response to it. I trust that this makes the position entirely clear.

Résidence Belplaisir
Cannes

Christmas morning

My dear Julia,

Having committed an act of negligence which she is otherwise unlikely to forgive for some considerable time, I shall have to ask you to intercede on my behalf with Selena: Terry has

225

escaped, insufficiently scolded and still uncommitted to any definite date for installing our bookcases. To say that his escape was unforeseeable and no fault of mine will do me, I suspect, no good at all.

As to the reasons for his sudden departure I can tell you, of my own knowledge, almost nothing. Quite early this morning, while I was making breakfast and Benjamin was in the bath, the telephone rang and was answered by Terry. The conversation lasted about two minutes, after which he came rushing into the kitchen, saying that he had to go back to England immediately and wanting to know about planes and taxis. An hour later he was gone, with not a moment to spare to be scolded about bookcases.

That, as I say, is all that I actually know of the matter. If invited to speculate on the basis of my impressions, I would say that the call was from the object of the attachment — offering, perhaps, a forty-first camel or an extra box of *marrons glacés*.

His departure reduces the number of houseguests to seven, including myself. How many more there may be for Christmas lunch is a matter of pure guesswork: Benjamin, of course, has no precise idea of whom he has invited. Still, I have put a very fine goose in the oven and washed and peeled large quantities of vegetables and filled the refrigerator with an ample supply of charcuterie — I am hopeful that no one will starve.

I feel free, therefore, to escape from the kitchen for a little while and give you the latest news of Selena's merchant bankers.

I mentioned, I think, at the end of my last letter, that I was becoming a little concerned about the noises from the next-door flat, where Natasha seemed to have abandoned one of her patients in a state of some distress. On my return from posting it I accordingly rang her doorbell. The door remained closed; but I quite distinctly heard a man's voice calling out, in English, for help.

Reluctant as I was to offend Natasha, I did not feel that this was something I could simply ignore. I went out on to the balcony and considered what I should do. The distance between the balconies is not more than two feet or so — at ground level, one would not think twice about crossing from one to the other. What made me slightly hesitant was the fact that we are on the third floor.

Still, I did not seem to have much choice. I took a deep breath, climbed up on to the balustrade with the aid of a chair, laid firm hold on a convenient drainpipe and stepped across. I arrived quite safely on Natasha's balcony, feeling rather foolish for having hesitated.

Opening on to the balcony was a most attractive drawing room, with a high ceiling, whitewashed walls and a polished wooden floor. The only ornaments were an interesting piece of abstract sculpture and a number of delightful watercolours — the work, I suppose, of Natasha herself. Since the room was empty, however, I did not pause to admire them but continued on into the hallway.

There were a number of doors leading from the hallway, all closed. I called out a little nervously "Hello — is there anyone at home?" and was answered by a sort of bellow — whether of pain or anger it was difficult to tell. Knocking on the door from behind which it came, I was answered by a further bellow. Construing this as an invitation to enter, I went in.

I found myself in a room not obviously set aside for the practice of medicine. It seemed quite simply to be a bedroom, opulently furnished in a style reminiscent of the 1920s. Instead of the narrow treatment couch which one might have expected, there was a double bed of luxurious proportions; nor could I see any form of medical equipment, apart possibly from something hanging from one of the bedposts, which looked, however, remarkably like a riding whip.

Lying on the bed was Edgar Albany.

"Lying" is perhaps not quite the mot juste, since it suggests some measure of comfortable repose: this was precluded in the present case by the fact that his wrists and ankles had been handcuffed together and secured to the bedhead. This arrangement looked to me to be a good deal more painful than anything I have ever known to be insisted on by even the most enthusiastic practitioners of osteopathy. I feel obliged to mention also that he was wearing nothing save a small frilly undergarment.

It occurred to me, I confess not quite for the first time, that the form of treatment offered by Natasha might not be exactly the sort of thing which one hopes to receive under our own dear National Health Service; and that when she spoke of specializing in pains of the lower back she had in mind their infliction rather than their alleviation.

Since he had presumably not merely agreed but paid to be put in this position, I thought it right to enquire whether he wished me to release him or to leave him undisturbed. His answer, however, left me in no doubt as to the sincerity of his desire for rescue. The key to the handcuffs was on the dressing table; I unlocked them as expeditiously as I could.

I would be, as you know, the last person to expect any effusive expressions of gratitude for so trifling an act of charity towards a fellow creature in distress. I was nonetheless a little surprised, having performed it, to be assailed with a torrent of abuse. Albany seemed to be under the impression that I was some sort of business associate of Natasha's, who was the primary object of his invective. He expressed himself in terms which I should not dream of repeating; but the substance of his complaint was that he had made it quite clear to her how far he wished her to go and she, with deliberate malice, had gone a great deal further.

Having been instrumental in his release, I could hardly leave him to wander freely about Natasha's flat. Deciding that the proper attitude was one of dignified indifference, I stood and admired the view from the bedroom window while he, rather painfully, resumed his clothing. By the time he was fully dressed, however, his remarks had begun to have a threatening quality which I felt could not simply be ignored.

"You can tell your precious girlfriend," he said as he fastened his tie, "that she isn't going to get away with this. She's going to be sorrier for it than she's ever been for anything in her life."

Hitherto, thinking to spare him embarrassment, I had refrained from addressing him by name. I now felt it prudent, however, to indicate that I was aware of his identity and that if he did not wish the morning's events to become known to his colleagues at Renfrews' he would be unwise to attempt any form of reprisal.

His response was to turn purple and accuse me of blackmail, making vague but disagreeable threats about what would happen if I said a word to anyone about the incident. He had friends, he said, who carried a good deal of weight with the local police authority; if I knew what was good for me I would forget all about it.

"Mr Albany," I said, "let me assure you that there is nothing I should like better than to erase from my memory all recollection of our meeting. Provided that you do not attempt to cause any unpleasantness for Mlle Natasha, you may rely on my discretion absolutely."

Still with no word of thanks, he finally left the flat. I watched from Natasha's balcony as he walked, rather slowly and stiffly, across the *place* in the direction of the villa. When I was sure I could do so without a further meeting with him, I also left the flat and went and sat in the café next door to wait, with some apprehension, for the return of Natasha.

Forgive me for describing this sordid episode in such distasteful detail. I have done so, of course, with the utmost reluctance and only because it seemed to me to have some possible bearing on the insider-dealing question. Selena once mentioned, I think, that Sir Robert Renfrew is thought to be something of a Puritan — if he is, then isn't the sort of thing that Edgar Albany appears to have a taste for exactly the sort of thing Sir Robert would be likely to disapprove of? And isn't it also exactly the sort of thing that someone like Isabella del Comino would have been likely to know about?

Natasha, I am relieved to say, took my intervention in good part, evidently regarding it as a matter for amusement rather than reproach. Indeed, though she made a good deal of fun of me for my soft-heartedness, she was perhaps quite pleased that I had saved her the possible unpleasantness of releasing Albany herself. He had spoken to her, I gathered, in a manner which she found lacking in respect; she had lost her temper and taken her revenge, without much thought for the consequences. When I enquired cautiously as to the nature of the insult offered her, it turned out that he had addressed her as *tu* rather than *vous*, not having, in her opinion, any right to do so. It just shows how careful one has to be — the French can be very touchy about these things.

My encounter with Albany was not quite the last I saw of the Renfrews' directors. Later that day, when I was sitting with Terry and Natasha in one of the cafés in the *place*, Natasha insisted on relating, for Terry's entertainment, a much embellished account of the events of the morning: halfway through her narrative, I heard someone laugh. Looking round, I realized that a man sitting a few tables away, whose face had been hidden behind the *Financial Times*, was none other than Geoffrey Bolton.

For a moment I felt profoundly embarrassed — apart from anything else, I had more or less promised Albany that he could rely on my discretion; but since she was talking quite rapidly in French, of which Bolton is notoriously ignorant, he cannot in fact have understood a word she said. I can only conclude that there was an unusually amusing editorial in the *Financial Times*.

All the guests at the villa left on Wednesday morning, not only Albany and Bolton but also Miss Tavistock — even an indispensable personal assistant, I suppose, is entitled to a Christmas holiday. They all drove off together in the Bentley, with a man at the wheel whom I assume to be Sir Robert's chauffeur, and have not been seen since. Since then I have several times seen Sir Robert sitting on the terrace, still looking in the pink of health — my misgivings on his behalf were obviously unfounded.

I must now return to my goose, which is beginning to smell delicious — almost as delicious, I hope, as the lunch you will shortly be enjoying with your aunt. With, again, my regards to her and warmest wishes to yourself,

Yours,

Desmond

♣ ♣ ♣

CHAPTER
FOURTEEN

24 High Street
Parsons Haver
West Sussex

Christmas Day

Dear Ragwort,

I write in some despondency, more for my own consolation than your entertainment. Maurice is quite ill, seriously enough to be in hospital, though not so close to death's door, according to my aunt and the doctors, as Daphne seems determined to believe.

The first sign we had of anything seriously wrong was yesterday morning. I had returned from posting my letter to you and acquiring, at my aunt's suggestion, some nice-smelling soap and bath oil for Daphne, and was being rewarded for my efforts with a largish gin and tonic as a prelude to our modest lunch. (Modest, that is to say, by Reg's standards, not by mine.) Then Daphne arrived, in a state of tears and agitation.

Discovering the cause of her distress, though it was immediately clear that it had something to do with Maurice, took some little time. Words and tears poured from her in more or less equal measure, but without actually explaining what was the matter. It eventually appeared, however, that Maurice had called at the Rectory as he said he would, on his way home on the previous evening; shocked to see him still out of doors on such a cold night, Daphne had gone into the kitchen to make him a hot drink, leaving him sitting in the drawing room; when she returned, she found that he had gone — simply left the house without saying good night, or in any other way signifying his intention to depart. Seeing that the lights were now on at the Vicarage, she had run across there and rung the doorbell, intending to ask him what was wrong; but though she rang several times, there was no answer. She had then returned to the Rectory and attempted to telephone him; the telephone remained equally unanswered.

Neither Reg nor I could suggest an explanation for behaviour on Maurice's part so entirely uncharacteristic.

"I know sometimes he doesn't answer the telephone," said Daphne, sitting on the sofa looking forlorn and liquescent. "When he's working hard on something very important and has to think a lot about it, he doesn't answer the telephone or the front door. But he'd only just got home, and he must have known it was me."

In the morning, after, she said, a sleepless night, she renewed her efforts, but Maurice's telephone and his front doorbell for some time continued to be unanswered. When at last she did obtain a response, it was a distressing one: he leaned out from an upstairs window and shouted to her to go away.

"He said he didn't want to see me," said Daphne, many times and with many sobs. "He said he didn't want to see me ever again. He sounded so angry, and I can't bear it, and I don't know what to do. I don't know what I've done — if I knew, I could say I was sorry, and it would all be all right, but how can I say I'm sorry when I don't know what it is?"

Please do not imagine that she said this only once, or only twice, or only three times. She repeated the same phrases, with variations of order and emphasis, over and over again, like the heroine of a grand opera delivering the principal aria, and conveyed a similar impression of being willing to go on doing so more or less indefinitely.

"Daphne," said my aunt, after the question "Why is he so angry with me?" had been repeated for the fourteenth or fifteenth time, and voicing a thought which had also occurred to me, but had seemed a little heartless to express, "Daphne dear, don't you think he may just have been a little irritated by your ringing so often at his doorbell when perhaps he didn't want to be disturbed? He has to take the midnight service tonight, you know."

"But he must have known it was me," said Daphne pitifully.

"Well, yes —" said my aunt, with a note of dubiety in her voice.

"And he must have known it was only because I cared about him, and wanted to make sure he was all right."

"Even so —" said my aunt, causing Daphne to burst into further floods of tears.

Although we all knew how unlike him it was to be unkind to anyone, it did not, I think, occur to any of us that his outburst might be a symptom of any physical illness. Reg, I need hardly say, invited Daphne to join us for lunch, and afterwards at long last persuaded her to return home, without making any further attempt to get in touch with Maurice. She would see him, said Reg, in the normal course of events, at lunch here on Christmas Day; by which time, if she did nothing further to remind him of it, he might well entirely have forgotten his vexation with her.

Thereafter the day passed peacefully until about half past ten, when Griselda and Ricky came round to be fortified for the midnight service with mince pies and mulled wine. When we had all consumed enough of these to be sure that our strength did not fail us, we trooped out into the churchyard and walked across to St Ethel's, which was looking very much at its best, ethereal and almost luminous in the bright moonlight.

We saw Maurice for a few moments on the way into church, but with no time for any proper conversation. We were all, I think, rather worried about how ill he looked — grey and gaunt and hollow eyed, much worse than he had the day before. There was a medicinal sort of smell about him, as of mothballs — I suppose from whatever he was taking for his cold — and he was trembling slightly as if he had a fever.

"Oh Maurice," said my aunt, "you ought to be at home in bed."

As a seasoned churchgoer, you will not wish me to describe the service in detail, save to the extent that it appeared in any way to depart from what is usual on such occasions. I would ask you to remember that St Ethel's, though small, is considered by the discerning to be an unusually fine example of early Norman architecture; that my aunt had been responsible for the decorations and the arrangement of the crib, which were therefore unusually charming; and that the choir, having practised the carols, I am reliably informed, with exceptional assiduity for the past six weeks, may be presumed to have sung them with unusual sweetness. Subject to that, I think I am safe in saying that everything proceeded in a perfectly usual manner until Maurice, in his long white robe, entered the pulpit to address the congregation.

He began by telling us that we had gathered to celebrate the birth of a child — a divine child, who would bring new hope to the world and salvation for our sins. This seemed to be thought an unexceptionable opening, and in accordance with what the congregation expected. From there he went on to speak of various references in pre-Christian writers which had from time to time been interpreted as prophecies of that event, with particular reference to the fourth Eclogue of Virgil, commonly known on that account as the Messianic Eclogue. This too the congregation seemed to find not unreasonable, no doubt feeling that an event which has been foretold by prophets must be of much greater significance than one merely recorded by historians.

238

"But we must beware of false prophets," said Maurice, with great solemnity, and the congregation seemed to become slightly uneasy.

He paused for a few moments, as if puzzled at what he had said and uncertain how to proceed further, but then began to explain, with wonderful lucidity, the historical background to the composition of the fourth Eclogue, establishing conclusively that it was intended to refer to the prospective first child of the marriage between Mark Anthony and Octavia, rather than to the Christian Saviour. It was a very learned explanation, but perhaps a little on the long side for so late an hour on an evening of festivity: I became aware of the rustlings and shufflings which are the sign of a dissatisfied audience.

Then he warned us again, with even greater fervour than before, to beware of false prophets, and the uneasiness became palpable. Ricky, in a rather too audible whisper, asked if my aunt thought that Maurice "had taken a drop too much". She shook her head and shushed him, but looked more anxious than ever.

It evidently occurred to Maurice at this stage that he might be thought to be accusing Virgil of being a false prophet, and the idea seemed to cause him much agitation and anguish. He had not, he said, at all intended to suggest that Virgil was a false prophet. There were false prophets and we must beware of them, but Virgil was not of their number — Virgil was a true prophet. If he had said anything to imply otherwise, then he was very sorry for it, and must ask us to excuse him for misleading us, as he had been rather ill. Virgil was a true prophet, and a great poet, perhaps the greatest who had ever lived, and we must never doubt that he was divinely inspired.

It became clear to me that this was not at all a usual way for the Vicar to address his congregation — not, at any rate, at St Ethel's. Several people had half risen from their places as if contemplating some kind of intervention.

And then, his arms raised high and spread wide in their loose white sleeves, Maurice began to read aloud from the fourth Eclogue — or rather to recite, since it was clear that he knew the lines by heart. His voice now lost all trace of hoarseness and the syllables rolled out clear and resonant into the church, filling the vaulted roof with their thunderous grandeur and reaching their majestic climax in the lines "*Aspice, venturo laetentur ut omnia saeclo.*"

There was for a few moments an absolute silence. He stepped down from the pulpit; stood for a moment facing us, looking down the aisle towards the main doorway; seemed to stagger; and lay prostrate, his arms still spread wide, looking like a huge white bird that has been shot down in flight across the sky.

Someone must have done something very efficient; an ambulance arrived in less than five minutes. To make sure that Maurice was promptly attended to when he arrived at the hospital, my aunt went with him in the ambulance.

It was the sound of the siren, I suppose, that made Daphne aware of something being wrong. Just as the ambulance was leaving she came running across the churchyard from the Rectory, already distraught and wild-eyed, wanting to know what had happened, and saying "It's Maurice, isn't it? Something awful has happened to Maurice." It would have been prudent, or so it seemed to me, to describe what had occurred in the least dramatic terms possible. Others, however, evidently did not share this opinion: she received a number of answers calculated to confirm her in the impression that Maurice was not merely ill but dying, if not already dead. These, as you may imagine, did not have a soothing effect.

Since she was wearing only her nightdress and a slightly moth-eaten woollen cardigan, it seemed likely that if she stayed out for long the next catastrophe would be her catching pneumonia. Eventually, however, Griselda and I persuaded her to come back here and wait for news and have some hot soup to warm her up.

We did our best to calm her down, but with little success. She continued to moan and sob and pummel herself with her fists, saying how terrible it was that Maurice was ill and she was not with him. She seemed to feel that someone should have sent for her to go with him in the ambulance: we ought to have known, she said, that she would want to be with him.

Reg arrived home a little after one in the morning. Ricky had driven to the hospital to collect her, stopping on the way to pick up various things that he thought Maurice might need, such as a pair of pyjamas. Ricky being Ricky, the package of essentials had included a bottle of whiskey.

By now almost convinced by Daphne's lamentations that Maurice was on the point of death, Griselda and I were disproportionately relieved to hear that the doctors did not agree. Although they were not quite sure what exactly was wrong with him — they said that it was probably some kind of virus — they thought that it would have been relatively harmless if his general health had been better. The real problem, they said, was that he was desperately malnourished: poor Maurice, I told you that he looked like a skeleton. They had attached him to some sort of plastic tube, designed to save him the trouble of eating, and hoped that he would soon show signs of improvement.

It was still some considerable time before any of us actually went to bed. Daphne apparently assumed that all other arrangements for Christmas Day were automatically cancelled and that my aunt would drive her over to the hospital first thing in the morning: when Reg explained to her that it would not be right to cancel a lunch for twelve guests on account of the illness of one, and that therefore she did not intend to visit Maurice again until the afternoon, there ensued a longer and more tearful argument than I have energy to relate. At long last, however, Daphne went home, with Griselda and me to escort her on her way and each other on the way back.

On my return, I found that Reg had poured herself a generous measure of whiskey and had laid out the cards for a rather complicated form of patience. These things indicated to me, on the basis of past experience, that there was some element in the situation which she found problematic.

"I think I ought to tell you," she said, having poured me a similar quantity of whiskey, "that I am not going to drive Daphne to the hospital tomorrow. Neither in the morning nor in the afternoon nor at any other time. Maurice doesn't want to see her — I don't know why, but he doesn't. And the doctors say he mustn't be upset."

I asked, rather foolishly, whether she was sure that she had understood him correctly.

"Oh yes," she said. "Quite sure, he said it several times. He was conscious, you see, by the time I left him, and able to talk a little, though he couldn't manage much more than a whisper. And one of the things he kept saying was, 'Please, Reg, don't let Daphne come here.' So of course I said I wouldn't. But I didn't want to tell Daphne about it tonight, when she's already in such a state."

I asked what else he had said.

"He kept saying," said Reg, "that he wished he could see Derek again."

She resumed her game of patience and I went rather anxiously to bed.

In the morning, however, she was in a much more cheerful mood, having already telephoned the hospital to find out how Maurice was: they had told her that he had spent a comfortable night and was as well as could be expected. Quite what this means I am never entirely sure — after all, there are circumstances in which one might be expected to be very ill indeed — but my aunt seemed sufficiently reassured to hum "Good King Wenceslas" while making the toast.

By nine o'clock Daphne was again on the doorstep, in what I now regard as her customary state of agitation: there were things at the Vicarage of which Maurice would have urgent need; only she knew what they were and where to find them; she had no way of getting in; she didn't know what to do. When my aunt admitted to having Maurice's keys, nothing would satisfy her but an immediate expedition.

Preparations for lunch were accordingly suspended while we all went across to the Vicarage to look for Maurice's favourite dressing gown and Maurice's favourite slippers. Not to speak of his favourite soap, his favourite toothpaste, his favourite cough mixture and his favourite paper handkerchiefs. It was essential, you understand, that each item taken should be the favourite in its category. Thus, instead of being content with the pair of blue slippers beside his bed, we were obliged to spend half an hour searching for a pair of green slippers which she believed him to be more deeply attached to and which turned out to be at the very back of the bathroom cupboard. Similarly with most of the other items, none of which seemed actually to be where Daphne had thought it was.

By the time we had found everything she considered immediately indispensable to his well-being and packed it safely in the boot of Reg's car, the arrangements for lunch were a little behind schedule.

Griselda, in the meantime, had ridden over to the hospital on her bicycle, laden with books and bottles of

244

burgundy, and also, after stopping on the way to give Christmas greetings to Mrs Tyrrell, with large quantities of gingerbread and home-made chocolate cake. She had found him, however, in no condition to enjoy either food or conversation — still attached to the tube and not allowed to eat anything.

Of lunch I shall say nothing, though it would have been in other circumstances a meal to be remembered in song and legend. Not only Maurice's illness, however, but the presence of Daphne, unkempt and red-eyed, still wearing her moth-eaten cardigan, silent and palpably resentful, detracted from the gaiety of the proceedings.

It was only when lunch was over and all the guests had left that my aunt told Daphne that Maurice did not want to see her.

It had of course been foreseeable that she would be upset. What I had not foreseen — though perhaps my aunt had — was that she would still insist, if possible with even greater vehemence, on being taken to the hospital.

Reg said that she would not take her. Daphne, in tears and rage, said that she must, she had promised. Reg denied having promised; Daphne continued to assert that she had.

"Daphne," said my aunt eventually, "there is no point in arguing. Maurice is my friend and he is ill and he does not want to see you — if I had given you such a promise, I should not dream of keeping it. Julia will give you some tea."

After which she walked briskly out to her car and drove away, leaving Daphne, although all too briefly, lost for words.

For half an hour or so I remained the vicarious object of furious and tearful reproaches, all on the theme that Daphne had never thought my aunt the kind of person who would break her promise. I made tea, however, as it seemed to me I had been instructed to do, and after she had drunk some of it she became slightly calmer and asked me to lend her the money for a taxi. I told her, untruthfully and with a degree of moral cowardice I am ashamed to admit to, that I had run out of money. She said she did not believe me. Becoming slightly braver, I said that even if I had the money I would not lend it to her. She said that I was a horrible person and she hated me and would never speak to me again. After this, I am afraid to my enormous relief, she marched out of the house.

Since it is Christmas Day, there are of course no trains or buses and I doubt whether anyone else will lend her the money for a taxi. It seems reasonable to hope, therefore, that she will not find any means of reaching the hospital today; what happens tomorrow is another question.

Christmas evening

I am no longer despondent. Perhaps it is not, after all, so unfestive a Christmas as I thought. Last night, it seems, after I had gone to bed, my aunt sat up finishing her game of patience and considering whether she should try to get in touch with Derek Arkwright.

Though she didn't have the name or address of his friend in London, she still had in her address book the telephone number which Maurice had given her last summer, for the place where he and Derek were staying in the south of France. She had no idea whether anyone would be there who knew where Derek was, or indeed knew him at all, at any rate by the same name that she did; but she decided, having brought her patience to a successful conclusion, that at least the attempt should be made.

She rang this morning, before I was even awake. To her astonishment it was Derek himself who answered; to her even greater astonishment he said he would come at once.

"He wasn't sure what flight he could get on Christmas Day, but he said he hoped he could be in Worthing by five and he would go straight to the hospital. I didn't dare tell Maurice when I saw him this afternoon, in case he didn't come after all. Poor Maurice, he was looking so fragile, I almost didn't believe he'd get better. I just sat by his bed and did some sewing and wished that Derek would come. And then he did. And Maurice said, 'Oh, Derek, I'm so sorry,' and Derek said 'So I should think, silly old thing,' and kissed him. So then I thought I'd come home."

And almost straight away, it seems, Maurice began to get better. When my aunt rang the hospital a few minutes ago, they said he was well enough to be taken off the plastic tube and be given some proper food. Derek's staying there overnight, of course.

We have been having a glass of champagne to celebrate and are feeling quite festive, after all.

26th December

I hardly know now whether to send this — poor Maurice died early this morning.

Julia

♣   ♣   ♣

Spring

CHAPTER
FIFTEEN

At this juncture, dear reader, you have, if I may say so, the advantage of me. You cannot have imagined me, I hope, so careless of the proper duty of an historian as to burden you with documents irrelevant to the subject of my narrative: you have therefore assumed, during your perusal of this exchange of letters, that there was some significant connection between the events related in them; you have drawn inferences which seem to you too obvious to be overlooked. Having had no grounds, however, for relying on the same premise, I would ask you not to judge me too severely for my slowness in arriving at the same conclusions.

Moreover, I first read these letters merely by way of diversion, while waiting in the Corkscrew for my friends on a cold evening in early February; I had no reason to subject them to the searching gaze of Scholarship, as evidence of something sinister and perhaps still dangerous. It is right to say, however, that even if I had studied them with the utmost care and at once reached all those conclusions which could correctly have been drawn, I would still not have known enough to prevent another death.

251

Julia arrived pink-nosed and shivering, having dressed with incurable optimism in expectation of spring, and purchased a bottle of burgundy as a precaution against pneumonia.

"I'm sorry to see," I said, "that your Christmas holiday came to such an unhappy end. Did you stay long in Sussex after Maurice's death?"

"About three days, which I shall look back on as entirely occupied with making tea for Daphne. Poor Daphne, she was terribly upset, of course. Well, as a matter of fact we were all rather upset, but Daphne seemed to have made her mind up to be more upset than anyone else. You see, she had the idea that it was all her fault that Maurice had died."

"Why should she think that?"

"Because of the Book. The Book, as you may remember, is kept in the drawing room at the Rectory. Daphne left Maurice on his own there while she went into the kitchen to make him a hot drink, and she thinks that he couldn't resist the chance to have a look at it. And that's why he died — no one must look at the Book except the Custodian and if they do something terrible will happen to them. So it was her fault for leaving him alone with it. We all did our best to reason with her, but reasoning with Daphne tends to be unproductive."

"And did you ever meet the interesting Derek Arkwright?"

"No," said Julia. "No, as a matter of fact I didn't. After Maurice died, he went straight back to London. He went down to Parsons Haver for the funeral, but that was after I'd left. I'd have stayed, of course, if I'd thought Reg wanted me to, but I had the distinct impression that she rather wanted some time to herself. I gather the funeral passed off without any major embarrassments." Julia paused and drew deeply on her Gauloise.

I refrained from asking what the minor embarrassments had been.

"And now I've just had this peculiar letter from Daphne — I don't quite know what to do about it."

The letter was written in large, childish handwriting on a rather grubby sheet of paper evidently torn from an exercise book.

Dear Julia,

It's horrible having to ask one's friends to do things for one but I don't know what else to do. I've got a legal problem and I don't know who else to ask and it's very urgent. Can you tell me please what happens if someone's quite old and very ill and someone makes them make a will that isn't right and not what they really want?

I'm sorry to trouble you when I know you're very busy and I can't pay you anything, but I know you're the sort of person who really cares about justice and doesn't only do things for money.

Please don't tell Reg that I have asked you about this as she doesn't want me to do anything about it and I don't want to upset her.

Gratefully remembering all your help and kindness in my time of terrible sadness,
Daphne

♣ ♣ ♣

"I suppose," said Julia, with a rather weary sigh, "that I ought to ring her up and try to find out what she's talking about. But the trouble is that when one starts a conversation with Daphne there never seems to be any way of ending it. So what I thought I'd do — ah, there's Ragwort."

His attention drawn by her welcoming wave, Ragwort joined us at our table.

"Now," said Julia, "let me pour you a glass of burgundy to keep the cold out and tell me all you know about the law on undue influence."

"By all means," said Ragwort. "But why do you want to know about undue influence? I wouldn't have thought it was the sort of thing that usually arises in tax cases."

"It isn't, that's why I'm asking you." She handed him Daphne's letter.

"Well," said Ragwort, having read it, "I suppose the Reverend Maurice must be the elderly testator in question?"

"I can't think of anyone else it could be. And I'm afraid the person she's accusing must be Derek Arkwright — it sounds to me as if Maurice must have made a will leaving him something quite substantial. And what worries me is that the most likely time for him to have done that is the night he died."

"Oh," said Ragwort, looking rather stern.

"Yes," said Julia, looking despondent.

254

"That is to say," said Ragwort, "when the Reverend Maurice was gravely ill in hospital and possibly disorientated, and Arkwright was virtually alone with him for several hours?"

"Yes," said Julia again, looking still more despondent.

"Well, it may be all right, of course, but on the other hand it may not. I really don't think you can just sit back and do nothing."

"No," said Julia, renouncing with manifest regret the course of action most congenial to her temperament. "No, I don't think I can. After all, I was rather fond of Maurice. If Derek really put pressure on him to do something he didn't want to —"

"And we already know that Arkwright is a rather dubious character — quite apart from his using a false name, there's the matter of the Virgil frontispiece."

"Yes. So now you know why I want to know about undue influence."

Ragwort's exposition of the law on this subject, which included numerous references to decisions of the Court of Appeal, *obiter dicta* in the House of Lords and comments on both by distinguished academic writers, would doubtless have been of the greatest interest to my readers; but considerations of space unfortunately preclude me from setting it out *in extenso*. Julia and I listened in increasing admiration.

"Ragwort," said Julia at last, "without doubting the depth of your learning on all matters of a Chancery nature, may I ask how you come to be so particularly well informed on this subject?"

"As it happens," said Ragwort, "I was looking up the authorities on it only this afternoon. Terry Carver rang me up this morning to ask if he could come and talk to me about a legal problem, so I said that if he cared to have lunch with me here tomorrow I'd see if I could help. I'm rather hoping it'll give me a chance to remind him about our bookcases."

"And Terry's problem also involves a question of undue influence?"

"Yes, it seems to. A friend of his has died and left him some money, and now some mischief-making harpy is trying to say the will is invalid. She's written to the executors making the most outrageous accusations and saying that she's taking Counsel's Opinion."

"Oh dear," said Julia. "Not the friend he was telling you about in Cannes? The one he was so badly treated by but went back to all the same?"

"Yes, it's all rather sad. It was because he was ill, you see, that Terry went back, and he died soon afterwards. I'm afraid poor Terry sounded very down about it all. And this unpleasantness about the will is obviously making it worse."

"Poor Terry, what a shame," said Julia. "If there's anything I can do to help —?"

With that warm camaraderie which is such an attractive quality of the Chancery Bar, my young friends agreed to combine their resources and in effect advise jointly on both problems: thus Terry would enjoy the benefit of Julia's thoughts on his case and Daphne of Ragwort's on hers. With this in mind, it was arranged that Julia should join Ragwort for his lunch with Terry on the following day.

Thinking that the lunch might prove to be an occasion of some interest, I enquired whether they would object to my being present.

"As long as Terry doesn't mind," said Ragwort, "we shall naturally be delighted. And I can't see why he should."

"We can tell him," said Julia, "that you're a distinguished academic lawyer whose advice we have sometimes found helpful. After all," she added, in a tone of some surprise, "there is a sense in which one could say that's actually true."

From a woman who but for my own investigations might still have been languishing in a dungeon on the wrong side of the Bridge of Sighs, my readers may think it a not unduly fulsome tribute.

Arriving in the Corkscrew on the following day a little after the appointed hour, I found Julia and Ragwort already installed there. Julia looked anxious; Ragwort looked severe. Between them sat the young man whom I had seen some months before on the floor of the Clerks' Room at 62 New Square, uncomfortably entangled with a merchant banker and a ladder. On that occasion, however, I had failed to appreciate the full charm of his appearance: the topaz-coloured eyes under long, dark lashes; the golden smoothness of the throat; the singular beauty of the mouth, putting one in mind of Leonardo's celebrated painting of John the Baptist.

"Hilary," said Ragwort, "allow me to introduce Terry Carver. Who has just told us, however," he added with the awe-inspiring severity of a judge about to pass the maximum sentence, "that he sometimes prefers, for reasons best known to himself, to be known as Derek Arkwright."

I was unable to show the degree of astonishment that Ragwort had apparently expected: it had for some time been as clear to me as it has doubtless been to my readers that Terry Carver and Derek Arkwright were the same person.

"How do you do, Professor Tamar?" said the young man. His smile, though of great sweetness, had also a certain satirical quality, attractive and slightly disturbing — one might almost have said dangerous. "It's very kind of you to take the time to talk to me. I must tell you straight away that I've behaved extremely badly and made myself an embarrassment to my legal advisers. I've been trying to explain —"

"It's no use trying to make light of it," said Ragwort sternly. "What sort of impression do you think it's going to make on a judge? There we shall be, putting you forward as a person of unquestionable respectability, and the first thing we have to tell him is that you've been using a false name. You must see —"

"Yes, Desmond, I do, truly I do, but when I told Maurice that my name was Derek Arkwright I wasn't actually thinking about what would happen if he died six months later and left me some money and there were legal proceedings and I had to make a good impression on the judge — I simply did it on impulse."

"But why? You talk as if it were a perfectly natural and reasonable thing to do on impulse — like eating a bar of chocolate or punching someone on the nose. Giving a false name isn't like that at all — I've never felt the slightest urge suddenly to tell someone that my name was Marmaduke Hackingbush, and neither has anyone else I know. I simply don't understand —"

"If you'd just let me explain, Desmond, it's really perfectly simple. I didn't want Daphne to know who I was."

"Daphne? What's Daphne got to do with it? Why should it matter to Daphne whether your name was Terry Carver or Derek Arkwright?"

"Because she's my cousin. My second cousin, I suppose — her mother and mine were first cousins."

I suggested that we should order lunch and that Terry should thereafter be permitted to tell his story without interruption.

"My mother came from a small town in Lincolnshire and all her family were very respectable and very boring. All except for wicked Cousin Dolly, who ran away to London and worked in a nightclub and was never spoken of again. At least theoretically she was never spoken of again — it all happened more than forty years ago, long before I was born, and I can't remember a time when I hadn't heard of wicked Cousin Dolly, so actually, I suppose, she must have been spoken of a good deal.

"And my mother and her sister Isabel must have heard a good deal about her too, while they were still

259

children, because as soon as she was old enough my aunt Izzie ran away as well and joined forces with her. So *she* was never spoken of either and my mother wasn't allowed to have anything more to do with her. My mother, poor dear, grew up to be respectable and married my father and in due course — well, became my mother. After their parents died, though, she and Aunt Izzie started writing to each other. They didn't see each other often — my mother didn't like coming to London — but they got on well enough for me to be allowed to come and stay with Aunt Izzie sometimes."

"And did you," asked Julia, "enjoy your visits?"

"Well, I think I enjoyed them more when they were over and I was safely home, if you see what I mean. Aunt Izzie was still living with Cousin Dolly, you see, and Cousin Dolly scared me out of my wits — I thought shc was going to eat me. Literally, I mean, once she'd got me nicely fattened up and while I was still young enough to be tender.

"I don't quite know why I thought so — I'd probably heard of wicked Cousin Dolly at about the same time as I heard of the wicked witch in Hansel and Gretel and I thought they did the same sort of things.

"But she was very fond of her food, and whenever I went there she used to pinch me, quite hard, as if she were wondering — well, that's what it seemed like. The grown-up half of me knew this was all nonsense, but the other half believed it absolutely — I always made sure to take plenty of exercise before I went there, so that I'd be too thin and stringy for her. I think she knew she frightened me, and was pleased about it.

"On the other hand, I got on rather well with Aunt Izzie. She was well into her forties by that time, but she'd taken much better care of her looks than Dolly had, and I thought she was tremendously glamorous and sophisticated. She told me all sorts of scandalous stories about people, quite famous people that I'd seen on television, and she took me to places that my parents would have been as shocked as anything about if they'd known — bars and nightclubs and so on."

"Places," said Ragwort sternly, "where it was quite illegal for you to be at that age."

"Yes, I suppose so, but some of the places Aunt Izzie went to didn't seem to mind much about things being illegal. And if she thought there was going to be a problem, she just dressed me up as a girl — like that I could pass for quite a fetching little eighteen-year-old." The young man smiled demurely at Ragwort, who looked more severe than ever.

"I take it," I said, "that Daphne was also part of this ménage? As I understand it, she was Dolly's daughter."

"Yes, that's right, but I'm afraid I didn't take much notice of her — she was about five years younger than me, and of course I never thought of her as being the same generation. Dolly had got married rather late in life, you see. To a man called Palmer, who died and didn't leave her any money — that's all I ever knew about him. That's when she and Izzie started the fortune-telling business. Cousin Dolly had always claimed to have some kind of psychic powers and done fortune-telling as a sort of hobby, Tarot readings for friends and so on, so she decided to try doing it professionally."

"I thought," said Julia, "that it was Isabella who claimed to be clairvoyant."

"Well, not in those days. What Aunt Izzie did was collect information. If you're going to be convincing as a fortune-teller you have to know things people don't expect you to know — Aunt Izzie was very good at finding out things like that. She'd kept all the contacts she'd made when she was working at the nightclub and she knew an awful lot of things about an awful lot of people. She was quite systematic and organized about it — she had a huge filing cabinet, which she used to call her little box of secrets, with files on all their clients and everyone who might be useful when they wanted to know something. And she always read the newspapers very carefully, especially the financial pages — they had a lot of clients who were stockbrokers and that sort of thing."

"In short," said Ragwort, "the whole business was based on a confidence trick?"

"Well, no, not exactly — I mean, I'm quite sure Cousin Dolly really believed in her psychic powers. What Aunt Izzie was doing, as far as Dolly was concerned, was help her to interpret what she read in the Book. There was an old book she'd got from somewhere, very large and bound in leather, which was what she used for the most important prophecies. Readings from the Book were incredibly expensive, but its predictions were always right — if they seemed to be wrong, you'd either asked the wrong question or misunderstood the answer.

"I tried to have a peep at it once, when Cousin Dolly had been doing a reading and seemed to have forgotten to lock it away afterwards. But she came back and caught me and asked if I'd read any of it. I said I hadn't, and she said she was glad about that, because one of the things it predicted was that any little boy who read it would be locked in the cellar and left there until the rats ate him, and wouldn't that be a pity for a pretty little boy like me? And she pinched my arm until my eyes watered."

Julia, much distressed, refilled Terry's wineglass and was rewarded with a Leonardo smile.

"I'd stayed with them several times and was beginning to think of it as a regular feature of my school holidays, when there was a terrible row between my mother and Aunt Izzie — I've no idea what it was about. But they never spoke to each other again and of course I didn't go and stay any more. Even when I grew up and came to live in London, I didn't try to get in touch again — I'd have felt I was being disloyal to my mother. Aunt Izzie sent us a card when Cousin Dolly died, and another with her new address when she moved down to Sussex, but my mother never answered. Then my mother died and I thought I ought to write and tell Aunt Izzie, but she didn't write back."

"And so," said Ragwort, "you never saw her again?"

"Well, only once, and I'm afraid I wished I hadn't. I suppose it was mostly curiosity, but — well, after a while it occurred to me that Aunt Izzie was the only close relative I had left and she'd been quite nice to me and I ought to find out if she were starving or anything. So I rang her up and suggested I might come and see her. She seemed quite keen on the idea, and down I went to Parsons Haver.

"She'd sent Daphne out for the evening and not told her I was coming — she seemed to think that Daphne would be jealous if she knew. So there were just the two of us, plus a rather disagreeable vulture, drinking champagne and trying to pretend this was just like the old days. Which of course it wasn't. She'd put on a lot of weight and her clothes were rather dirty and her stories were all about people who didn't matter any more. The horrible thing was that she seemed to have got so much more like Cousin Dolly — not just the way she looked but the way she talked. She'd decided that she had psychic powers as well and she obviously took it all seriously. It was as if, when Dolly died, Izzie had somehow inherited her personality."

"Still," said Julia, "at least you didn't think she was going to eat you?"

"Well, no, I didn't exactly think that, but — well, you see, she'd always sort of flirted with me a bit — it didn't mean anything, it was a kind of game. And she was still doing it, but somehow I felt it wasn't quite a game any more — she seemed to keep wanting to touch me. And I didn't want her to.

"Still, I did my best to be amusing and she evidently enjoyed the evening and expected me to come back again. I was still wondering how long I could leave it without hurting her feelings when I saw that she'd died

— Daphne didn't write to me, I saw it in the newspaper. Poor Aunt Izzie, I'm afraid I felt rather relieved. So I thought the least I could do was go to her funeral.

"I didn't particularly think about what I'd say to Daphne — I suppose I meant to go up to her at some point and say, 'Hello, I'm your cousin Terry.' But for some reason she seemed to take an instant dislike to me — she was simply radiating hostility all through the service. I don't know why — it can't have been that she recognized me, I'd changed far too much. So I thought the best thing would be to slip away quietly. But then there was this clergyman, you see, with a face like an eagle and the most beautiful voice I'd ever heard, and I —" He sighed. "Silly, isn't it?

"When it was all over, he came over to talk to me and asked who I was. I'd just begun to tell him when I realized that Daphne was only a few feet away, still oozing hostility from every pore, and if I said 'Terry Carver' she'd know I was her cousin and everything would be spoilt. So I said my name was Arkwright — I'd seen it on one of the tombstones. As I say, it was just an impulse — I'm sorry if it makes things difficult."

"We can all understand," said Ragwort magnanimously, "that sometimes on the spur of the moment one does things one afterwards regrets. But surely, once you and the Reverend Maurice were on terms of friendship, you could have explained the position?"

"You're perfectly right, Desmond, as of course you always are — that's what I ought to have done. But you see, I rather enjoyed being Derek Arkwright. I somehow thought of him as someone slightly different from me — someone travelling light, with no past, no responsibilities, no bookcases to make, no VAT forms to fill in. It was rather delicious. And I felt that it was part of my — what was that discreet phrase of yours? — my being on terms of friendship with Maurice. I felt that as long as I was Derek I could keep it as something secret and special, but if I turned back into Terry I'd somehow be breaking the spell. And as it turned out, I was absolutely right.

"Poor Maurice, I didn't really mean to mislead him about the kind of person I was. I never told him anything about myself that wasn't true — I just didn't tell him very much at all. But he must have built up some extraordinary fantasy about me as someone terribly glamorous and interesting — God knows exactly what. And when he found out that I was just an ordinary, boring sort of chap doing an ordinary boring sort of job, he felt terribly hurt and disillusioned."

"My dear Terry," said Julia, "no one could conceivably think you either ordinary or boring."

"Your profession is one," said Ragwort, "which a clergyman should hold in particular esteem. And Benjamin thinks you one of the finest craftsmen in London."

The young man shrugged his shoulders and smiled his satirical smile.

"It was my impression," I said, "that the Reverend Maurice never knew any more about you than you had told him yourself. How did his disillusionment come about?"

"I don't know — I just know that it happened. I mean, I don't know who told him about me or what they said exactly. We'd been away on holiday together and everything was marvellous — at least I thought it was. I did have a few anxious moments, because it turned out that Selena was staying at the house opposite. I was afraid we might run into her in one of the cafés or somewhere and she'd say, 'Hello, Terry, why aren't you working on bookcases?' before I had a chance to ask her not to."

"Yes," said Ragwort. "Yes, I dare say she would have said that."

"But she wasn't there very long and she seemed to be working the whole time, so it didn't happen. And the weekend after we got back to England I went and stayed with Maurice again and everything was still marvellous, or at least I still thought it was. I was beginning to feel quite serious and long-term about things. And then two days later I had a letter from him — it was the only one he ever sent me. It was a terrible letter, all about me deceiving him and not being the person he thought I was — he practically made it sound as if I'd done something criminal."

"But he didn't make any specific accusation?"

"No, I suppose not — but he made it clear enough that he didn't want to see me again."

"He made no mention of the Virgil frontispiece?"

"No," said the young man, with every appearance of bewilderment. "Why should he mention that?"

As frequently happens when the heart's affections are engaged, there seemed to have been a misunderstanding: Terry until now had known nothing of the theft of the frontispiece.

Nor was he able, after hearing Julia's account of the matter, to suggest any explanation for its disappearance. He had a perfectly clear recollection of the last evening he had spent at the Vicarage: he remembered seeing Maurice put it back in the drawer where it was usually kept.

"And I can't be mixing it up with another evening, because I remember him putting the photographs in the same drawer — the ones he'd taken while we were on holiday — and we'd only collected them that day. And there was no one else in the house, so if the frontispiece was missing next morning — poor Maurice, no wonder he was upset with me. And I've no idea how it can have happened — I only know I didn't take it."

"It's extraordinary," said Julia. "But there must be some explanation."

"Julia dear, from everyone's point of view except mine, the explanation is perfectly simple — I took the frontispiece and now I'm lying about it."

The Leonardo smile was infinitely disarming.

CHAPTER
SIXTEEN

"I don't suppose," said Selena wistfully, "that you felt able, at any stage of this conversation, to allude to the bookcase question?"

"Just sort of casually," said Cantrip. "You know, like saying you couldn't advise Terry about his case because you couldn't find the right books and why you couldn't find them was because all our books are in chaos and why they're in chaos is that we haven't got any bookcases to put them in."

In the coffeehouse on the following morning, Ragwort's account of our meeting with the young carpenter was proving something of a disappointment to an audience who had evidently had high hopes of it: there was in the air a sense of not quite unspoken reproach.

"One must remember," said Julia, "that the making of bookcases is a creative process, similar to painting a picture or writing a poem. You can't expect Terry to work on it when he's still so upset about Maurice."

"Quite so," said Ragwort. "And I'm afraid the recovery of his usual spirits is being impeded by this unpleasantness about the will. Until it's resolved, I doubt very much whether he will be able to concentrate properly on our bookcases."

"But Ragwort," said Selena, turning pale, "contested probate proceedings might take years."

"He assured us," said Ragwort, "that the will was not made in his presence and indeed that until about two weeks ago he had no idea of its provisions. I would hope to persuade the executors, in these circumstances, that any suggestion of undue influence is manifestly absurd and they can safely disregard it, without the expense and delay of a full-scale probate action."

"Right," said Cantrip. "And I suppose they're professional executors, so before they decide if they can or not they'll spend two years looking up their insurance policies and getting Counsel's opinion from everyone in sight and in the meantime we still won't have any bookcases. No, what we've got to do is shut up this Daphne bird. So what you've got to do, young Larwood, is write and tell her she's talking codswallop and if she doesn't stop she'll get put in prison for slander."

"I have a feeling," said Julia apologetically, "that it might not be entirely proper for me to write to her in quite those terms. I'm proposing to tell her that Derek Arkwright turns out to be someone I know and that means I can't advise on the matter, even on an informal basis. Moreover, I think that you underestimate the difficulty of making Daphne shut up about anything — she's the sort of girl who tends, once started, to go on. And indeed on. I had a letter this morning from my aunt which you may all find instructive."

270

24 High Street
Parsons Haver
West Sussex

Thursday, 3rd February

Dear Julia,

I do wish people wouldn't die, it makes things so complicated. Poor Maurice was always such a considerate person, but his will is causing all sorts of trouble.

It leaves everything — well, not everything, because there are legacies and so on, but everything left over — to "the person whom I know by the name of Derek Arkwright" — so it looks as though he knew or suspected that that wasn't Derek's real name. Apparently he's really called Terence Carver, and the solicitors in charge want me to go up to London to meet him at their offices and sign something confirming that he's the right person. They've suggested the 17th or 18th of this month — I thought we could meet for lunch, so do let me know which would suit you better.

That's not what I mean by trouble, of course — I'm rather looking forward to it. What I mean by trouble is the effect on Daphne, who's worked herself into a quite appalling state about it. She disliked Derek enough, heaven knows, simply as Derek Arkwright — as Terence Carver she detests him even more, because he turns out to be her second cousin. I did once tell you, didn't I, about

Isabella having had a sister, whom she'd quarrelled with and never spoken to again? The sister died and Terence is her son, and Daphne seems determined to keep the quarrel going.

They hadn't met since they were children, so it isn't surprising that Daphne didn't recognize him. Perhaps subconsciously she did — I suppose that might account for her taking such an instant dislike to him. Anyway, she's now more convinced than ever that her dislike was justified — he was a horrible, sly, deceitful boy, she says, and it just shows how right she was when she said he was that kind of person.

And she simply won't believe that Maurice meant to leave him everything he had. She's got some idea in her head that Maurice was somehow tricked or hoodwinked into doing it and she keeps saying that we owe it to his memory to make sure Derek doesn't get away with it. It's all complete nonsense — the will was drawn up by Maurice's solicitors in London and signed and witnessed in their office — but she's quite beyond reasoning with on the subject. She's already written the solicitors a very silly letter — she didn't show it to me before she sent it — implying that she knows a lot of things they don't about the background and telling them that they mustn't apply for probate. I'm hoping that they'll ignore it, but I suppose they'll probably think they have to investigate.

I have a feeling, from one or two things she said, that she may try to persuade you to advise her about all this — if she does, do for heaven's sake do your best to discourage her.

The fact is, when one tries to pin down exactly what it is that she's accusing Derek of, that it comes down to nothing more than pretending to be nicer than he really is. I've told her that a great many people (including me and I dare say you as well) spend most of their time pretending to be nicer than they really are. A very good thing too — if they didn't life would be quite impossible. Daphne seems to think this very cynical of me.

Poor Daphne, I suppose what's really upsetting her is not being mentioned in the will. I don't mean that she's mercenary, just that it is rather wounding for her. It was made quite recently — last October, when she was spending a lot of time with Maurice and doing all his shopping and so on — and it does seem rather strange that he didn't think of giving her anything. It almost looks like a deliberate unkindness — after all, he left legacies of two thousand pounds each to Griselda and Mrs Tyrrell, and I'd have thought he'd have realized how hurt Daphne would be — but it would be so unlike him to be deliberately unkind to anyone.

Some people might also find it odd of him to leave everything to Derek just after that beastly business about the Virgil frontispiece, but as a matter of fact I don't think it was. Maurice was an incurable romantic — even worse than you — and I can just imagine him wanting to make some sort of gesture to show that he cared more about Derek than anyone else, however badly he had behaved. After all, he didn't really have anyone else to leave it to — his earlier will left everything to various charities — and it wasn't an enormous amount, I think about twenty-five thousand pounds, mostly in building societies.

I suppose Derek really did take the frontispiece — I wish that I could think it was all some kind of mistake, but I don't see how it can have been.

What I got under the will was Maurice's personal chattels, as defined by Section whatever-it-is of some Act or other, and that's another complication. You see, we had an arrangement. Maurice didn't like the idea of a stranger going through his personal things after he was dead, and he asked me ages ago if he could leave them all to me, so that I could sort through them and do what I thought was best. I said yes, thinking it would all be quite straightforward. He gave me a list of things he wanted particular people to have, and from time to time he'd say, "I'd like so-and-so to have such and such when I die," and I'd add it to the list. But I didn't really expect it to happen, not for years — after all, Maurice wasn't old, only a year or two older than me.

You wouldn't believe how much trouble I've had over that wretched list. I thought it was all perfectly clear and businesslike, but when you start trying to work out whether "clock on the mantelpiece" means the one in the study or the one in the dining room, and exactly how many glasses Ricky's supposed to get with the cut-glass decanter, it turns out not to be easy at all. Several people one would have expected to know better have really been quite unpleasant. Mr Williams who plays the organ and Mrs Jarvis from the library who helps with the flowers have practically come to blows over the record player and —

Well, I didn't mean to bother you with all that. What I meant to tell you was that Maurice had a rather nice little rococo looking-glass, not really valuable but very pretty, which he'd inherited from a great-aunt and wanted you to have. But then Daphne was looking so hurt and miserable about not being mentioned in the will that I just couldn't bear to tell her that there wasn't anything on the list for her either, so I told her he wanted her to have the rococo looking-glass. I'm sorry, I should have asked you first, of course, but I had to say something right away or it would have seemed odd, and the looking-glass was the only thing I could think of. I do hope you don't mind too much — I'll find something nice for you in the antique shop to make up for it.

Daphne seems to be here most of the time at the moment. She comes round in the morning and asks me if I want any shopping done and if I say yes she goes out and does it and brings it back and stays until lunchtime. And if I say no, she just stays until lunchtime. So, one way or the other, it always ends with my feeling that I have to offer her lunch, and she always accepts. Poor girl, I can't really blame her — I know she can't afford to feed herself properly — but the fact is, of course, that making a meal for someone else is always more trouble than making it just for oneself. And somehow or other, by the time we've finished, the best part of the day has gone and I haven't really done anything with it — haven't painted anything or read anything or even written any letters. And yet I feel quite tired.

I've once or twice tried hinting — rather more heavily in fact than I'd usually think polite — that there are things I'd like to be getting on with. She doesn't seem to understand, though, that that means I'd like her to go. It's odd, she's not the sort of girl one would call sociable, but she doesn't seem able to imagine that anyone could sometimes prefer solitude to company.

Even the most sparkling company, which, to be candid, Daphne's isn't. She just sits there looking mournful and talking endlessly about Maurice, as if he were some kind of saint — quite a different sort of person from the one I was friends with. She keeps saying that I'm the only person she can share her grief with. The trouble is — I dare say it's very selfish of me — but I don't want to share mine, I want it all to myself. After all, I was friends with Maurice long before Daphne even knew him.

When she isn't talking about how wonderful Maurice was she's talking about how wicked Derek is, and how she isn't going to let him get away with it.

On the subject of Derek, she's really not quite rational. She's absolutely convinced that someone's prowling round the Rectory at night and spying on her and either it's Derek himself or he's responsible for it. She's even begun to suggest that he had something to do with the burglary last summer and the stone that was thrown at her through the kitchen window. Of course, it's absolute nonsense — what earthly reason could he have? — but the poor girl does seem to be quite seriously frightened about it. She's insisted on giving me a spare key to the Rectory, so that if she doesn't come round here in the morning I can go and find out what's wrong.

Again, I'm sorry about the rococo looking-glass, but I knew you'd understand. Don't forget to let me know which day would suit you for lunch.

Yours with much love,

Reg

♣   ♣   ♣

"So you see," said Julia with a sigh, as she finished reading the letter, "that when one's dealing with Daphne one has to bear in mind that she is — how can one put it?"

"Not entirely well balanced," said Selena.

"Disposed to paranoia," said Ragwort.

"Nutty as a fruitcake," said Cantrip.

A certain despondency fell upon the gathering. If the revival of Terry's enthusiasm for his work depended on

Daphne's ceasing to make trouble, it seemed likely to be long delayed. Moreover, tolerant as she hoped she was of other people's little weaknesses, Selena had begun to reflect with some anxiety on the possible disadvantages of employing a carpenter with a tendency to steal antique manuscripts.

Though Ragwort and Julia both firmly maintained their belief in Terry's innocence, it soon became apparent that their confidence was founded, in Ragwort's case, on personal friendship and, in Julia's, on length of eyelashes. Selena found these arguments unpersuasive.

I thought it right to say that I also, for less sentimental reasons, did not believe that Terry had stolen the frontispiece.

"If you can suggest any other explanation of the evidence," said Selena, "then please do so, Hilary, and we shall all do our utmost to be convinced. Why don't you believe that Terry stole the frontispiece?"

"Because I don't believe," I said, "that the frontispiece was stolen."

"Hilary," said Selena, "you're making this rather difficult for us."

"I believe that it was not the frontispiece that was stolen, but the photographs. That is to say, the photographs were the object of the theft — the frontispiece was taken only because it was in the same drawer and the thief had no time to sort out what he wanted from what he did not."

"The photographs? Do you mean the photographs that the Reverend Maurice had taken on holiday in

278

France? Why on earth should anyone want to steal those?"

"I rather think," I said, "because they included one or more photographs of the man in the black Mercedes."

They ordered further cups of coffee and indicated that I had their attention.

"I would invite you," I said, "to consider a number of significant facts, and to do so with that scrupulous attention to the chronology of events which was always insisted on by the immortal Bentley." The name of that great progenitor of the art or science of textual criticism carried, I fear, less weight with them than it deserved.

"The first significant fact is that the Reverend Maurice was the only person in Parsons Haver who had seen and could recognize the man in the black Mercedes — to whom, for the sake of brevity and in accordance with established convention, I shall refer to as X. We know, of course, that X was supplying Isabella with information known only to the directors of Renfrews' Bank and that he must therefore be either Edgar Albany or Geoffrey Bolton. Remember, however, that the Reverend Maurice did not know that. All he knew about X was what he looked like — he did not know his name, address or profession or anything else which would have enabled him to find X if he wished to do so."

"We know all that," said Cantrip. "Come on, Hilary — how about cutting to the action?"

"By all means," I said. "Forgive me if I have trespassed unduly on your patience. The position, then, was as I have described it until September of last year, when a very significant event occurred: the Reverend Maurice went to France on holiday and while there saw and recognized X."

"Hang on a minute," said Cantrip. "Is that just a guess, or have you found out something you haven't told us about? Because if you have it's cheating and you don't get points for it in the ace detective stakes."

"My dear Cantrip," I said, "I assure you that I have no more information than you do on the subject. When I say, however, that while on holiday the Reverend Maurice saw and recognized X that is so far from mere conjecture as to be a virtual certainty. We now know, which we did not at the time, that he was a guest at Benjamin Dobble's flat in Cannes, where Ragwort stayed during Christmas. And unless, my dear Ragwort, I have much misunderstood your account of the place, anyone staying there would be likely to spend at least part of the day sitting on the drawing-room balcony?"

"Yes," said Ragwort, "I suppose they would. It's very comfortable and has a quite superb view of the Mediterranean."

"And also of the roof terrace of Sir Robert Renfrew's villa, where Selena and the directors of Renfrews' Bank spent several days during the same period. And since we know that X must be either Albany or Bolton, it is almost inconceivable that the Reverend Maurice should not have seen him."

From that point my reasoning became, of necessity, somewhat more speculative. I could not pretend to know precisely what thoughts had passed through the clergyman's mind on seeing the man who a few months before had been the object of so much interest in Parsons Haver.

I imagined, however, that he had found himself in a dilemma. He realized, as we knew from his conversation with Julia at Christmas, that X's connection with Isabella had in some way involved the crime of insider dealing; but he was uncertain of the moral gravity of the offence. To bring disgrace and punishment on someone he did not think guilty of any serious wrongdoing would have been repugnant to him. Ought he to take steps to identify X and expose him as a criminal, or should he take no action?

He would not have wanted to make an immediate decision — he needed time to reflect and perhaps seek the advice of others. Besides, he would have been reluctant to be distracted from his idyll with Terry. But he would have seen that X was merely a temporary visitor at the villa, as he himself was at Benjamin's flat, and might leave at any moment. If he did nothing now, how would he find X again if he decided that he ought to do so? What would enable him to act later without committing him to act at once? He had his camera with him and he was an enthusiastic photographer. His solution would have been to take a photograph.

With a photograph, he could reasonably expect to have little difficulty in identifying X. Once he showed it to someone familiar with people in financial circles — someone, for example, like Ricky Farnham — he had every chance of learning not only the man's name, but enough about him to judge what action to take.

281

But before he could show the photographs to anyone —

"They were stolen," said Julia.

"Crumbs," said Cantrip, "you mean it was X who swiped them?"

"From the sequence of events that Hilary has described," said Ragwort, "that certainly seems a reasonable conclusion."

Selena gave a deep sigh.

"You all seem to have forgotten," she said, "that the theft took place at night, when Terry and the Reverend Maurice were the only people in the house."

"My dear Selena," I said, "the security arrangements in a country vicarage are unlikely to be comparable to those of the Bank of England. It would require, I imagine, very little skill in housebreaking to obtain entry by a downstairs window."

"And to find what one wanted in a strange house, at night, without making a mess of anything or disturbing the occupants?"

"Maurice and Terry looked at the photographs in the study, which faces on to the street, and afterwards put them away in a drawer in the same room. Someone who had been watching through the window from the darkness outside would have had little difficulty in finding them."

"And how would X even know that Maurice had taken his photograph or that it was anything for him to worry about?"

"A man with a crime to conceal notices when he is being watched, even more when he is being photographed. Once X discovered, as he could have done by a few very simple enquiries, that the person taking the photographs had an address in Parsons Haver, the danger would have been clear to him. You seem determined, if I may say so, to dislike my theory."

"On the contrary," said Selena, "I like it very much. I think it's a perfectly charming theory. That's why it seems such a pity that there isn't any evidence for it."

Selena is sometimes inclined to take a rather narrow view of what constitutes evidence: it was hardly reasonable to expect me, in all the circumstances, to provide bloodstains and fingerprints. I had not said that the matters I had referred to were conclusive; I had said merely that they were suggestive.

And, in addition, there was also the matter of Daphne's burglary.

"Do explain, by all means, what Daphne's burglary can possibly have to do with the matter."

"We have been told by Terry that Isabella kept a filing cabinet, which she called her little box of secrets, containing documents which she used for the purposes of fortune-telling. And also, no doubt, for the purposes of blackmail. The filing cabinet is presumably in Daphne's possession and still at the Rectory. If X was being blackmailed by Isabella, the filing cabinet almost certainly contains documentary evidence of whatever it was that she knew to his discredit. In short, it appears probable that the victims of the theft and of the attempted burglary both had something in their possession which X would have wished to destroy. Do you think it unduly fanciful to suggest a connection?"

283

"Well," said Selena, sighing again, "if I say to myself every night before I go to sleep, 'The frontispiece was not stolen by Terry, but by a man called X,' I dare say I may come to believe it."

The others, however, embraced my theory with more wholehearted enthusiasm, too pleased with it for exonerating Terry to observe that it might also have less agreeable consequences. I felt obliged to draw their attention to a further sequence of events, which if subjected to such reasoning would point to a similar but more sinister conclusion.

"We must remember," I said, "that the loss of the photographs did not quite restore the position to what it had been before. The Reverend Maurice now knew something — that is to say, an address at which X had at least stayed for a few days — which would have given him, had he been determined to identify X, a possible avenue of enquiry. He might, for example, have written a discreetly phrased letter to the owner of the villa. In fact, however, his distress at the loss of the frontispiece drove the whole matter from his mind. We can safely assume that he took no further action until shortly before Christmas."

"Why should we think that he did anything then?"

"A few days before Christmas he had a conversation with Julia, in which he seemed anxious to learn whether the man in the black Mercedes was guilty of a serious crime. Julia's answers would evidently have confirmed that he was. On the following day, at the same time that Julia was posting a letter to Ragwort, the Reverend Maurice also posted a letter. On the morning that

Ragwort received Julia's letter, Sir Robert Renfrew, in the same postal area, apparently received a communication which caused him suddenly to summon his fellow directors to Cannes. I am suggesting that it was the letter posted by Maurice."

"Oh nonsense," said Selena. "He summoned his fellow directors because he'd decided that the time was ripe for the takeover of a company called Lupilux — as it happens, I'm working on the documents now. There's nothing secret about that — the bid became public nearly a month ago, and has been widely commented on in the financial press."

"I am suggesting that that was merely a pretext for the invitation. I cannot say, of course, exactly what the Reverend Maurice may have said in his letter, but it must have been enough to indicate to Sir Robert that one of his co-directors had been seen in Parsons Haver in circumstances which seemed suspicious. He naturally concluded that this had something to do with the insider-dealing business which had been worrying him for so long."

"So he decided to get them both down to Cannes," said Cantrip, "and then just sort of casually mention Parsons Haver and see how they reacted?"

"Something, no doubt, very much along those lines. It appears that he did not succeed in identifying the culprit — if he had, Selena would be aware of it. On the other hand, it is likely that whatever he said would have been enough to warn X of the danger. Albany and Bolton returned to England on 22nd December. On

Christmas Eve the Reverend Maurice was taken ill. By the morning of Boxing Day he was dead."

"But Maurice was at home by himself all day on Christmas Eve," said Julia. "Hilary, you talk as if X could walk through locked doors, and come and go without anyone seeing him."

Poor Julia is of an imaginative and superstitious disposition. I perceived that she was alarmed by the image of a nameless and faceless figure, gliding silent and unseen through the night, leaving death behind.

"My dear Julia," I said. "I am not suggesting that X has any supernatural quality. He is invisible only in the same way as any other stranger whom you might pass in the street without taking any particular interest in. One must imagine him, of course, to be a man of some ability — not only physically agile, but quick-witted and decisive, always ready to calculate risk against opportunity."

"It's pure moonshine," said Selena, with unusual asperity, "and high time that we went back to Chambers and did some work." Of the two men who might be X, I had not described the one she liked least.

I myself would have preferred not to reach the conclusion I had; but two people who had known something that X would have wished to conceal had met unexpected deaths. I could no longer feel confident that Isabella and Maurice had died of natural causes; nor did I think it unreasonable for Daphne to be afraid.

CHAPTER
SEVENTEEN

Though my academic duties called me back ineluctably to Oxford, these matters for some days lingered in my mind. I had little hope, however, that further speculation would prove fruitful: my present information was insufficient for me to determine the identity of X; without meeting personally either of those I suspected I could see no way of adding to it. I tried in vain to think of anyone in banking circles whom I knew well enough to ask to arrange an apparently casual meeting.

My college was at this time engaged — as nowadays, indeed, when is it not? — in what the Bursar referred to as a resources enhancement exercise; that is to say, we were trying to raise money. To this end, a reception was to be held by the Senior Common Room for a carefully chosen group of former students whose success in later years might be supposed to have inspired them with gratitude for their education and provided them with the means to express it in concrete form.

The Bursar, I need hardly say, regarded this project as far outweighing in importance the pursuit of any scholarly research or the tuition of our present students. By St Valentine's Day he had already circulated three memoranda advising us how we should dress, what we should talk about and generally as to our conduct and demeanour. Finally, evidently suspecting that I had not read these with the care they deserved, he called on me in my rooms to give me my instructions in person and to hand me a typewritten list of those guests to whom I was to pay particular attention.

The venue chosen for what he termed this exciting project was the library. Though not in truth among the most ancient of the college buildings, it has undeniably a grandeur and elegance suggesting centuries of learning and civilized discourse — made possible, we were to remind our guests, by the liberality of various distinguished benefactors. Moreover, its high Gothic windows command an admirable view of our picturesque fourteenth-century chapel, behind which, as we gathered, a pale and graceful moon had obligingly risen.

Noting on my arrival that the Bursar was in the north-east corner of the room, I made my way towards the south-west. Not wishing, however, to be thought neglectful of my responsibilities, I joined a group which included two of the eminent barristers mentioned on his list and was soon sufficiently absorbed in anecdotes of judicial indiscretion to become oblivious of him.

It was thus a rather disagreeable surprise suddenly to hear his voice immediately behind me, braying about the bottom line or the interface or something of that sort. Fearing that he might add me to his audience, I was careful not to turn my head. He was interrupted by an attractive baritone voice saying, "But Bursar, if you knew anything about economics —"

"As it happens," said the Bursar, with an unspontaneous laugh which failed, or perhaps was not intended, to conceal the degree of offence taken, "I am the senior Economics Fellow of this college."

"Yes, I know," said the baritone voice cheerfully. "But that only explains why the students here don't know anything about economics."

Unable to resist observing the Bursar's response to this, I risked a backward glance. I saw to my astonishment that the other party to the conversation was Geoffrey Bolton. Though admittedly I had seen him only once before, I did not think it possible that I could be mistaken; but what was he doing in the library of St George's? And why had I heard no trace in his voice of the north-country accent on which all accounts of him had commented? The scholar in pursuit of knowledge will make almost any sacrifice: with scarcely a moment's hesitation I turned and greeted the Bursar.

Though his response was less than cordial, he could not well avoid effecting an introduction. I had not been mistaken — the owner of the attractive voice was indeed Geoffrey Bolton. I was able, however, to exchange no more than a few words with him before the Bursar, whispering furiously, "That's not one of yours, Hilary, that's one of mine," led me away, more or less by force, to meet yet another eminent lawyer.

Still, I supposed that I had ample time to contrive another and more fruitful encounter, especially since I saw shortly afterwards that Bolton was engaged in conversation with our Romance Languages Fellow, Felicity Dorset, an amusing and attractive woman whom I regarded as a friend and ally. I could not imagine that a man of taste and judgement, having secured a place at her side, would relinquish it in less than twenty minutes: nothing would be easier, once I was able to conclude my present conversation, than to cross the room and join them.

My feelings need not be described — they will be all too easily imagined — at seeing, a mere five minutes later, that Felicity was talking to someone else, having nothing whatever to do with my investigation, and that Geoffrey Bolton was in the doorway, unmistakably making his farewells to the Warden.

This development took me entirely unawares: it had not occurred to me that a man who had come so far for such an occasion would not stay to the end. To attempt to speak to him now would be worse than useless: a breathless pursuit across the quad would not be a convincing prelude to an apparently casual conversation.

Moreover, the eminent lawyer was telling me what turned out to be a rather long story about his most recent forensic triumph: to leave him before he reached the climactic line would be the gravest discourtesy. I listened with increasing impatience, unreasonably vexed with him for not being Geoffrey Bolton. To have had so unexpected and promising an opportunity and been unable to profit by it was almost beyond enduring.

Eventually, it occurred to me that all might not be lost: if Bolton had thought it proper to offer the Warden any explanation for his early departure, he would almost of necessity have mentioned where he meant to spend the rest of the evening. But had the Warden been listening? An astronomer by training, he tends to pay little attention to his immediate surroundings. And even if he had, how long would he remember what he had been told? I felt that I could wait no longer for the eminent lawyer's story to reach its climax.

"Dear me," I said, "the Warden seems to want me urgently for something — what a pity, I'm afraid I shall have to leave you."

The Warden said that Bolton had intended to take the next train to London. It was possible, as I knew all too well, that he was thinking of someone else, or of some other occasion, or of some quite different universe. Resolutely dismissing these possibilities from my mind, I hastened forth in search of a taxi.

By the time the clerk in the booking office handed me my ticket, the London train was already at the platform. I had no opportunity, before boarding it, to ascertain whether Bolton was among my fellow passengers. I began to wonder, as it drew out of the station, whether I had not been a little overprecipitate.

I had conscientiously — and, as it now seemed to me, improvidently — returned my keys to Timothy's flat. If he did not happen to be at home, or if he did not consider it his duty, at quite such short notice, to provide his former tutor with a bed, I would be obliged to return to Oxford that night — by a slow train, almost certainly with no buffet car. Moreover, if I failed to find

Geoffrey Bolton, I should have squandered in vain the return fare from Oxford to London.

By fortunate accident, rather than by design, I had entered the train at the foremost carriage: I would thus, without retracing my steps, be able to walk the length of it in search of him. By the time I was halfway along, however, I was feeling a little discouraged. This was partly, no doubt, because I remembered that the Warden habitually used the expression "London" to denote anywhere that was not Oxford; but I thought it might also be due to lack of food. I decided to fortify myself, when I reached the buffet car, with a sandwich and a glass of wine.

And there at the counter, amiably scolding the barman for the prices, was the man I had been seeking. I prepared to remind him who I was, but found there was no need.

"Professor Tamar, how splendid — I'd no idea you were taking this train. I don't know if you'll remember me — I'm Geoffrey Bolton. We were introduced about an hour ago by that pompous idiot — oh dear, I'm sorry, is he a friend of yours? No, of course he isn't — look, why don't you find us a table while I see to the drinks? What are you having? No, no, nonsense, Professor Tamar, I wouldn't dream of it."

High-handedness in such generous guise could be neither resented nor resisted. Having told him what I would like, I withdrew to the adjoining carriage to find a table — not, in truth, an onerous task, since it was almost empty.

Soon afterwards he joined me, bearing a bottle of wine and two plastic glasses.

"I'm sorry I've been so long — the barman couldn't find his corkscrew. And I'm afraid he's run out of sandwiches." He sat down on the seat facing me and carefully filled the two glasses. "By the way, I hope I'm not imposing myself on you?" He spoke, however, with the cheerful confidence of a man accustomed to being liked.

I could well imagine that his company would not often prove unwelcome. It was not precisely a question of looks: his features, though of a style usually attractive to women, had not the perfection of regularity which provokes the resentment of men; his complexion was rather pale, accentuating the blackness of hair and eyelashes; his eyes very bright, of the colour generally called hazel; his mouth rather narrow, turning up at one corner and down at the other, as if in habitual scepticism. The attractiveness of his face lay rather in its expression — one of alertness and vitality, as if he expected life to be interesting and would encourage it, if necessary, with the occasional prod in the ribs, to come up to that expectation.

I myself, I confess, was already disposed to like the man: his liberality in the matter of the wine; his soundness of judgement in the matter of the Bursar; his presence on the train when I had almost despaired of it — these things combined could not fail to produce a favourable impression on me. I said with perfect sincerity that I was delighted to have his company.

We spent a pleasant few minutes exchanging, with sympathy and candour, our views on the character of the Bursar.

"He's the sort of man," said Bolton, "who somehow always makes me want to do the exact opposite of what he wants me to do. It's rather a disadvantage in a fundraiser. As a matter of fact, I don't in the least mind giving something for the upkeep of the library or whatever it is, but I can't stand him telling me it's my duty. Why the devil should it be my duty?"

"The idea is," I said, "that those who have benefited financially from an Oxford education have some sort of obligation to make repayment in kind. But perhaps you don't feel that applies to you?"

The question seemed to amuse him, as if reminding him of some very private joke.

"As it happens, I could make out a fair case for saying that in my present circumstances, my Oxford education is a financial disadvantage." He smiled and refilled my glass.

"You provoke my curiosity," I said. "What are the present circumstances?"

"Well, if you'd like to hear about it I'll tell you, but I must warn you, Professor Tamar, that it's really a very simple story — you may find it tedious."

I assured him that I would not.

"I must begin by explaining that I was born and brought up in Lancashire and educated at —" He named a grammar school well known to me for the excellence of its academic record. "Oh, you've heard of it? Yes, of course, we've always done rather well in the

Oxford entrance exams. So you won't find it at all surprising that in due course I got a scholarship to Oxford. I read PPE, concentrating on the Economics rather than the Philosophy or Politics. It was a bit of a toss-up between that and French and German — I've always had quite a good ear for languages — but my headmaster told me I could do those on my own and I took his advice.

"When I came up to Oxford, I spoke, as you'd expect, with a Lancashire accent. Of which, by the way, I wasn't in the least ashamed — I didn't make any conscious effort to lose it. But when I went home at the end of my first term, my mother nearly threw me out of the house for talking posh and giving myself airs. So after a while I got quite used to switching from one to the other — a Lancashire accent at home, and what southerners call an educated accent when I went back to Oxford.

"I began to be interested in the way people reacted to me, depending on which I was using. I wasn't unduly surprised, of course, that they thought me better educated and of a higher social class when I was using my southern accent. What rather surprised me was that when I used the northern accent they were more inclined to trust me."

Again he refilled my glass, brushing aside my protest that I was taking more than my fair share of the wine.

"After I graduated, I joined an investment bank which had its headquarters in Paris and for the next twenty years or so I mostly worked outside England — first there and later in New York. During that time,

when I talked English it was with my southern accent
— it came to me more naturally by that time, and the
French and Americans can't tell the difference anyway.
But when I was dealing with the British, and wanted
them to feel that I was a sensible, down-to-earth sort of
chap who wouldn't pull any fast ones, I used a rather
mild version of my Lancashire accent.

"And then one day I was offered a job by an English
company. I'd been involved in some negotiations with
the Chairman and apparently he'd taken a liking to me.
I was very keen to accept — it was a good job, and I
wanted to get back to England. I never thought of there
being a problem about the accent."

I quite saw that if, when he first met the Chairman,
he had spoken with one accent he could hardly, on
taking up his new appointment, immediately begin
speaking with another; but I would have supposed that
over a period the northern accent could be
imperceptibly eliminated.

"That's what I meant to do. But I hadn't realized,
you see, how important it was to him — not the accent
itself, but what he thought it signified. He assumed that
someone who spoke with that accent couldn't have
been to university — not to Oxford or Cambridge, at
any rate. I did mention that I'd been to grammar
school, but he's a public school man himself, of course
— that simply made him think I was educationally
deprived. He imagines me as a barefoot urchin walking
the streets of Manchester, going without food to buy
books and studying by candlelight after fourteen hours'
work in the mill.

"And he'd given the same idea to the people I was going to be working with, who happened to include a man I find rather irritating. He's also a public school man. He couldn't resist sneering at me for being an ignorant working-class northerner and I couldn't resist teasing him by living down to his expectations. So instead of toning down the accent, I found myself making it broader. And the worst of it was that I somehow developed a persona to match — I began to turn into a sort of caricature of the kind of person he assumed I was. I suppose I was trying to find out how far I could go before he realized I was teasing — but he never did. So the result is that I've turned myself into this appalling stereo-typical northerner — I hate foreigners and I don't hold with books and I probably beat my wife if she's late getting my supper on the table. It's like Jekyll and Hyde, and I simply don't know how to get out of it."

He did not appear, however, to be unduly cast down by the thought of this: indeed, he gave every sign of regarding it with the liveliest amusement. I reminded him that he had spoken of his Oxford education as a financial disadvantage.

"Well, it would be if the Chairman found out about it. You see how dangerous it would be to spoil his illusions. They're not just illusions about me — they're illusions about himself. He prides himself on having recognized my abilities in spite of my having no formal qualifications — it would take the gilt off the gingerbread if he ever discovered that I had quite a good degree from Oxford. Well, a First actually." He sighed. "If he found out, I don't think he'd ever forgive me."

He again refilled my glass. I protested again that he should not give me all the wine. I saw that his own glass, though he had not replenished it, was still three-quarters full.

"Oh, I can't drink much this evening. I have an urgent meeting — with the Chairman, as it happens — first thing in the morning. It wouldn't do to have a hangover. So you see what I mean when I say that my Oxford education, in my present circumstances, is a financial disadvantage rather than an asset? Absurd, isn't it?"

"It would be going rather far to blame St George's."

"Oh, certainly. Besides, St George's was not my college."

"Wasn't it?" I remembered a fragment of conversation reported by Ragwort. "I suppose you're a Worcester man?"

"Yes, that's right. How did you know? Oh, I was forgetting that you're a detective."

I was disconcerted, almost unpleasantly so. My renown in the field of criminal investigation is not so widespread that I could expect my name alone to be sufficient to inform him of my connection with it: I had supposed him to know nothing more of me than might have been gathered from our meeting and conversation that evening.

"I can lay no claim," I said, "to any such description."

"My dear Professor Tamar, you are too modest. Felicity has told me that you have successfully investigated several mysterious crimes."

"Felicity?" I said, increasingly bewildered. "Do you mean Felicity Dorset?"

"Yes, of course." He laughed. "Oh, perhaps you didn't know, in spite of being a detective — I'm Felicity's husband. That's why I was at this evening's do."

I had known, certainly, that Felicity had a husband somewhere or other, whose name she did not use in her professional capacity; I must also have known, since I had imagined him to be American, that she had met him some years before while teaching at Columbia. The discovery that he was Geoffrey Bolton astonished me almost as much as the idea that Felicity was Bolton's socially disadvantaged wife.

Bolton showed a flattering interest in what he termed my detective activities. He began to ask me about my previous investigations and whether I believed that there was any quality which all murderers had in common — whether there was such a thing as the homicidal character.

"Character is a myth invented by novelists for the sake of adding interest to the narrative. Human beings are not so different one from another as the authors of fiction would have us believe. Some people do kind things and are described as kind, but they are not incapable of acts of cruelty. People who shrink from danger are described as cowardly, but they may be capable of acts of heroism. In real life almost anyone might do almost anything."

"Do you mean that perfectly ordinary people whom one meets every day are capable of murder?"

"Why not? We know that in wartime most people are quite capable of killing other human beings."

"Is there no common factor?"

"I think it's a question of knowing what they most care about. It is always a dangerous thing to come between anyone and the thing they most desire."

To my regret, I was finding it increasingly difficult to concentrate on what he was saying, even more so to answer with any degree of coherence. I seemed to be curiously disoriented by the movement of the train as it rattled and lurched through the night and the unfathomable darkness outside.

He seemed particularly interested in knowing whether I was currently engaged in any such investigation. These enquiries, which in other circumstances I would have found pleasantly flattering, were in these something of an embarrassment. I told him that at present I was engaged in nothing of that kind and that all my time and energies were required for my academic duties; but he gave me a smile which seemed to express a degree of disbelief.

My head ached and my perception of things seemed to be in some way slightly distorted. The reflection of Bolton's face in the window beside him looked strangely different from the reality: the crooked smile that had seemed so attractive now had a slightly malicious, almost diabolical quality. It seemed important to persuade him that I was telling the truth when I said that I was not at present engaged in any investigation.

"My dear Professor Tamar," he said with apparent concern, "you are very pale — are you feeling quite well?"

"Yes," I said with some effort. "Yes, perfectly well, thank you."

I felt as if I were suffering from a fever of some kind. I could scarcely remember where I was or what I was doing there. I reminded myself with what seemed enormous difficulty that I was travelling on a train, somewhere between Reading and London, and that in quite a short space of time I would arrive at Paddington Station. I knew that I was there because I particularly wanted to talk to Geoffrey Bolton, but I could no longer remember why. Eventually I recalled that it was because he was the principal suspect in a case of poisoning.

The bottle stood empty on the table between us. Bolton's glass was still half full.

Timothy, I am the first to admit, has all the qualities which one would most hope to find in a former pupil: in particular an unhesitating readiness, upon unexpectedly finding his former tutor ill and exhausted on the doorstep, to offer a bed and a modest supper.

He has also developed, perhaps even to excess, that questioning and independent attitude of mind which as his tutor I had always striven to encourage. When I explained to him that I had been poisoned, he chose to attribute my symptoms to a combination of excessive alcohol and auto-suggestion.

"My dear Timothy," I said, "if you wish to take that view, I fear that I am in no state of health to argue with you about it. If you see nothing strange or sinister in the fact of Bolton, having purchased a whole bottle of wine, electing to drink less than half a glass of it . . ."

"If he'd put anything really lethal in it, surely he wouldn't have drunk even that much? And as I understand it, he didn't actually force you to drink the rest of the bottle. But of course, if you're really feeling ill, I'll drive you over to the Emergency Department at St Thomas's."

I explained the unwisdom, weakened as I already was, of my undertaking such a journey. Moreover, I feared that the poison used would be identifiable only after numerous tests, possibly in themselves dangerous, and too late for any effective antidote to be administered. We were dealing with a man of intelligence and sophistication: he would not have poisoned me with anything commonplace or obvious.

If he had indeed poisoned me. By the following morning I was sufficiently recovered not only to accept Timothy's offer of scrambled eggs but to consider the possibility that he might be right in his opinion of the causes of my malaise. My consumption of alcohol had been, I need hardly say, in no sense immoderate. I remembered, however, that I had set out for London having eaten nothing since lunch; in the expectation of dining, I had drunk freely of the sherry provided at the reception, which owing to one of the Bursar's more ludicrous economies was of indifferent quality; and the wine on the train was perhaps also somewhat inferior to what I am accustomed to: all these factors might have affected me more than I had realized.

"Yes, exactly," said Timothy.

On the other hand, I had unquestionably been extremely ill and was even now feeling very far from robust.

"What a pity," said Timothy. "I was hoping you'd be well enough to join us for lunch."

"Lunch?" I said. His tone had seemed to suggest an occasion of festivity.

"Julia's aunt is coming up to London this morning to see some solicitors in the Gray's Inn Road. They want her to swear a statutory declaration identifying Terry Carver as the person she knows as Derek Arkwright. Terry'll have to be there as well, of course, and Selena thought it would be a nice idea to invite them both out to lunch — she thinks it will be an ideal chance to talk to Terry about bookcases. We'd all be delighted if you were able to join us."

I assured him that if my strength permitted I would be happy to accept his invitation.

CHAPTER
EIGHTEEN

The table in the Italian restaurant was laid for eight: covered by a cloth of cream-coloured damask and set with sparkling glass and silverware, it had an encouragingly festive look. Timothy and Julia were already present and drinking champagne, in celebration of Julia winning a large sum of money on a horse called Vagrant Folly.

Since the race in which this animal was to triumph was not to be run for another three hours the celebration seemed to me to be slightly premature; but Julia said that the running of the race was a mere formality. She had backed the horse on the advice of a destitute Irishman whom she had met that morning in High Holborn and to whose living expenses she had made a modest contribution.

"And in this morning's *Scuttle* Madame Louisa said that I should not ignore advice, even from a total stranger, because it might prove unexpectedly helpful. So I regard success as assured."

I perceived, however, that Julia had not that expression of unclouded contentment which might have been expected in such circumstances.

"I'm feeling slightly worried about Reg. When she first arranged to come to London she was planning to stay for a night or two and go to exhibitions and so on, but she rang me yesterday to say she was going to go straight back to Sussex after she'd seen the solicitors — she said she was feeling under the weather. I managed to persuade her that she ought at least to stay for lunch, but it's made me rather anxious. It isn't at all like her to give way to feeling ill."

But if Regina was feeling at less than her best, there was, when she entered the restaurant, no immediate sign of it. She was laughing as she came in, looking back over her shoulder at Terry Carver, who had evidently said something to amuse her. Dressed in turquoise and black, a silk scarf draped round her shoulders and fastened with an antique brooch of silver and amber, her smooth dark auburn hair framing her slightly medieval features, she gave an impression of easy and comfortable elegance. The Italian waiters, with welcoming murmurs of "*Buon giorno, signora,*" gathered round her to take her coat, pull back her chair and fill her glass with champagne.

She and Terry, it was clear, were delighted to be in each other's company: any embarrassment there might have been about the Virgil frontispiece was forgotten or resolved. They had spent a satisfactory morning with Maurice's solicitors, who had given them sherry and biscuits, thanked Regina very nicely for her help and assured Terry that they would complete the administration of the estate as soon as possible. There was now, they said, no obstacle to their doing so, other than the

305

unpleasant insinuations which continued to be made by his cousin Daphne.

"But Terry," said Julia, "if Maurice instructed them in person and executed the will in their office, they must know the whole idea of undue influence is absolute nonsense."

"Oh yes," said Terry. "And they've told Daphne that, so now she's suggesting something much more sinister. She's written them a letter going on about how suddenly he died and me being the last person to see him. She's practically saying that I made away with him to get my paws on his savings. It's all rather upsetting."

"It's perfectly monstrous," said Julia. "But never mind — no one takes any notice of anything Daphne says. Did you tell her, Reg, that you were coming to London to give evidence for Terry?"

"Certainly not," said Regina. "She'd have made a scene about it and I really didn't feel like coping with one of Daphne's scenes. I just told her that I was going to London on business. And even so, she was quite difficult about it. She's been having an attack of the Cassandras — she keeps saying she's afraid something awful is going to happen to me and she can't bear it and she doesn't know what to do. Telling her I was coming to London seemed to be the last straw — she got into a terrible state and said I mustn't. I'm afraid I had to be rather sharp with her."

"Why? What does she think will happen to you in London?"

"My dear Julia, I've no idea — you know what Daphne's like. She seems to think I'm too old and silly and feeble to be allowed out in the big city. She keeps telling me I'm ill and not as young as I used to be."

"Reg," said Julia anxiously, "are you sure you're not really ill?"

"Don't be ridiculous, Julia," said her aunt briskly. "I have a cold, that's all, like half the population at this time of year. The fact is, I think the poor girl is really rather nervous about my being away. With no one at the Vicarage, I'm her nearest neighbour. Now, for heaven's sake, do let's stop talking about her and think about food and wine. Oh, Julia, before I forget — I have a present for you."

She had with her a small valise, of which she had not permitted the waiters to dispossess her. From this she now took and handed to Julia a flat rectangular package, wrapped in green and gold paper and tied with tinsel ribbon. Julia regarded it with pleasure and perplexity.

"It isn't from me, it's . . . well, it's from Maurice. I was clearing out his desk the night before last — I ought to have done it sooner, but I'd been putting it off — and I found his Christmas presents still in the bottom drawer, all wrapped up and ready to give to people on Christmas Day. So I spent yesterday morning running round Parsons Haver giving everyone their presents from Maurice. There were quite a lot of them — mostly just small things, you know, for people he wanted to give something a bit more than a Christmas card."

"Oh dear," said Julia, presumably thinking of the rococo mirror, "I do hope there was one for Daphne."

"Yes, thank heavens — she'd have been terribly upset if there hadn't been. Well, this is yours — are you going to open it now, or are you going to wait until after lunch and not risk spilling anything on it?"

Not the most decisive of women, Julia was still debating this question when Ragwort and Cantrip arrived. They advised us not to wait for Selena before ordering lunch.

"I was in the Clerks' Room twenty minutes ago," said Cantrip, "and Selena's big-shot banker rolled up, all of a tizzwoz, with his solicitor in tow and wanting an urgent conference. So of course Henry said, 'Yes sir, certainly sir, anything you like sir, and who gives two hoots about Miss Jardine's lunch?' Or words to the like effect."

"We must try to console ourselves," said Ragwort, "with the hope that Henry will charge a fee which reflects the starvation factor. Did you happen to gather any hint of why the matter was so urgent?"

"Well, I couldn't say for certain, but what it sounded like to me was that they'd got another insider-dealing problem."

Though we ordered and ate our meal at a leisurely pace, it was not until we were halfway through the second course that Selena at last arrived. She was obliged even now to eat in uncomfortable haste: her conference was not over but adjourned to the afternoon, and she had to be back in Chambers by quarter past two.

At ten past two she sighed and rose from her chair, gulping a last mouthful of black coffee. Finding myself in need of a little fresh air, I offered to keep her company on her way back to New Square.

"This is most kind of you, Hilary," said Selena, as we stood waiting to cross Chancery Lane. "So few people would have worried about how lonely and miserable I might get walking back through Lincoln's Inn all by myself — almost no one, in fact. Do you happen to have any particular topic of conversation in mind which might enliven our journey?"

"I was wondering," I said, "if you might like to tell me about the insider-dealing problem at Renfrews' Bank, relating to the most recent takeover."

"My dear Hilary, whatever makes you think there is any such problem?"

"My dear Selena," I said, "few questions are impenetrable to the mind of the trained scholar."

"You mean it's your usual mixture of eavesdropping and guesswork. Well, I'm willing to admit it's quite a good guess."

"It seems likely, then, that the person who previously acted improperly for Isabella's benefit has now decided to do so for his own. I suppose there is still no way of knowing which of them it was?"

"As it happens, that is a rather less good guess. As you know, Sir Robert made his decision to go ahead with the takeover just before Christmas, when he was at the villa in Cannes. He asked his two co-directors to join him there to discuss the steps to be immediately taken. Until they arrived at the villa, they didn't know what the meeting was about. It wasn't the sort of meeting where they needed lawyers present, but apart from that conditions were much the same as when I was there in the summer — that's to say, all calls and fax messages from the villa were automatically recorded."

We walked through the gateway into Old Buildings.

"Well, up to a point it all seemed to have gone smoothly. They had a busy day on the Tuesday, buying up the maximum number of shares permitted without making a public announcement, and the share price hardly moved at all. Which meant, of course, that there was no reason to suspect that there'd been any insider dealing. But in the past week someone did a more or less routine analysis of the dealing pattern in the period before the takeover and the results were rather disquieting. It showed, of course, a large number of purchases on the twenty-first of December, most of which were purchases by Renfrews' clients in pursuance of their advice. But one of them wasn't."

"Ah," I said, since some such comment seemed to be called for.

"You may well say so — the chances of its being a coincidence are almost non-existent. The records don't show the identity of the purchaser, only his stockbroker. The stockbroker wouldn't disclose the identity of his client without a court order. And even then, it would probably be a nominee company registered in the Channel Islands or Liechtenstein or somewhere like that. But what it does show is the time the bargain was struck. And it shows that this particular bargain was struck at twenty to ten on the morning of the twenty-first of December."

"Which in France would have been twenty to eleven?"

"Quite so. Which would mean, according to my instructions, that the order was placed immediately before that — at the outside, not more than ten minutes. And at that time, one of Sir Robert's fellow directors was under surveillance and could not have made a telephone call. And the other wasn't."

We had reached the steps of 62 New Square.

"Sir Robert thinks the case proved. But I've told him that the first thing to do is put the accusation to the person he suspects. He wants to have his lawyers present when he does that, so he's told the director in question to be here this afternoon."

"But which of them is it?"

"Really, Hilary," said Selena, pushing open the heavy oak door leading to the Clerks' Room, "I would have thought that the trained mind of the Scholar . . . oh, bother."

The entire floor space of the waiting room being at present occupied by piles of books, the accommodation provided for visitors consisted of two rather uncomfortable chairs in the corridor outside the Clerks' Room. One of these was occupied by Edgar Albany, who rose, however, on observing our presence, or rather on observing Selena's — mine he seemed content to ignore.

"Ah, Miss Jardine. I want a word with you, young lady."

"Good afternoon, Mr Albany. I'm afraid I can't discuss anything with you until Sir Robert arrives — he should be here very shortly."

"Now look here, that just isn't good enough, you know. I get a telephone call from the Chairman telling me to drop everything and be here straight after lunch because he has 'a very grave matter' to discuss with me and when I get here I'm kept hanging around in this bloody corridor like some bloody fourth-former outside the headmaster's study being given time to think about what's coming to him."

"I'm sure," said Selena, "that Sir Robert had no deliberate intention of keeping you waiting. As I understand it he asked you to be here at half past two. Naturally, I am extremely sorry that we can't offer you a more comfortable place to sit, but our refurbishments —"

"I don't give a damn about your bloody refurbishments. I just want to know what's going on, and if the Chairman's got a bone to pick with me about something why he has to do it in some damned lawyer's office instead of back in his office at Renfrews'. And don't tell me you don't know, because I bloody well shan't believe you."

"I have no intention of telling you anything of the kind. Sir Robert has a matter which he wishes to discuss with you and feels it desirable to do so in the presence of his lawyers — that is to say, Mr Vavasour and myself. If, having heard what he has to say, you feel that you don't wish to make any comment until you can instruct lawyers on your own behalf . . ."

"Christ Almighty, you sound like a policeman saying anything I say may be taken down and used in evidence. Anyone would think I'd done something criminal. Well, let me tell you —"

He broke off suddenly, making a curious noise which was not precisely a gasp nor exactly a groan nor strictly speaking a rattle but somehow participating in the qualities of all these, and stood staring with an expression of alarm at the doorway behind us, as if some hideous spectre had appeared there.

Upon following the direction of his gaze, I saw nothing more alarming than the graceful figure of Ragwort.

Sir Robert and his solicitor were mounting the steps behind him. Becoming aware of this, Ragwort stood courteously aside to allow them to precede him through the doorway.

Selena greeted them with perceptible relief and proposed that they should all now proceed to her room.

"I'm not going anywhere," said Albany, "until I know what's going on. And what that man is doing here. And what lies he's been telling about me."

Sir Robert gazed at him with astonishment and a measure of disapproval.

"What man? My dear Edgar, you seem to be overwrought."

"I'm not going another step till you tell me what this is all about."

"Well, Edgar, if you insist on my telling you in this not very private place, then I have to tell you that it is my painful task to enquire into an incident which occurred on the morning of the twenty-first of December. When, as you may recall, you and Geoffrey Bolton were visiting me in Cannes."

Albany's response to this was to lunge forward and attempt to strike Ragwort on the nose. Ragwort moved adroitly aside. Albany overbalanced and fell to the ground. He appeared, having done so, unable or disinclined to rise.

"Edgar," said Sir Robert, "have you gone quite mad?"

"I don't know what he's told you, but whatever it is I deny it. He's a liar and a blackguard."

Though I felt little inclination to sympathize with Albany, the duty of the Scholar is to the Truth. I felt it my duty to intervene.

"Mr Albany," I said, "before you deny what Mr Ragwort has to say, do you not think it prudent to find out what it is?"

"I know damn well what it is, and it's all lies. And who the hell are you?"

"My name," I said, "is Hilary Tamar. Professor Hilary Tamar, of St George's College, Oxford. I am a friend of Miss Jardine and Mr Ragwort, with whom I have been lunching. I do, however, have some knowledge of legal matters, and I would strongly advise you to find out what you are accused of before you attempt to rebut the accusation."

"Get stuffed," said Albany.

"Sir Robert," I said, unsurprised by Albany's ingratitude, "I believe that Mr Albany may be labouring under a misapprehension. I suggest that you tell him the precise nature of your accusation."

"Professor Tamar," said Mr Vavasour icily, "I am sure that you mean well. But Sir Robert is not in the habit of taking the advice of total strangers on the conduct of his affairs."

Sir Robert's reaction to this was rather curious. He stood as if struck by some sudden revelation and a gentle smile spread over his chubby features.

"No," he said at last. "No, as Mr Vavasour says, I do not usually do that. And yet ... really, how extraordinary. Yes, in spite of that, Professor Tamar, I shall take your advice. Edgar, on the morning of the twenty-first of December, a purchase was made of shares in a certain company. The evidence compels me to ask you whether you were the purchaser."

"What evidence? What shares? I'm sorry, Uncle Robert, but I haven't the faintest idea what you're talking about."

"A significant number of shares in the company which we discussed the evening before over dinner at El Maroc. I'm sure you will realize how unlikely it would be for anyone to have bought those shares, by pure coincidence, who was unaware of the decision reached during that discussion."

"Oh, I get it." Albany pulled himself up to a sitting position and sat with his back to the wall, staring at Sir Robert with an expression of bitterness in his round blue eyes. "Oh yes, now I get it — someone's done a spot of insider dealing and I'm the main suspect. Just as a matter of interest — I mean, I know you've only known me since I was born, I know I'm only the great-grandson of one of the bank's founders, I know I only went to a decent school and a decent university instead of going to evening classes, so I quite see I'm the number-one suspect — but just as a matter of interest, do you mind telling me why that little bounder Bolton isn't even in the frame?"

"The purchase took place at twenty to eleven, which means, as you know, that instructions must have been given immediately before that time. Geoffrey Bolton was with me throughout the morning, and almost continuously engaged in making telephone calls in connection with the proposed takeover, all of which were recorded. It would not have been possible for him to have given instructions for any private purchase without my knowledge. You, on the other hand, went out at about ten o'clock, saying that you didn't feel you had anything to contribute to the proceedings, and after that . . ."

"Well, I didn't, did I? Bolton obviously thought he could handle the whole thing on his own, and you obviously agreed with him, so there wasn't much point in me hanging around, was there?"

"I'm not criticizing you for going out. I am saying merely that your movements during the morning are unknown to me. Miss Tavistock happened to be doing some shopping in the square and she has told me that you were sitting in a café there until about quarter past ten. After that she unfortunately lost sight of you and you did not return to the villa until after twelve. Are

316

you prepared to tell us what you were doing during that time?"

"I . . ." Albany was plainly having difficulty in deciding whether Sir Robert would disapprove more of his exchange with Mlle Natasha than of insider dealing. "I . . . I was walking about."

"In an area," said Mr Vavasour, "where it would not be difficult to find a public telephone? I'm afraid, Mr Albany, that that is not a very satisfactory alibi."

"I didn't make any telephone call — I couldn't have made a telephone call. Why can't you just take my word for it?"

"I'm afraid," said Sir Robert, "that in the circumstances . . ."

"He knows," said Albany, suddenly pointing at Ragwort. "That man — he knows I couldn't."

"My dear Edgar, you seem to be under some extraordinary delusion about this young man — I have no reason to think that he knows anything whatever about the matter."

Ragwort had for some minutes taken no apparent interest in the conversation, but had stood smiling gently towards the ceiling, as if communing on matters spiritual with the celestial host of saints and seraphs.

"As it happens," said Ragwort, "I was in Cannes during the Christmas holidays and might have some knowledge of the matter. It was my impression, however, that Mr Albany did not wish me to mention the events of that morning."

"Well, no need to go into details, old chap. If you could just tell Sir Robert and Mr Vavasour that I

317

couldn't possibly have made a phone call any time between ten-thirty and twelve that morning . . ."

"But they may not believe me, Mr Albany. You have told these gentlemen within the past five minutes that I am a liar and a blackguard and that they should not believe a word I say. We can hardly expect them, in those circumstances, to accept a bare statement with no corroborative detail."

"My friend Mr Ragwort," said Selena, "is a member of the Bar and of these Chambers — his evidence may of course be relied on without question. Nonetheless, in a matter of such delicacy and importance, it would be unsatisfactory for Sir Robert to be asked to rely on a bare assertion, with no explanation of the facts on which it is based."

"And indeed," said Ragwort, "it would be an embarrassment to me to ask him to do so. So do you wish me, Mr Albany, to explain the circumstances of our meeting in Cannes or do you wish me to keep silent on the matter? It is entirely for you to say, but there is no middle course."

"Oh God," said Albany, slumping despondently against the wall. "All right, go on then, tell them."

Ragwort appeared to reflect for a few moments.

"I happened, during Christmas, to be staying with a friend in a block of flats in Cannes. My friend's next-door neighbour is — I won't call her a doctor, since it may well be that she has no formal qualification — a specialist in pains of the lower back. Mr Albany, I gather, has the misfortune to suffer from a problem of that sort, and on the morning after his arrival in

Cannes found himself in urgent need of treatment. From ten-thirty until eleven-thirty that day he was undergoing a form of treatment which I think would effectively have precluded him from making a telephone call. He asked me not to mention the matter to anyone — at a certain age people become absurdly embarrassed about these physical infirmities."

"A back problem?" said the Chairman. "Oh, my dear chap, you should have told me. I have a simply splendid man in Harley Street . . ."

I did not stay to hear more. It seemed to me that my enquiry could be more fruitfully pursued in the Sir John Soane Museum.

CHAPTER
NINETEEN

It was not the season for tourists or schoolchildren: Miss Tavistock's, until I added my own, was the only name in the visitors' book.

She was not to be found in the Picture Room; nor in the New Picture Room; nor in the Breakfast Parlour; nor in any other of the upstairs rooms. Concluding that today she was not in the mood for paintings or antique furniture, I descended the narrow staircase leading to the basement — the area which the distinguished founder of the museum, in gentle mockery of the fashion for the Gothic in art and literature, had designated the crypt. Through silent, dimly lit chambers filled with sarcophagi and funeral urns, I came finally to the small chapel-like room known as the Monk's Parlour.

She was sitting almost in darkness: the stained-glass window behind her, looking on to an enclosed courtyard furnished with picturesque ruins, afforded at that time of year but little illumination. Though presumably she had chosen the place for the sake of solitude, she seemed pleased, albeit surprised, by my intrusion, evidently now remembering me as a friend.

320

We sat together in the recess below the window, not quite side by side: between us was a marble-topped card table, on which stood a rather charming bronze statuette representing, I believe, the god Hermes. I admitted that I had come there in hopes of finding her; she responded with a look of innocent enquiry.

"I thought it right to tell you," I said, "that I have been visiting friends in 62 New Square and was present at a conversation involving, among others, Sir Robert Renfrew."

"Oh," said Miss Tavistock, "what an interesting coincidence."

"And that matters have not turned out as I believe you were expecting. Edgar Albany has been cleared of the suspicion of insider dealing."

"Oh," she said again, adding after too long a pause, "I'm very pleased to hear it." She was not an accomplished liar.

"Yes, it has been established that Mr Albany has what is termed an alibi for the period during which instructions were given for the share purchase . . . As of course you know, since you were careful to make the telephone call at a time when you had arranged for him to be kept fully occupied by your friend Mlle Natasha."

"Oh dear," she said, looking disconsolate. "So you know all about it — oh dear. I thought it was such a good plan. And so did Natasha — such a kind girl, and really very talented. You see, we never thought Mr Albany would be prepared to admit — oh dear, I seem to have made a complete mess of things, don't I? I suppose you must think me very stupid, Professor Tamar."

She sounded so much like an undergraduate admitting with excessive contrition to some minor misdemeanour that I could not resist the impulse to comfort rather than reprove.

"Not at all, Miss Tavistock. It was a most intelligent plan, but you were very unlucky. The young man who released Mr Albany from Mlle Natasha's flat is a member of the same Chambers as Selena Jardine. He happened to be present this afternoon when the accusation was made and despite Mr Albany's own initial reluctance provided him with an alibi. It was a contingency you could not have foreseen."

"It's kind of you to say so, Professor Tamar," she said sadly.

"It's a pity, of course, from your point of view, that Geoffrey Bolton also has an unimpeachable alibi, but of course you must have known that he would."

"Oh," she said, turning towards me with a rather shocked expression, "I wouldn't have risked Mr Bolton being blamed. The whole point was to make it look as if Mr Albany had done it. I hope you don't think, Professor Tamar, that I acted from motives of personal gain?"

I admitted that some such thought had occurred to me.

"Oh no, I wouldn't have done that, it would have been very wrong. I just wanted to make sure Mr Albany never became Chairman of Renfrews'. You see, Sir Robert is bound to retire quite soon and I'm afraid, as things stand, Mr Albany is almost certain to succeed him. Oh, I dare say Sir Robert would prefer Mr Bolton, but after all, Mr Albany is a relative and in the end blood's thicker than water, isn't it? So unless something happens to discredit him completely, I'm afraid he'll be the next Chairman. And that'll be a disaster, you must see that."

"I can imagine," I said, thinking that I now understood her, "that you would not find him a congenial person to work with."

"I don't just mean for me, Professor Tamar, I mean for the bank. The trouble with Mr Albany as an investment banker is that he's — well, that he's hopeless at investment. And he won't admit it — his great-grandfather was a successful merchant banker and he thinks that must mean that he has a natural flair for it. So if he becomes Chairman, he won't just sit back and leave things to people who know how to do them, he'll want to run everything. It'll be ruinous."

It was not then, after all, for her own sake, but for the sake of the bank that she had gone to such lengths. I confessed to some surprise that such an institution should inspire such a degree of affection.

"Well, I've worked at Renfrews' since I was twenty, and generally been very happy there, so I suppose I do feel rather fond of it. But that's not exactly — oh dear, I told you that I didn't do it for motives of personal gain, but I suppose I did in a way. You see, we've always had very generous profit-sharing schemes and I've always exercised the option to take shares rather than cash, so I've built up quite a nice little holding. And they've done terribly well, much better than I expected. And I've rather got used to the idea that they're my guarantee for old age — that whatever happens I'll be quite comfortably off. But if Mr Albany becomes Chairman —" She sighed.

I did not doubt for a moment the truth of her explanation. Plainly it could apply only to the most recent incident, not to the previous episodes of insider dealing which had left Albany and Bolton equally under the shadow of suspicion; but I had already accepted that for those some other person must be responsible. I had never supposed that the naive and diffident Miss Tavistock was capable of the bold and ruthless actions which I had ascribed to X. Moreover, the one thing certain from the Reverend Maurice's description was that the occupant of the black Mercedes was a man.

And yet I was troubled by a curious sense of having overlooked some vital point — a conviction that something I had learnt that day would be, if correctly interpreted, of crucial significance to the solution of the insider-dealing problem and that Miss Tavistock somehow held the key to it.

"And now I've made such a mess of things, Mr Albany will become Chairman. And I suppose I'll be disgraced and have to resign straight away. And Sir Robert — oh dear, poor Sir Robert, is he very upset? About me, I mean?"

"When I left New Square, the idea that you might be the person responsible had not yet occurred to him. Though one might think it an obvious conclusion to draw from the fact that neither Albany nor Bolton could have done it, I am somehow inclined to think that he will regard you as above suspicion."

"And Mr Albany, I suppose, regards me as beneath it."

She rose from her chair and stood gazing pensively out of the window at the picturesque ruins, absent-mindedly fingering the bronze statuette. There was no museum official at hand to reprove her: the crypt was as empty of staff as of tourists.

"So actually, Professor Tamar," she said in a more cheerful tone, "you're really the only person who knows it was me?"

I acknowledged that I was.

Now that she was standing I could see her more clearly — tall, athletically built, large-featured, dressed as usual in a tailored trouser suit, her hair severely drawn back. I felt, for the first time in her presence, a qualm of apprehension. Seeing her across the street from the window of his study, by the light of the lamp over the front door of the Rectory, could the Reverend Maurice have made a mistake? Could she after all be the person whom he had described as "a middle-aged man in a City suit"? Had I perhaps been a trifle unwise to seek her out in such a secluded place?

But no — plausible as it might seem, I knew at once that there was something false about the idea, something indefinably wrong. My conviction nonetheless persisted that the solution to the insider-dealing mystery was almost within my grasp — that if only I knew the right question to ask she could give me the answer. On a sudden random impulse, I adopted what might be termed the Cantrip method of questioning.

"Miss Tavistock," I said, "do you happen to know a place called Parsons Haver?"

"Well, yes," she said, with perfect composure. "As a matter of fact, until a few months ago I used to drive Sir Robert down there quite regularly. Why do you ask?"

"Sir Robert —?" I found that I was at a loss for words. A monstrous suspicion had all at once begun to form itself in my mind: a suspicion impossible to believe, and yet once thought of impossible to doubt.

The silence was broken by the sound of footsteps.

"Katharine? Katharine, are you there?" The rotund figure of Sir Robert Renfrew appeared in the doorway. "Ah, Katharine, my dear, I was hoping I might find you here — I know it's one of your favourite places."

"Sir Robert," she said, turning towards him and blushing. "Sir Robert, I'm so sorry — I didn't think you'd need me until at least half past three."

"Neither did I, my dear, but our conference ended unexpectedly early, so I thought I'd come and look for you. Good heavens, isn't that Professor Tamar? What an extraordinary coincidence — are you a friend of Katharine's?"

"I hope," I said, "that I may say so."

"I am very pleased to have the opportunity of thanking you, Professor Tamar, for your timely intervention — you have saved me from committing a grave injustice. Katharine, my dear, you will be pleased to hear that Edgar Albany has been entirely exonerated

— he has a problem with his back, poor fellow, and was receiving medical treatment throughout the morning when the call was made. And Bolton was with me, of course, so he can't have made it either."

"I'm so glad, Sir Robert." Like almost all human skills, her lying had improved with practice.

"So the purchaser must have been someone who had nothing at all to do with Renfrews'. Miss Jardine has pointed out that by the time it was made our client had already placed several orders for the purchase of shares in the company — an alert stockbroker could well have read the signs and decided to back his judgement. I'm sure she's right."

"Oh, Sir Robert, this is good news."

"And all thanks to your friend Professor Tamar here. Advice from a total stranger — really, quite remarkable. It troubles me to think, though, how nearly I came to making a terrible mistake. I sorely miss the guidance of — well, Katharine, you know the person I mean."

"Yes, of course. Oddly enough, Professor Tamar asked me a few moments ago whether I knew Parsons Haver at all, and I was explaining — oh dear." She blushed again. "Perhaps I shouldn't have said anything about it."

"Oh, I think we can trust Professor Tamar with our little secret. It wouldn't do for it to be known in the City, of course, but — I'm sure, Professor Tamar, that you are not one of those people who deride as superstition everything that is beyond our limited human understanding. If you have friends in Parsons

Haver, perhaps you had the privilege of knowing Signora del Comino?"

"No," I said, perceiving that my appalling suspicion was about to be confirmed. "No, alas, I had not."

"A woman of remarkable gifts, Professor Tamar, quite remarkable gifts. For some years I took no major step without her guidance. Katharine used to drive me down to Sussex almost every month to consult her. But she died last year. Since then — ah well. Katharine, my dear, I'm afraid that you and I must be getting back to Lombard Street."

He turned, with the self-confidence natural in a man who controls the financial destinies of men and institutions, and led us out through the museum into Lincoln's Inn Fields. Miss Tavistock and I followed a few paces behind him.

"Professor Tamar," said Miss Tavistock, "I ought to thank you for not mentioning — well, you know what I mean. I'd somehow assumed you wouldn't, but I realize, when I think about it, that it was rather presumptuous of me."

"My dear Miss Tavistock," I said. "I should like to think that we are friends. You may count on me to conceal almost any crime you commit — short, that is to say, of murder."

She smiled at the notion.

"But Hilary," said Selena, looking at me reproachfully over her liqueur glass, "I've just begun to believe in X and I want to go on believing in him. This is no time to tell me that he does not exist."

328

Having said my farewells to Miss Tavistock and Sir Robert, I had returned to the restaurant and found the lunch party still in progress. Understandably anxious, however, to witness the triumph of the horse recommended to her by the destitute Irishman, Julia had adjourned with Cantrip to a downstairs room containing a television set. They had been joined there by Selena, set free by the early conclusion of her conference for a leisurely liqueur. It was to this latter group that I announced my solution to the insider-dealing problem.

Selena, however, now seemed displeased by the non-existence of X. I enquired why she had become attached to him.

"Because if X doesn't exist he can't have stolen the Virgil frontispiece, and if X didn't steal it then it must have been Terry after all. And at this very moment Julia's aunt is having a conversation with Terry which is designed to lure him into making a firm promise to install our bookcases on a specified date within the reasonably foreseeable future. And since she clearly has a lifetime's experience of persuading men to do what she wants them to I have every confidence that she will succeed. And if she does, I don't want to have to start worrying about what we have to lock up while Terry's working in Chambers."

"I'm afraid," I said, "that there is nothing I can do. Now that we know that every important decision taken by Sir Robert Renfrew over the past two years was taken after consultation with Isabella, we can't doubt that he was her source of information."

"Look here," said Cantrip, "are you saying no one's been blackmailed and no one's been murdered and nothing exciting's been happening at all?"

I was obliged to admit that that was my conclusion.

"But look, no one said there were two people in the Mercedes. If there were two of them someone ought to have told us, otherwise it's not fair play."

"The Mercedes, you will remember, had tinted windows and was driven through Parsons Haver at considerable speed — it is understandable that no one realized that there were two occupants."

"And the Reverend said that the chap in the Mercedes was middle-aged. Sir Robert Whatsit's a hundred if he's a day — you can't call that middle-aged."

"He is in his late sixties. The Reverend Maurice, who was only a few years younger, would have described him as middle-aged. The only person he would certainly not have so described was Miss Tavistock. The thought did briefly occur to me that he might have mistaken her for a man — but it would have been for a young man. Transvestism, whether deliberate or accidental, invariably has a rejuvenating effect on women and an aging effect on men."

"You haven't explained," said Selena, with a slight frown, "the most recent incident. Surely my client hasn't found another psychic counsellor?"

Fearing that Selena might be placed in some embarrassment if I asked her not to mention it to her client, I had said nothing of the confession made to me by Miss Tavistock.

"I understand," I said, "that you yourself suggested an explanation for that, which Sir Robert found entirely satisfactory."

"Yes," said Selena, "yes, I did, but — well, as you say, my client seems to be satisfied with it. And he evidently thinks it covers the earlier incidents as well, so he's perfectly happy. It would be rather a shame to upset him all over again by pointing out that they were all his own fault."

"As it turns out," said Julia, "it's rather a pity that you decided not to tell your client that the source of the leaked information seemed to be in Parsons Haver — if you had, he would presumably have realized that Isabella was a person not entirely to be trusted."

"No, Julia," said Selena with some asperity, "that, if I may say so, is not what turns out to be rather a pity. What turns out to be rather a pity is that I ever believed a single word of what my client told me. He told me, clearly and firmly, looking me straight in the eye, that the information needed for the insider dealing was known only to his co-directors, himself and Miss Tavistock. If he had added 'And of course my shady fortune-teller in Sussex' I might have had rather less difficulty in assisting him with his problem."

I sympathized with her feelings on the subject. In constructing my own hypothesis I had assumed that Sir Robert's decisions concerning the investment of enormous amounts of other people's money were reached on the basis of careful research and sophisticated analysis by a highly paid staff of qualified economists, rather than by methods which might have been adopted in the early years of the seventeenth century by a more than usually gullible peasant girl trying to choose a husband. This assumption being false, I had been led to erroneous conclusions.

"We quite understand," said Julia, "that in the face of the irrational even the methods of Scholarship are powerless. You were not to know that Sir Robert was the sort of man who consults fortune-tellers."

I was compelled, however, to decline her kindly meant exculpation: I knew that if I had studied the evidence with the care which I would have devoted to a medieval manuscript, I would long ago have realized that Sir Robert was incurably superstitious.

All the things he had done which appeared to be capricious — his sudden requests for conferences and equally sudden cancellations, his apparently irrational confidence that Selena could solve a problem quite outside her province, his decision just before Christmas to proceed with the acquisition of Lupilux — all these were the result of acting in accordance with his horoscope.

"But Hilary," said Julia, "how do you know?"

"My dear Julia, from what you have told me. Sir Robert is clearly born under the same sign of the zodiac as you are — and has even greater faith in the predictions of Madame Louisa."

On the television screen, the horses were lining up for the race.

"I can't understand it," said Julia, two and a half minutes later. "I was sure that Madame Louisa was referring to the destitute Irishman. She must have meant someone entirely different."

We returned to the table, where Julia was consoled with grappa for the disappointment of her financial hopes.

The lunch, it seemed, had been a success. Terry had the dazed expression of a carpenter who has made a firm promise to begin installing bookcases on the following Friday.

Moreover, it appeared that Regina was feeling much improved in health and spirits: the air of London, polluted as it was, had evidently a more beneficial effect on her than the air of Parsons Haver. It now seemed to her to be absurd to return straight home: she decided that after all she would remain in London for a day or two to visit exhibitions and theatres.

"Julia," she said, as we rose to leave, "aren't you going to open your present from Maurice?"

Julia took the flat, rectangular parcel from the shelf on which she had placed it and began carefully to undo the ribbon with which it was tied. She removed the festive wrapping and found within a white envelope some sixteen by nine inches, and a smaller envelope. She opened the smaller and read out the note which it contained.

"'Dear Julia — This has brought me so much unhappiness that I can no longer bear to keep it, but I hope that you may find pleasure in it."'

She took from the larger envelope a rectangle of cream-coloured parchment, a little scuffed at the edges, but now safely enclosed in a clear plastic folder.

Between margins garlanded with vines, an ornate initial *F*, Etruscan red edged with gold, almost filled the page; a landscape of fields and mountains glowed green and blue in the space between its two horizontal arms; in the foreground a grey-haired shepherd gazed wistfully at a beautiful young man, lightly clad in a loose, diaphanous tunic; the young man looked back at him with a teasing, equivocal smile. Penned, no doubt, by a master of calligraphy, the only line of text took little effort to read: *Formosum pastor Corydon ardebat Alexim* — "The shepherd Corydon was on fire with love for the beautiful Alexis."

The opening line, as my readers will doubtless recall, of the second of Virgil's Eclogues.

Having no reason to return immediately to Oxford, I yielded to the temptation to spend the weekend in London, where spring seemed at last to be in the air: the pale sunshine had begun to hold a suggestion of warmth and the lawns of Lincoln's Inn were scattered with daffodils.

There prevailed among my young friends a general sense of joie de vivre, due chiefly to the fact that Terry Carver was at last going to install the bookshelves. Moreover, it was no longer necessary to suspect him of stealing the Virgil frontispiece. How it had come to be lost — whether it had slipped behind the back of a drawer or been absent-mindedly misplaced by the Reverend Maurice we could only speculate; but whatever the explanation, it seemed clear from the fact of its reappearance that it had never left his possession.

334

It was also gratifying — at least to most of us, though I have to say that Cantrip seemed just a trifle disappointed — to have established that in the present case the unpleasant crime of murder had not after all been committed. Since Sir Robert's visits to Isabella had been made not under the compulsion of blackmail but in innocent confidence in her psychic powers, there was no reason to attribute her death, or that of the Reverend Maurice, to anything but natural causes.

On the Sunday evening, since Regina's train left from Victoria, we gathered — all or most of us, I forget quite who was there — for a final glass of wine together in the bar of the Grosvenor Hotel. Regina was in excellent spirits: three days of shops, exhibitions and theatres and a chance encounter with her favourite ex-husband had left her refreshed and invigorated. She had entirely recovered from her cold. She declined, however, to prolong her visit further, though pressed by Julia to do so: when the time for her train drew near, she made her farewells and left us.

"Julia," said Selena, observing that her friend seemed uncharacteristically downcast, "why are you looking as if she'd left on a three-year expedition to the Amazon jungle? She's only going to Parsons Haver."

"I know," said Julia. "I wish she weren't."

"Well, she has to go back sometime. It's where she lives."

"Yes, I know. But everyone seems to keep dying there. Daphne's always saying that something awful is going to happen to people and then it always does."

I left it to others to reason with the poor creature: I also had a train to catch.

On my return to Oxford, hoping to avoid a tiresome encounter with the Bursar, I dined at a modest Indian restaurant close to the station and returned late enough, as I hoped, to avoid him. On my way back to my rooms, however, I had the ill fortune to encounter him in the quad — he had been lying in wait for me, for all I know, throughout the weekend — and was obliged to listen to ten minutes of his thinly veiled reproaches for my defection on the previous Thursday. He had a heavy cold and smelt of mothballs.

"Bursar," I said, "forgive my asking, but are you using some interesting kind of aftershave lotion? There is a most curious aroma in the air — not unwholesome, not by any means, but decidedly pungent."

Tactfully as I had phrased it, the question seemed for some reason to annoy him; still, he did not decline to answer.

"Well, if you must know, Hilary, and since you plainly find the subject far more interesting than my views about the future of our college, I suppose that I may smell somewhat of camphor. I have been rubbing it on my chest — as you may have observed, I have a rather bad cold."

"My dear Bursar," I said, "I am so sorry. It's most thoughtless of me to keep you talking out here on such a cold night — do go back to your rooms and straight to bed with a large whiskey."

And yet when I had made my escape the smell of camphor lingered in my nostrils, like the tune of a song long after it has been played. It haunted me even in sleep: I had a nightmare in which the Bursar was rubbing my chest with camphor and Julia was telling him to stop or something awful would happen.

I have rooms on the same staircase as our Junior Chemistry Fellow, a pleasant young man despite his having spent his formative years at Cambridge. Thinking that by eight o'clock he would certainly be awake and that soon indeed he might have gone out, I descended at that hour in my dressing gown and knocked with apologetic urgency on his door.

"Hilary," he said, evidently surprised, "what are you doing up so early?"

"I'm very sorry," I said, "to disturb you so early, but there is something I have to ask you. Is there a poison that smells like camphor?"

"Camphor?" he said doubtfully.

"Yes," I said, "camphor."

"Camphor," he said again, as if attempting to familiarize himself with a newly learnt word in a foreign language.

"Yes, camphor," I said again. Scientists are not like us: one must be patient with them.

"Hilary," said my young colleague, "is this one of those questions people keep asking in Oxford about the Provost of Oriel?"

"My dear boy," I said, "what has the Provost of Oriel to do with it?"

"I mean, is it one of those questions about whether if I say that I saw someone going into Blackwells who looked like the Provost of Oriel and it actually was the

Provost of Oriel, it's true or not to say that he looked *like* the Provost of Oriel? Because if it's that sort of question I honestly don't think I'm up to it at this hour of the morning."

"Do you mean," I said, "that camphor is itself a poison?"

"Well, yes, of course. Didn't you know?"

"No," I said. "No, I had always supposed its qualities to be medicinal."

"Moths don't think so," said the scientist, laughing uproariously. "Anyway, any medicine's a poison if you take too much of it. Camphor does have therapeutic uses, of course. I believe it was used quite a lot in traditional Chinese medicine — the natural form of it's made from the bark of a Chinese tree — and there was a bit of a vogue for it as a tranquillizer at the end of the nineteenth century. But it turned out to be rather unpredictable, so nowadays it's only used externally."

"But if you swallowed it, what effect would it have?"

"Oh, quite unpleasant, I should say. Vomiting and convulsions and so on. And possibly a certain amount of delusion. People would probably think you were drunk."

"When you say it's a poison — do you mean that someone could die of it?"

"Oh, absolutely. There've been quite a few cases of people taking oil of camphor by accident, because they thought it was supposed to be taken internally. It doesn't taste all that unpleasant, you see — no more unpleasant than people expect medicine to taste."

"How much would it take to kill someone?"

"For heaven's sake, Hilary," said my young colleague rather peevishly, "I'm a chemist, not a pharmacist — I haven't the faintest idea. Anyway, it would depend on all sorts of things — if you're in the prime of life and reasonably good shape physically, it'll take a lot more to kill you than if you're a child or an elderly invalid."

"And I suppose it would not be unduly difficult to obtain?"

"Oh, I shouldn't think so. If you went to one of the Chinese shops in Soho —" He paused and regarded me with a rather stern expression. "Now look here, Hilary — trust me, this is not the right solution to our problems with the Bursar."

Assuring him that nothing had been further from my mind, I thanked him for his advice and hastened back to my room.

There had been a smell of camphor in the drawing room of the Rectory on the morning after Isabella had died there: Isabella, I recalled, had been suffering from a cold; Daphne had been looking after her. The Reverend Maurice had also been suffering from a cold shortly before his death; the cough mixture Daphne had brought for him tasted of mothballs. Sir Robert's clothing had smelt of mothballs on the evening he was taken ill: though the incident had occurred many hundreds of miles from Parsons Haver, I supposed that so ardent a devotee of Isabella would keep himself well supplied with a stock of the natural remedies which she had advocated — and which Daphne had no doubt assisted in preparing.

I searched my address book for Regina's telephone number. But though I rang several times, her telephone remained unanswered. It was not until after midday that I discovered why.

On her arrival home on the previous evening, Regina had seen lights on at the Rectory and considered telephoning Daphne to announce her safe return. It occurred to her, however, that if she did so Daphne might come round and have to be given supper; there was a television programme that she was interested in watching; she yielded to the temptation of solitude.

In the morning, seeing that the lights were still on, she began to wonder if anything were amiss. After an unsuccessful attempt to telephone, she walked across and rang the doorbell; there was no answer. At last, with some reluctance, she made use of the key which Daphne had given her. Having called out to Daphne several times, she made her way through the house to the long black drawing room, where once again an unpleasant experience awaited her.

Daphne by now had been dead for three days; and this time there had been no one to discourage the vulture.

CHAPTER
TWENTY

The Bursar had received by the morning's post a remarkably large donation from Geoffrey Bolton, who was kind enough, in the accompanying letter, to attribute his generosity to certain remarks of my own, made in the course of our train journey together. I regret to say that the Bursar was disappointingly unexcited by my success in fund-raising: the few meagre words of congratulation which he felt obliged to offer me were spoken with difficulty, apparently through clenched teeth.

Weary, by the end of the week, of meeting his furious and resentful glare whenever I dined on high table or entered the Senior Common Room, I decided to escape once more to London: on Friday, therefore, I was again among those gathered for lunch in the Corkscrew.

The mood was one of cautious optimism: in accordance with the timetable agreed to a week before, Terry Carver had appeared that morning in Chambers and was even now diligently engaged in his final preparations for installing the bookshelves. Our spirits, I have to say, were only a little subdued by thoughts of Daphne's death. None of us but Julia had known the poor girl, and Julia not well. We could feel no more than that vague sense of *lacrimae rerum* which is customary on hearing of any unexpected and premature death.

I asked Julia whether her aunt had recovered from the unpleasant experience of discovering the body. Julia replied that she was displaying her customary fortitude, but would no doubt feel relieved when the cause of Daphne's death had been formally established by the inquest, which was to be held on the following Monday.

"In re which, Hilary," said Cantrip, turning towards me in a rather accusatory manner, "haven't you got just the itsiest bit of explaining to do? What you said last week was that we'd all been wasting our time and Isabella and the Reverend had both just died of old age and there was nothing sinister going on at all. So if nothing sinister's going on, how come this bird Daphne's suddenly popped her clogs?"

"It seemed not improbable," said Ragwort, "that the deaths of Isabella and the Reverend Maurice, who were in indifferent health and not in the first flush of youth, should be attributed to natural causes. Daphne, on the other hand, was in her twenties and not known to be suffering from any illness. Her sudden death does seem to require an explanation."

"Right," said Cantrip. "So you'd better come up with one pretty fast, Hilary, or we're not buying you any more booze."

"My dear Cantrip," I said kindly, "the insights of Scholarship are neither to be purchased by bribes nor compelled by threats. As it happens, however, I have formed an hypothesis, which explains, as I believe, all the events under consideration, and which I shall be happy to share with you. I must warn you, however, that my explanation has little of the Gothic and sensational element which you may be hoping for."

They filled my glass and assured me that I might proceed without fear of disappointing them.

I accordingly explained the process of reasoning whereby I had concluded, some days before, that Isabella and the Reverend Maurice had both died of camphor poisoning and that Sir Robert's illness had been similarly caused; that the camphor had been contained in medicine which they were taking for their colds; and that it was Daphne who had added it.

"Hang on a minute," said Cantrip. "If your theory is that everyone was poisoned by Daphne, isn't it a bit of a snag that she's been poisoned as well?"

"By no means," I said. "I had never imagined that Daphne poisoned anyone deliberately. We must remember that Daphne thought of herself as a disciple of Isabella and that Isabella claimed, among other things, to be a healer. I have no doubt that her medical supplies included camphor: it is made, as I dare say you know, from an oriental tree — she would have regarded it as a natural remedy. She, I imagine, would have used it with discretion, but Daphne was clearly the sort of person who believes that if one teaspoonful is good for you two teaspoonfuls will be twice as good — remember what everyone said about her cooking. So when she used Isabella's recipe for treating coughs and colds, she tried to improve on it by adding more camphor."

"Yes," said Julia. "Yes, I can imagine her doing that."

"And last week, I suppose, she found that she herself was suffering from a cold, as so many people are at this time of year. What could be more natural than to take a large dose of the medicine she had such faith in? I see no point in taking any action in the matter — the inquest will no doubt establish that that was how she died."

"But she didn't," said Julia.

"Didn't? My dear Julia," I said, a little disconcerted, "whatever do you mean?"

"Didn't die of camphor poisoning." Julia looked apologetic. "My aunt's doctor is a friend of the pathologist who did the post-mortem. He says that the poison she died of was hemlock."

For a moment, I confess, I was rather taken aback. The explanation, however, was not far to seek: having previously used camphor, Daphne had decided to experiment with hemlock. Though how even she could have thought of hemlock as a plant noted for its therapeutic qualities —

"You don't suppose," said Selena, "that she might have done it on purpose? If you're right, Hilary, then she was responsible for the deaths of the two people to whom she was most attached. If she suddenly realized what she'd done —"

Selena paused, evidently more distressed by this idea than by the fact of Daphne's death. So indeed were we all — despair somehow seems more poignant than death.

"I gather," said Julia, "that the police have ruled out suicide. There was no suicide note. And they didn't find the container which held the poison, so it looks as if she washed the glass or whatever it was in and put it tidily away. They say that if she'd done it on purpose she wouldn't have bothered to do that — she'd just have sat and waited for the poison to take effect."

We sipped our wine and ordered our salads, cheered, perhaps irrationally, by the thought that Daphne had not died by choice.

"It's curious, isn't it," said Selena, "how everything to do with this business seems to turn on whether someone would have washed a glass? Now that I come to think of it, I still don't know who washed the glasses on the night Isabella died. I wouldn't have said that Sir Robert was at all the sort of man to do it — people have been washing glasses for him all his life. Do you think it was Katharine Tavistock?"

"No," I said a little absent-mindedly. "No, I think not. I asked her when we were walking back from the museum whether she'd ever met Isabella and she told me that she hadn't. During Sir Robert's consultations she always stayed in the car."

A slightly inconvenient thought now occurred to me. There emerged from somewhere in the depths of my unconscious mind a recollection of the moment, many months before, when I had first learnt the name of Selena's merchant banking client. I had seen Sir Robert's photograph on the City page of the *Scuttle*, over a report of a dinner at which, on the previous evening, he had been the guest of honour. Searching my memory with a certain reluctance, I was compelled to admit that this had occurred on the morning of the day on which we heard the news of Isabella's death: if the report was to be relied on, Sir Robert could not have been her visitor.

"Hilary," said Selena, "this way madness lies. You established last week, to our complete satisfaction, that the man in the black Mercedes was Sir Robert Renfrew. If you're now going to try to persuade us that there was also an entirely different man in an entirely different Mercedes, I shall put my hands over my ears and refuse to listen."

"My dear Selena," I said, "I would be as averse as you are to reaching any such conclusion. I think the explanation must be that Isabella's visitor on the evening of her death was not, after all, the man in the black Mercedes."

No one, so far as we knew, had actually seen the Mercedes on the evening of Isabella's death. Regina had not: she had inferred its presence from the fact that Daphne had said that her aunt was giving a Personal Reading. The Reverend Maurice had not: he had expressly said that by the time he took Daphne home there was no sign of it. There were no other witnesses.

"So what you're saying is," said Cantrip with some indignation, "that all this time we've been worrying about a chap in a Mercedes washing up the glasses we needn't have been worrying at all, because it wasn't him but some other chap in a second-hand Toyota who probably does it every day?"

"That," I said, "is entirely possible. We know nothing whatever about Isabella's visitor on the evening of her death. We know only that he, or indeed she, was not Sir Robert Renfrew, and therefore not the man in the black Mercedes."

The question was in any case immaterial: the identity of Isabella's visitor on the night of her death did not affect the theory that I had proposed. And yet I was unable to dismiss it from my mind. I felt as one does when, after sending an article for publication in some learned journal, one comes across some reference one has overlooked. I fell for a time into an abstraction.

When my attention returned to the conversation around me, it was no longer concerned with Daphne but with a case in which Cantrip and Ragwort had that morning been appearing against each other in the High Court. Following some rather severe hints from the judge that it ought to be settled, they had conscientiously tried to reach an equitable compromise. Their efforts had been thwarted, however, by the absurd obstinacy of one of their clients — Cantrip's according to Ragwort, Ragwort's according to Cantrip. This meant, among other unhappy consequences, that they were unable to linger over lunch: they had to be back in court at two o'clock.

"Ah well," said Selena, "into each life some rain must fall. Console yourselves with the thought that good times are just around the corner. Any day now we'll have our bookshelves and life will be wonderful."

"I wouldn't bet on it if I were you," said Cantrip, evidently resolved on pessimism. "The way I see it is, now Terry's in the money, he's not going to be too fussed about getting our bookshelves finished. He'll probably go off on a world cruise or something and forget all about it."

"In the money?" said Ragwort, looking surprised. "My dear Cantrip, whatever do you mean?"

"Well, he's the rezzy benny under Isabella's will, isn't he? And that means that now the Daphne bird's snuffed it he'll get the lot. And that means he'll get the Rectory. And according to Julia's aunt Reg the Rectory's worth between three and four hundred thousand smackers. Which is what I call not at all bad going. And now Daphne's not around to make trouble, he won't have any problem getting the cash from the Reverend's estate as well. So I'd say he was pretty nicely fixed."

"Cantrip," said Ragwort, "have you noticed the time?"

"Crumbs," said Cantrip. "All right, I'll race you — last one in court's a sissy.

Their departure left the best part of a bottle of excellent claret to be shared among three of us, none of whom that afternoon had any such pressing obligations; the circumstances should have been propitious to convivial relaxation. Cantrip's final remarks, however, seemed somehow to have cast a kind of shadow over the afternoon: nothing so definite as to be called a suspicion, but rather an uneasy sense of ambiguity. Though well aware of the matters of which Cantrip had reminded us, we had none of us, I think, considered consciously until then how profitable the sequence of events had proved to be to the attractive young craftsman. We seemed, without speaking of the subject, to reach an understanding not to do so; but our conversation became desultory, as if each of us were thinking of something other than what we talked of.

"Julia," said Selena, when the wine was finally disposed of, "if either of us is going to get any work at all done this afternoon, isn't it time we thought of getting back to Chambers?"

Julia conceded that it was.

"I'll walk back with you," I said. "There's something I should like to ask Terry."

Terry, however, was no longer working diligently on preparations for the bookshelves. There had been a telephone call (said Selena's clerk Henry) from Miss Larwood's aunt, who seemed to know that Terry was likely to be found at 62 New Square. She had asked to speak to him and said that it was urgent. Not being in the habit (said Henry) of listening in to other people's telephone conversations, Henry did not know what they had said to each other. He only knew that Terry had left immediately afterwards, saying that he would not be back that day. Henry had not asked him where he was going, which was none of Henry's business; but he had seemed to be in a hurry.

I felt as if the room had turned suddenly cold. I could imagine no subject upon which Regina could have wished to speak urgently to the young craftsman save in connection with Daphne's death. Had she remembered something about it which she found perplexing or significant? Something perhaps which she felt that she should include in her evidence at the inquest? And why, if so, had it been to Terry that she had felt she ought to mention it? Was it something that she thought, as a matter of fairness, she should offer him a chance to explain? And for what purpose, when she had done so, had he left in such haste?

From the anxious exchange of glances between Julia and Selena, I perceived that I was not alone in my disquiet.

"Hilary," said Julia, "what was it you wanted to ask him?"

"I wanted to ask him," I said, "when exactly he visited Isabella. I rather think that it may have been on the night she died."

"Henry," said Selena, "Miss Larwood and I are going to Sussex. Perhaps you would be kind enough to tell Miss Larwood's clerk."

From central London, in the middle of a Friday afternoon, not even Selena, for all the dexterity and insouciance of her driving, could make a rapid departure. I had ample time, as her Ford Escort edged its way along the Strand behind a convoy of double-decker buses, to explain why I now believed that it was Terry who had visited Isabella on the night of her death.

"When he told us of his visit to her, I assumed, I confess too readily, that it had taken place some weeks, if not months, before she died. Upon more careful reflection, I realize that he did not in fact say that. He did say on the other hand, that on the evening of his visit Daphne was sent out of the house."

"Yes," said Julia. "I remember him saying that."

"We know, however, that when that happened it was usually because of a visit from the man in the black Mercedes — that is to say, as we have now established, Sir Robert Renfrew. The only occasion that we know of on which Daphne's exile to the Newt and Ninepence cannot have been on account of a visit from Sir Robert was on the evening of Isabella's death."

We joined the slow-moving stream of traffic crossing Blackfriars Bridge.

"Even if that was the evening that Terry went to see her," said Julia, drawing deeply on a Gauloise, "it doesn't follow that there was any causal connection between the two events. She may still have died, as you suggested earlier, of an accidental overdose of cough medicine. Or even of natural causes."

I agreed that it was not impossible.

"And if Terry was her visitor," continued Julia, with renascent optimism, "then there's nothing in the least sinister about him washing up the glasses. A nicely brought-up young man who'd been having drinks with an elderly relative — it would be the most natural thing in the world."

"No doubt you are right," I said. "There is nothing at all sinister about the situation. Except that Isabella and Daphne are both now dead and Terry will in consequence inherit a property worth three or four hundred thousand pounds."

351

We had now for some minutes remained stationary in the Elephant and Castle, where someone had for some reason decided to dig up the road: little of Selena's attention was required for her driving.

"Of course," said Selena thoughtfully, "Terry could have inherited without Daphne dying. Under the terms of Isabella's will, she'd have forfeited her interest in the estate if she'd simply stopped living at the Rectory . . . I suppose the first idea one would have in those circumstances, if one happened to be the residuary beneficiary, would be to try and frighten her away. Let's say, for example, by burgling the house or throwing stones through the window."

"Terry didn't know the terms of the will until after Isabella died," said Julia.

"He says he didn't," said Selena.

Julia made no direct answer, but enquired if it might not be quicker to take the train. Selena, having considered this, thought that it would not.

"It's five miles to Parsons Haver from the nearest mainline station and it might take ages to get a taxi. Don't worry, it won't take long once we're out of London."

London, however, seemed endless, spreading southwards from the Thames in an almost infinite succession of suburbs, some affluent, some dilapidated, some quietly genteel, some noisily bohemian, but all filled with a sluggish stream of motor vehicles, moving with the utmost slowness in the direction of the coast.

My thoughts grew increasingly confused. At times I was convinced that the case against Terry was overwhelming and Regina in the gravest danger; at times that the evidence against him was merely circumstantial and there was no reason at all for the urgency of our journey.

I remembered, with relief, that he had no motive at all for doing any harm to Sir Robert, but then with anxiety that he was in Cannes at the time the poisoning had taken place and indeed an habitué of the restaurant where it had occurred.

Brixton seemed gradually to become Streatham, but with no perceptible diminution in the stream of traffic.

I recalled that he had been far from Parsons Haver at the moment when the Reverend Maurice was taken ill during the Christmas service; but if the clergyman's illness had been due to natural causes, Terry had been at his bedside the following night when the illness had been fatal.

Streatham at last became Croydon.

I knew of no specific occasion when he would have had the opportunity to administer poison to Daphne; but the contrivance of such an occasion was not beyond human ingenuity, and he was the only person to profit by her death.

Croydon with the utmost reluctance became Coulsdon.

By the time we reached open country and roads on which Selena could drive at a speed she considered reasonable the sun was already low in the western sky. Long before we completed our journey, the voluptuous curves of the Sussex countryside were hidden in darkness. Had it not been for the reduction of our speed to one more suited to a village high street, I would scarcely have realized that we had reached our destination.

There was no light to be seen upstairs or downstairs, either in the windows of Regina's house or of the house next door. A thin white mist was creeping up from the river, obscuring the edges of things.

Julia's ring at the doorbell produced no answer, no sound or sign of movement within.

We stood shivering on the narrow pavement, after all the urgency of our journey uncertain what to do next. Having somehow assumed, despite our fears, that we would find everything as usual and Regina, smiling and offering drinks, at the door to greet us, we had made no plans for any other contingency. Perhaps, suggested Julia, we would be able to see something from the back of the house.

We followed her down a narrow passageway, feeling our way cautiously between rough stone walls, and emerged to find ourselves beside the gate leading into the churchyard. From here we could see that the windows at the back of the house were as dark as those at the front.

Ahead of us, however, on the far side of the churchyard, the darkness was broken by an angry copper-coloured glow.

"Julia," said Selena, "is that the Rectory?"

I saw now that the glow, which I had at first perceived as formless, had the outline of a large and imposing house, its windows blazing with orange and crimson light: if it were not a mirage, it must be the

Rectory. One might perhaps have imagined that what we were seeing was merely the reflection in its windows of a more than usually spectacular sunset; but the sun, as I have said, had long since fallen below the horizon.

"Oh my God," said Julia.

We began to run across the churchyard, none of us doubting, I think, that the Rectory was the scene of whatever catastrophe we had come in time or too late to avert.

The lamp above the doorway of the church barely served to show us the way between the gravestones, round which white skeins of mist wound shifting and deceptive spirals. We were running, as it seemed, in a world of darkness and silence, hearing hardly even our own footsteps on the soft grass and no other sound at all.

It occurred to me, as we drew nearer, that there was something more than natural about the silence. Should we not be hearing a hiss and crackle of flame, the crashing and tearing of timbers? Could any building burn without a sound? I became conscious also of the absence of smoke and heat.

It was Selena, outdistancing Julia and myself, who was the first to perceive the truth of the matter: it was not the Rectory that was burning — someone had lit a bonfire in the garden at the back.

But February is not the month for bonfires.

Standing outside the high uncurtained windows and gazing through the long black drawing room, we saw that the fire was still some sixty or seventy feet away, beyond the conservatory. It was a well-constructed bonfire, ten feet or more in height, built in the shape of a pyramid round a tall stake planted firmly in the ground, as bonfires were built in the days when their purpose was more serious and sinister than the destruction of a rag-filled effigy for the entertainment of children. The flames leapt up towards the starless sky, filling the room before us with a grotesque pavane of endlessly moving shadows.

Between the bonfire and the house a figure ran to and fro, assiduously nourishing the voracity of the flames. Distorted by the firelight, it seemed constantly to change in shape and size, to be sometimes something more, sometimes something less than human. Its face, however, when I saw it at last, was the beautiful, dangerous face of Terry Carver.

Pushing in despair or irrational optimism at the front door, Julia found that it was open, as if we had been expected.

CHAPTER
TWENTY-ONE

There were four people in the long dark drawing room, silently watching the flickering light of the bonfire. On one of the black chaises longues, two young women sat hand in hand, one red-haired and of boyish appearance, the other fair, with a pleasing roundness of face and figure. On another, facing them, was a heavily built man with a handlebar moustache. Sitting next to him was Regina, who rose, smiling, and asked us what we would like to drink.

"You seem," said Julia, "to be expecting us."

"Yes, of course," said her aunt. "I rang your Chambers to ask your advice about something and your clerk said you were all on your way down here. He didn't seem quite to know why, but I thought you must have guessed what we were doing and decided to come and help."

"No," said Julia. "Not exactly — what are you doing?"

"Burning papers," said Regina. "You know — the way they do in embassies."

It had occurred to Ricky Farnham that morning that the inquest on Daphne might end in an open verdict, or even a verdict of murder; that the police, in that event, might think it their duty to examine in detail any letters and other documents to be found at the Rectory, in case these contained some clue to the identity of the culprit; that these would include any papers kept by Isabella for the purpose of her blackmailing business; and that distress and embarrassment might be caused by these finding their way into, as it were, the public domain. Having thought of this, he went round to High Street to talk to Regina.

Regina still had the key that Daphne had given her: once Ricky had explained the problem, they had gone round to the Rectory with the intention of removing anything which could prove embarrassing. They had been thwarted, however, by the volume of documents involved: there were several dozen boxes of files, all at a rapid glance containing material which might be compromising.

"So we decided to burn them," said Regina, "and Griselda said she'd build a bonfire. But then it occurred to us that now Daphne's dead everything at the Rectory belongs to Terry and perhaps we ought to tell him what we were doing. And I knew he was working at New Square this morning, so I rang up and explained it all to him and he said he'd come down."

Regina explained these matters with the confident serenity of a high-principled woman who knows that she is doing the right thing; I did not believe for a moment that she was telling the entire truth. She could not have failed — indeed, it was clear that she had not failed — to see the possible relevance of Isabella's files to the mystery of Daphne's death: if she had agreed to

358

destroy them, it must mean that to her the death was no longer mysterious. Either she knew for certain that it had not been murder — but I did not see how she could be certain of that — or, knowing that it was, nonetheless thought it right to protect the person responsible.

Looking from one to another of them, I wondered which of her friends she would think it right to protect, even if guilty of murder. The devoted Ricky? The impulsive Griselda? The gentle Mrs Tyrrell?

But then at last the truth became clear to me and I knew that it was none of these.

"The letter," I said. "You mustn't burn the letter. There must have been a letter from Maurice — you haven't burnt it?"

"Not yet," said Regina. "We thought we ought to ask Julia whether anyone could say we were doing something illegal. That's why I tried to ring her."

Christmas Eve

Dear Daphne,

It may seem unkind, some may even think ungrateful, but I am going to kill you. You have left me with —

No, it would not be true to say that I have no choice. The alternative would be to kill myself. That indeed was my intention when I prepared the poison — it was for myself, not you, that I chose hemlock. I would not have chosen it for you.

359

It was one of the plants that Reg and Griselda rescued from the physic garden at the Rectory. About a week after my Virgil frontispiece disappeared I went out late at night and dug it up by the roots: I had read in some learned journal or other an article about the death of Socrates, which mentioned that the root is the most poisonous part. The writer was a scholar of considerable eminence — I am sure that he can be relied on. I ground it up into a powder and prepared a decoction in the way he described. I had begun by meaning to take the poison straight away, but found when I had made it that I felt better and no longer wanted to. I put it in a bottle with an airtight stopper and hid it away in a cupboard in my bedroom, taking great comfort from the thought that it was there if I needed it.

But please understand that even then it was your presence, not Derek's absence, which had made my life seem insupportable. By the time I knew him, you had already begun to make me feel a little desperate; you brought me presents that I did not want and you could not afford; you insisted on doing things for me which I would much rather have done for myself; you praised me in immoderate and embarrassing terms for qualities I do not have and achievements of which you are no judge. In return, you seemed to feel entitled to make demands on my time and emotional energy more absolute and more implacable than a newborn baby could reasonably make of its mother. Where I went, you followed; I could not go out without meeting you; I could not stay at home without your ringing my doorbell. I could see neither how to endure nor how to escape your endless, stifling thereness.

And then there was Derek and life became bearable again. Oh, more than bearable — golden, delightful, like the first day of spring after a long, dark winter, full of laughter and pleasure. I thought that I had never been so happy, not even when I was very young. I almost imagined that God was rewarding me for being patient with you and I thought how generous it was, when all I had prayed for was a little peace and privacy.

It ended, as you know, very painfully for me, but I have no wish to say any more about that.

While I was grieving for my loss and had no strength to protect myself, nor any consciousness of the need to do so, you somehow took possession of my life. It became an accepted thing that I was a kind of invalid and you were looking after me. You cooked and cleaned and shopped for me; you even did something you called looking after my garden — oh, my poor garden. You stayed with me all day from morning till night to make sure that I should not be lonely — though you quickly made other visitors feel that they had stayed inconsiderately long.

And I only wanted you to go away.

The more I was with you, the more I longed for Derek. I regretted bitterly the letter I had written him; I wished that I'd pretended not to know who had taken the frontispiece. I no longer cared if he was a thief, a liar and insincere in his affection for me; I would rather have lived in a world of absolute illusion than one from which irony and elegance had so utterly perished.

I still felt that I ought to try not to hurt your feelings. My life became a series of tactful excuses. I said that I had lost my appetite, rather than admit that the food you cooked disgusted me; that I was too tired to sit up in the evening, rather than let you see how weary I was of your company; that I was too unwell to go out, when the only way I could avoid you was to stay at home and pretend not to hear the doorbell.

But when the effort became too much and I began to say things that were unkind, quite seriously unkind, I found that it made no difference. You understood, you said, that it was "the pain talking". By defining me as ill, you somehow managed to convert everything I said into its opposite; you construed expressions of anger as signs of affection; you translated every plea for solitude into an appeal for company.

I became more and more unkind to you — I said things more wounding than I had ever imagined saying to anyone. I told you that your conversation bored me, that your voice set my teeth on edge, that I found you personally distasteful. You cried; but you did not go away — this, it seemed, was your idea of friendship.

And something horrible began to happen to me.

Though I know all too well that I am often less thoughtful, less generous, less actively kind than I ought to be, I have always believed myself incapable of deliberate cruelty; I found it incomprehensible that anyone could take pleasure in causing pain. But now I began to find that I enjoyed hurting you; when I said something particularly wounding, I no longer felt remorse but a kind of loathsome satisfaction. Sometimes the desire even to hurt you physically was so powerful that I trembled with the effort of resisting it. I no longer found it extraordinary that people might take pleasure in tormenting a child or a helpless animal: I saw that they were merely like me and moved by the same impulse.

And if this impulse was simply a part of human nature, I wondered if it was also a part of the nature of God. I had from time to time, of course, the usual doubts about the existence of God, especially as I could never really solve the problem of why, if He exists, He should allow the innocent to suffer; but I had never doubted that if He existed, He was benevolent. But it now occurred to me that perhaps He enjoyed our suffering — that perhaps, indeed, He had created us for that purpose — it would explain everything. I thought that if I believed this I would not wish to go on living.

But until last night I never dreamt of killing you.

No, that's not true. I did dream of it, every night, and by means far more painful and violent than poison. But in my waking hours I knew that it was out of the question: you meant well and were doing your best and it was not your fault that I had become a monster. If death was the only solution, I quite accepted that it must be mine, not yours.

Until last night.

How did you ever come to let me find the frontispiece? You thought, I suppose, that it was quite cleverly hidden in the middle of the pile of old newspapers that you keep to line the floor of the aviary. But did you really imagine, even though only an edge of it was showing, that I would not see and recognize a thing I had so much loved and valued? And why hide it at all? Why not merely destroy it? Surely not because it was beautiful? You knew, I suppose, that it was worth money — was it merely its commercial value that saved it from destruction?

Perhaps a psychoanalyst would say that when you left me alone there, in that hideous black drawing room, you subconsciously wanted me to find it. But even so, with what motive? From a sense of guilt, or one of triumph?

I hardly understood at first what it meant to find it there. And yet after a few moments I saw how easy it must have been for you — a question merely of leaving my back door unlocked when you put out the rubbish that morning. You would have known how unlikely I was to notice. And that night creeping back into the house in the darkness, while Derek and I were already in bed upstairs —

I felt sick at the thought of it — at that moment, it would have been physically impossible for me to speak to you. I took the frontispiece and left, leaving you still busy in your kitchen with whatever nauseating beverage you were preparing for me as yet a further symbol of your devotion and concern.

And now I do not see why I should die rather than you. You have taken from me the thing that I held most dear; you have stolen all the hope and pleasure from my life; you have made me hate God. You are destroying me by inches like some horrible disease — why should I not defend myself?

By the time you read this you will have eaten, I suppose, at least half of the chocolates I am giving you for Christmas. I think it is safe to tell you that they are poisoned. I spent what remained of the night filling and refilling my fountain pen, as if with ink, from the little bottle of hemlock and carefully discharging it into the base of each chocolate. I did it, I think I may say, quite neatly — I am sure you will not notice anything odd about them.

I shall not give them to you today — I should not like anything to happen to spoil the midnight service. I suppose it will be my last — I should like it to go well. I shall take them to you tomorrow morning, before we go to lunch with Reg, and tell you that I want them to be all for you — I know how greedy you are about chocolates and how pleased you will be not to be expected to share them. And when you go home in the evening you will open the box and eat them, as you always do, one after another until they are all gone.

I intend to place this letter at the bottom of the box. It may be that you will notice it soon after you have finished the top layer of chocolates and that you will still have strength enough to summon help. I do not think, however, that it will be in time to save you; the Athenians, in whom I have great confidence, considered hemlock a most reliable poison.

You may also, of course, have time and strength to denounce me. Even if you do not, I think it unlikely that I can retrieve this letter before it falls into the hands of the police. I suppose that they will put me in prison: but I'm unable to care very much about that — I feel you have made me accustomed to imprisonment.

I do not know if you will suffer much. It was suggested in the article I mentioned that death by hemlock might be less painless than Plato would lead us to believe. You cannot expect me to care a great deal about that: I am human; and God, who delights in suffering, has made me in His own, unspeakable image.

Maurice

♣　♣　♣

His friends all said that the letter should be burnt.

"You see," said Regina, "we all know he wouldn't really have done it. It's quite absurd to think that Maurice could poison anyone. If he hadn't been taken ill on Christmas Eve, he simply wouldn't have given Daphne the chocolates. But of course when I found Maurice's Christmas presents in the drawer of his desk, I gave Daphne the one with her name on it, just as I did with everyone else. So her dying was really just an accident and Maurice is no more to blame for it than I am."

"What I don't quite understand," said Selena, "is how the letter comes to be in your possession."

"Well," said Regina, looking slightly surprised, "it was beside the poor girl's body when I found her. And I didn't want the police to find it, so I put it away in my handbag before they came. And the empty chocolate box and all the wrappings, of course."

"Oh dear," said Julia, turning rather pale. "I'm not entirely sure you should have done that, Reg. I think they might call it tampering with the evidence."

"Oh nonsense, Julia," said her aunt. "How could it possibly be right to let the police find something which would only mislead them? I knew perfectly well that Daphne's death was simply an accident, but if the police had seen Maurice's letter they'd have been bound to say that he poisoned her on purpose. And then there'd be horrible stories in all the newspapers and that's how everyone would remember him, not as the kind of person he really was at all. And it simply wouldn't be fair."

It was with some difficulty that I persuaded them of the dangers of burning the letter; the danger that the inquest would find on the following Monday that Daphne had died by some criminal act: the danger that some innocent person would be suspected of the crime: the danger, in particular, that the person suspected would be Terry himself. They finally agreed that it should be placed in a sealed envelope and lodged in the custody of some respectable bank.

The documents in Isabella's filing cabinets I did not attempt to save from the bonfire: though their destruction caused me, as an historian, a certain pang of distress, I supposed that it would add to the sum of human happiness. Besides, I could not think quite what else could be done with them.

The only remaining object of contention was the Book; impressively large and bound in leather, as Regina had described it, it still occupied, as it had when she first visited Isabella, the display cabinet at the end of the long drawing room. While disclaiming any superstitious belief in its malevolent powers, they all seemed curiously reluctant to handle it. At length, since books are not among the things I am afraid of, I offered to take custody of it.

On the Wednesday before Easter there was champagne in the Corkscrew: the bookshelves had finally been installed; subject only to the return of the electrician to fit the lights, the refurbishment of 62 New Square was complete.

Several weeks had by now elapsed since the inquest on Daphne's death. Griselda had given evidence that hemlock was one of the plants which had once grown in the physic garden of the Old Rectory and perhaps still survived there; she had also drawn attention to the similarity in appearance between hemlock and parsley. The jury had taken no more than a few minutes to return a verdict of death by misadventure.

In the meantime, thinking it prudent to recommend the destruction of any medicines acquired from Isabella which Sir Robert might happen to have in his possession, I had telephoned Miss Tavistock. She told me that Isabella had indeed from time to time given him medicine for various ailments; but he had used the last of it the previous summer, when he had been in France and caught a heavy cold. My theory regarding the deaths of Isabella and the Reverend Maurice could have had no clearer confirmation.

One aspect of the affair, though of no intrinsic importance, had for some time continued to puzzle me: the letter which Maurice had posted shortly before Christmas, apparently as a result of his conversation with Julia about insider dealing, and which I had supposed to have been addressed to Sir Robert Renfrew. To whom had it been written? What had it said? Was it after all entirely unconnected with the insider-dealing business? I became almost resigned to never knowing the answer to these questions.

A few days before Easter, however, I had happened to encounter Benjamin Dobble on the steps of the Bodleian Library. Our conversation had turned to Terry Carver and we spoke of his attachment to the Reverend Maurice.

"He must have been a dear old thing," said Benjamin. "I wish I'd met him. He wrote to me once, you know."

"Wrote to you? Why?"

"Oh, it was a rather strange letter. He wanted to know the name of the man who lived opposite my flat in Cannes, but I imagine he just wanted an excuse to get in touch with me in the hope of getting in touch with Terry again. But before I had time to ask Terry what he'd like me to do about it there was a telephone call saying he was ill and Terry went back anyway. And then of course I heard he'd died, so there was no point in doing anything about it."

I now felt able, therefore, not only to share in the general rejoicing at the completion of the bookcases but also to reflect with modest satisfaction on the successful completion of my investigation.

"I am not entirely sure," said Selena as she filled my glass with champagne, "in what sense precisely you are using the word 'successful'."

"I mean," I said, "that the truth has been established."

"Yes," said Selena. "Yes, I suppose it has. But not exactly as a result of your investigation — as a result of Maurice's letter."

370

"That, certainly, was of great assistance in establishing how Daphne died. Daphne's death, however, was peripheral to the main subject of my investigation — that is to say, the deaths of Isabella and Maurice and the insider-dealing problem."

"But Hilary, most of your theories about those matters have turned out to be entirely wrong."

"My dear Selena," I said, "to be always right is the claim of the charlatan, not of the Scholar. The mark of true Scholarship is a fearless and unflinching readiness to modify one's theories in the light of new evidence."

"So when you finally decided that the deaths of Maurice and Isabella had nothing to do with the insider-dealing problem, that was a modification of your theory that they had both been poisoned by the person responsible for the insider dealing?"

"Exactly."

"Which in turn was a modification of the theory that they had both died natural deaths?"

"Quite so." I paid no heed to her slightly satirical tone: to a woman who has spent the year dealing with builders much may be forgiven. "I fully concede that in the course of my investigation I have frequently been in error. My cardinal mistake was my failure to attach the proper significance to the affair of Mrs Tyrrell's ring."

"I will admit," said Selena, "that I don't see what relevance Mrs Tyrrell's ring has to anything at all."

"Unless you mean," said Julia, who had settled in prudent proximity to the champagne, "that you believe Daphne really did have some kind of prophetic powers?"

"On the contrary, the one thing of which I have throughout been entirely certain is that she did not. I should therefore have reflected far more carefully than I did on the alternative explanation. It was, after all, a perfectly simple one: Daphne had seen the ring lying on the washbasin or some such place and recognized it as Mrs Tyrrell's. But instead of simply saying, as most people would have done, 'I think Mrs Tyrrell has left her ring in the bathroom,' she had seen an opportunity to demonstrate her psychic powers."

"And I suppose," said Selena, "that there is some equally simple explanation for her remark about Ricky Farnham being paid for some medicine he'd sold?"

"She could have known in any number of ways that he had shares in a particular pharmaceutical company — he'd probably mentioned it himself sometime in the bar of the Newt and Ninepence. To find out when it was due to pay a dividend she had only to look at the financial page of the newspaper."

"You make it sound," said Julia, "as if she were quite clever. That wasn't my impression of her."

"You underestimated her, my dear Julia, because she was not interested in the same things that you are interested in. In some ways she was really quite clever, as indeed Isabella must have been. Moreover, children generally acquire the skills of those they grow up with, even without any conscious effort to learn or teach. Daphne had acquired the skills of a professional fortune-teller. These include, I need hardly say, the art of collecting small scraps of information, perhaps in themselves entirely trivial, and presenting them as extraordinary and mysterious. If I had given proper consideration to the affair of the ring, I should soon have seen that certain other events, apparently mysterious, also bore the hallmarks of Daphne's authorship. Instead, having allowed my attention to become concentrated on the insider-dealing question, I mistakenly attributed them to the man in the black Mercedes."

"You are referring," said Selena, "to Daphne's burglary and the stone-throwing incident? I take it that she simply invented them?"

"Undoubtedly. The story of the burglar was invented by Daphne to make herself an object of sympathy and interest, in particular to Maurice, but by telling it at midnight on the doorstep of the Vicarage, dishevelled and apparently terrified, she lent it a plausibility it might not otherwise have had. The stone-throwing incident was a repetition of the same effect, with a certain amount of embellishment — she threw the stone herself, of course, from inside rather than outside the Rectory garden, and then scraped her head with it until she drew blood."

"Just to make herself interesting?" Julia turned pale and hastily lit a Gauloise.

"People have been known to go to greater lengths."

"And you think that was also her reason for claiming to have the power of prophecy?"

"That, I would say, did rather more than make her interesting. If she could persuade people to believe it, it provided her with a means of influence, even of control, over people and events. Having even less power than most of us to have any effect on the world around her, she had a correspondingly more desperate desire to do so."

"Hilary," said Julia, drawing deeply on her Gauloise, "you seem to be saying that everything Daphne did was a conscious and deliberate deception. But you never met her — you don't know how appallingly earnest she was about everything. I'd have sworn that she really believed every word she said — that she had the power of prophecy and all the nonsense about the Book and so on."

"My dear Julia," I said, "I have no doubt that she believed in them absolutely. In order to deceive others, it is necessary also to deceive oneself. The actor playing Hamlet must believe that he is indeed the Prince of Denmark, though when he leaves the stage he will usually remember who he really is. On the other hand, when someone's entire life is based on pretence, they will seldom if ever return to reality. That is the secret of successful politicians, evangelists and confidence tricksters — they believe they are telling the truth, even when they know that they have faked the evidence. Sincerity, my dear Julia, is a quality not to be trusted."

"What I find curious," said Selena, "is her prediction about animals. Why did she risk her credibility by making it? After all, it was pure chance that it actually came true."

"Well, perhaps. You will remember, however, that it came true, so far as Griselda was concerned, as the result of an accident of which Daphne was the indirect cause. The primary purpose of the stone-throwing

374

incident was no doubt to inspire the interest and concern of the Reverend Maurice. But was it, I wonder, entirely by chance that it occurred at a time when Griselda was sitting out of doors and the notoriously nervous Tabitha was asleep on the roof of the potting shed and the traffic in the High Street was at its busiest?"

"You surely don't think she did it on purpose?"

"My dear Julia, who can fathom the workings of the subconscious mind? She would not, I imagine, have admitted to herself that she was hoping to cause an accident. The fact remains that she achieved what she wanted — her prophetic powers were vindicated and Griselda was prevented from looking after Maurice's garden. Which was the motive for the prophecy in the first place — she was hoping, quite absurdly of course, to frighten Griselda into giving up working at the Vicarage. Reference was made, you remember, to the bad-tempered Alsatian in the garden next door."

"But Hilary, why on earth should she want to do that?"

"Because no one was to do anything for Maurice except Daphne herself. She not only wanted to play a part in his life, she wanted to be the only person who played any part in it. She was determined that he should need her — and that he should need no one else. She succeeded, as I have said, in replacing Griselda as his gardener. She hinted to Mrs Tyrrell that he could no longer afford to pay for cleaning, so Mrs Tyrrell tactfully stopped cleaning for him and was also replaced by Daphne. By her constant presence and her exaggerated devotion she began to separate him from his friends. And when Terry came on the scene, she naturally took steps to get rid of him — hence the theft of the frontispiece."

"Even so," said Selena, "one could hardly have foreseen that she'd be the death of him."

"Not quite that, perhaps. But one might have foreseen, I think, that if he was ill she would tamper with his medicine — she could not have borne the idea that she played no significant part in his treatment. There was one thing at least, you see, about which she had been entirely truthful: she wanted what she always said she wanted — to feel that she was caring for someone who really needed her."

Epilogue

There is little to add that is material to my narrative. At the next annual general meeting of the shareholders of Renfrews' Bank, Sir Robert announced his retirement from the chairmanship and proposed the appointment of Edgar Albany as his successor. This proposal, I need hardly say, was carried without opposition: a significant number of the shares were still held, after all, by family trusts of which Albany was a beneficiary. Shortly afterwards, Geoffrey Bolton resigned from Renfrews' and joined what is called an international conglomerate. I felt at this juncture some concern for the safety of Miss Tavistock's nest egg; but upon reading, a few months later, that the same conglomerate had taken over Renfrews', I concluded that it was in no danger.

I would have liked to tell my readers that the refurbishment of 62 New Square is now complete and that my young friends are enjoying the comfort and elegance to which they have so long aspired. This, unfortunately, is not quite the case, since as yet the lights are not working: the light fittings originally supplied proved to be of the wrong size, certain delays were experienced in obtaining the right ones, and by the time they were delivered the electrician who was to install them had emigrated to Australia. Still, Selena appears confident that the problem will be solved very shortly.

My possession of the Book, I am happy to say, has thus far brought no misfortune on my head; on the contrary, it constitutes a pleasing addition to my modest personal library. It is a legal lexicon, entirely in Latin, published in Paris in the early seventeenth century — there is much in its pages that is of interest to me. I do not attempt, however, to read the future in them.

Also available in ISIS Large Print:

The Complete Hilary Tamar Series
by Sarah Caudwell

"Imbued with poised wit, written in flawlessly judged prose." **The Times**

"An utterly delightful book . . . it will be irresistible to all." **New York Times Book Review**

"Superbly constructed . . . fine mystery, it keeps the reader guessing until the very end." **Faye Kellerman**

Dame Sarah wrote four outstanding mysteries before her early death in 2000. Narrated by a legal historian, Hilary Tamar, the books centre around an office of young attorneys of his acquaintance. Caudwell's dry British wit, combined with her background in law, bring these book on par with the best in the mystery genre.

THE SIRENS SANG OF MURDER

Sarah Caudwell

Young barrister Michael Cantrip is off on a jaunt to the sunny Channel Islands to take on a tax law case that's worth a fortune — if Cantrip and his tax-planning chums can locate the missing heir. But it soon transpires that Cantrip has waded in way over his head. Strange things are happening on these mysterious, isolated islands and something — or somebody — is bumping off members of his legal team, one by one.

Very soon, young Cantrip is calling upon the aid of his colleagues back at Lincoln's Inn and it's up to mentor and amateur investigator Hilary Tamar to get Cantrip back to the safety of his Chambers — alive!

ISBN 0-7531-6989-4 (hb)
ISBN 0-7531-6990-8 (pb)

THUS WAS ADONIS MURDERED

Sarah Caudwell

For young barrister Julia Larwood, it was to be a vacation in pursuit of romance, and a flight from the tax man . . . in short, an Art Lover's Tour of Italy. Reduced to near penury by the Inland Revenue, Julia could hardly afford such luxury but she'd be in hock to the Revenue either way so why not? But poor, deluded Julia — how could she have known that ravishing Art Lover for whom she had conceived a fatal passion was himself an employee of Inland Revenue? Or that her hard-won night of passion would end in murder — with her personal, inscribed copy of the current Finance Act found lying a few feet away from the corpse . . .

ISBN 0-7531-6841-3 **(hb)**
ISBN 0-7531-6842-1 **(pb)**

THE SHORTEST WAY TO HADES

Sarah Caudwell

It seemed the perfect way to avoid three million in taxes on a five-million-pound estate: change the Trust arrangement. Everyone in the family agreed to support the heiress, Camilla Galloway, in her court petition — except dreary cousin Deirdre, who suddenly demanded a small fortune for her signature. Then Dreary Deirdre has a terrible accident, which is the moment when the London barristers handling the trust — Cantrip, Selena, Ragwort and Julia — decide to summon their Oxford mentor Professor Hilary Tamar to Lincoln's Inn.

And when deadly accidents in the family escalate, Hilary is dispatched on the most perilous quest of all: to find the truth and unmask the killer . . .

ISBN 0-7531-6839-1 (hb)
ISBN 0-7531-6840-5 (pb)